Outstanding Praise for the Granny Reid Mysteries!

Murder at Mabel's Motel

"Readers will hope this series has a long run."
—*Publishers Weekly*

Murder in the Corn Maze

"Offers welcome insight into the woman Stella is and the woman Savannah is destined to become. Sure to please McKevett loyalists and other fans of plucky women."
—*Kirkus Reviews*

"Small-town Southern life, friendship, close family ties, and a mature female protagonist add to the appeal of this satisfying cozy, which is a kind of prequel to McKevett's ongoing Savannah Reid series, starring the adult Savannah."
—*Booklist*

"The conclusion is chilling, but readers will be hungry for the next installment of this warm-hearted, 1980s-set series."
—*BookPage*

Murder in Her Stocking

"For a glimpse into small-town life, where the neighbors squabble, gossip flies, everybody knows your business before you do, and when times are hard but everyone pulls together, this Christmas tale will warm your heart."
—*King's River Life Magazine*

"McKevett gives us a sometimes sassy and sometimes stern yet always relatable protagonist in Stella, whose juxtaposition of strength and vulnerability beautifully embodies the complexities and dynamism of real, everyday women. Be forewarned: You'll laugh, you'll cry, and you'll probably curse the fact that you have to wait a year for the next book."
—*Criminal Element*

"Readers will look forward to Stella's further adventures."
—*Publishers Weekly*

Books by G.A. McKevett

Savannah Reid Mysteries

JUST DESSERTS
BITTER SWEETS
KILLER CALORIES
COOKED GOOSE
SUGAR AND SPITE
SOUR GRAPES
PEACHES AND SCREAMS
DEATH BY CHOCOLATE
CEREAL KILLER
MURDER À LA MODE
CORPSE SUZETTE
FAT FREE AND FATAL
POISONED TARTS
A BODY TO DIE FOR
WICKED CRAVING
A DECADENT WAY TO DIE
BURIED IN BUTTERCREAM
KILLER HONEYMOON
KILLER PHYSIQUE
KILLER GOURMET
KILLER REUNION
EVERY BODY ON DECK
HIDE AND SNEAK
BITTER BREW
AND THE KILLER IS . . .
A FEW DROPS OF BITTERS

Granny Reid Mysteries

MURDER IN HER STOCKING
MURDER IN THE CORN MAZE
MURDER AT MABEL'S MOTEL
MURDER MOST GRAVE

Published by Kensington Publishing Corp.

G.A.
McKevett

Murder at Mabel's Motel

A Granny Reid Mystery

www.kensingtonbooks.com

KENSINGTON BOOKS are published by

Kensington Publishing Corp.
119 West 40th Street
New York, NY 10018

All Kensington titles, imprints, and distributed lines are available at special quantity discounts for bulk purchases for sales promotion, premiums, fund-raising, educational, or institutional use.

Special book excerpts or customized printings can also be created to fit specific needs. For details, write or phone the office of the Kensington Sales Manager: Attn.: Sales Department. Kensington Publishing Corp., 119 West 40th Street, New York, NY 10018. Phone: 1-800-221-2647.

First Kensington Hardcover Edition: February 2021

ISBN-13: 978-1-4967-2908-8 (ebook)

ISBN-13: 978-1-4967-2907-1

First Kensington Trade Paperback Edition: December 2021

10 9 8 7 6 5 4 3 2 1

Printed in the United States of America

For Juliana,
who has poured so much love
into so many other people's children.
Including ours.
You are forever "Our Juli."

Acknowledgments

Thank you, Leslie Connell, my dear friend, faithful copyeditor, and First Reader. What would I have done without you all these years?

I wish to thank all the fans who write to me, sharing their thoughts and offering endless encouragement. Your stories touch my heart, and I enjoy your letters more than you know. I can be reached at:

sonja@sonjamassie.com
and
facebook.com/gwendolynnarden.mckevett

Murder at Mabel's Motel

Chapter 1

"Woo hoo! Git a load of Granny!"

"She's got lipstick on!"

"*Red* lipstick! Looks like she's been suckin' on a red lollipop!"

"That's 'cause she's goin' on a date!"

"Granny and the sheriff, sittin' in a tree. K-i-s-s-i-n-g!"

"Yeah, she's gonna get red lipstick all-l-l over his face!"

"Hush up, the lot of you! That'll be quite enough!" As Stella Reid looked around her kitchen table at her snickering grandangels, she tried her best to fake a frown to go with the command. But, in spite of her best efforts, a grin slipped through.

For a moment, she locked eyes with her oldest, Savannah, and saw the knowing smirk on the child's pretty face. Much to Stella's sorrow, Savannah was mature, far beyond her thirteen years. The residue of having lived her formative years in the household of a mother who made poor choices. Usually, right in front of her children.

The result of those foolish decisions was Shirley paying her debt to society in a Georgia penitentiary and her brood eating all of their meals and sleeping every night in the custody of their grandmother.

Raising seven children was a mighty task that didn't leave a lot of free time for outings of any sort. Let alone of the romantic type.

So, tonight was special. Very special. In fact, it scared Stella to even think what Sheriff Manny Gilford's invitation to dinner and a walk by the river might mean.

"Gran and the sheriff aren't going on a date," Savannah was telling her siblings in a tone that sounded as insincere as that of any grown-up trying to convince children of some falsehood. For their own good, of course. "They're just going to the Burger Igloo for a hamburger, so they can have some peace and quiet to discuss business."

"*Monkey* business!" squealed Marietta, the second oldest. Like her sister, the girl knew far more about activities between the sexes than Stella would have liked, but Miss Mari had none of her big sister's common sense or respect for privacy.

Marietta was, as Pastor O'Reilly would say, Stella's "thorn in the flesh." But being considerably less spiritually minded than the good reverend, Stella simply called Marietta a "pain in the hindquarters." But never to her face.

Like her brother and the rest of her sisters, Mari had been called far too many names, much worse ones than that, by her own mother. Often while dancing at the end of Shirley's belt.

Stella was determined to not repeat her daughter-in-law's mistakes. The children deserved a peaceful, steadfast, loving hand to guide them for the remainder of their childhoods, and she was determined to supply that.

But looking down at her sometimes thorny, pretty much always butt-pain granddaughter, Stella could see the child's mental wheels turning as she considered her next comment. The mischievous sparkle in her eyes warned Stella it would be a doozy.

"I heard what you said to Savannah when the two of you was sittin' out there in the porch swing on her thirteenth birthday." Marietta looked around the table, making sure everyone within earshot was listening. "You told her she was a lady now and had to watch out for boys."

"Marietta, you stop right there, gal. That was a private conversation, and you shouldn't've been sneakin' around, listenin' with your ears out on stems—"

"Hey, you hear all sorts of good stuff that way!" Marietta shoved a spoonful of carrot slices into her mouth, pushed them to the side of her mouth, like a squirrel filling up its cheek pockets, and continued to talk around them. "You told her they're only interested in one thing and—"

"Don't you say another word, Marietta, or I swear I'll stick you in your bedroom till you're thirty-eight."

"Good idea. Then you won't have to worry about her, and boys, and what it is they're so interested in," Savannah mumbled, buttering her bread.

"What they're so interested in," Marietta continued unsubdued, "is suckin' on your face, then gettin' your clothes offa ya and wrasslin' you onto a bed so they can—"

"Marietta Reid!" Stella was around the table and had a firm hold on Granddaughter #2, thankfully, before she could finish her sentence.

As Stella pulled the girl from her chair and onto her feet, she glanced around the table and saw the startled, wide-eyed expressions on the faces of her four younger grandgirls: Vidalia, Cordele, Jesup, and Alma. She could tell that they sensed they had been about to hear something their grandmother didn't want them to, which, of course, made the missing information fascinating, even unheard.

Savannah, who was seldom rattled by anything or anyone, even Miss Contrary Mari, looked mortified. In Stella's home, such intimate conversations about delicate topics were limited to the front porch swing and only with the older siblings. Stella figured such information was to be disclosed strictly on a "need-to-know" basis.

Her hand tightened around Marietta's arm as she felt the girl trying to pull away from her. Even the pertinacious Marietta knew when she'd gone too far and was about to "get her comeuppance."

Stella led her away from the table and through the humble, shotgun house to the girls' bedroom with its three sets of bunk beds. Turning on a plug-in nightlight, Stella waved a hand toward the top bunk on the far side of the room. Mari's bed.

"Yank off them shoes of yours and crawl up there onto that bed, young lady."

"I ain't tired!"

"Well, I am. I'm plum wore out with your shenanigans. I'm in desperate need of a time-out, so you're fixin' to take one."

Stella gave her a less than graceful boost up onto the bunk, where the girl sat, huffing and puffing like a river toad with a chest cold.

"I didn't finish my supper! I'm still hungry!"

For a moment, Stella considered telling the child she was going to bed without eating the rest of her meal. But Stella couldn't bring herself to exact that particular punishment. She knew far too well how many times her daughter-in-law had sent the children to bed hungry, and it had nothing to do with misbehavior . . . except Shirley's.

In the little town of McGill, Shirley Reid was famous for three things: having more children than she knew what to do with; her addiction issues; and being unfaithful to her long-distance trucker husband when he was out of town, being unfaithful to her.

On rare occasions, when Shirley Reid managed to get her hand on some money, she seldom bought food for her children. Most of her cash was spent on mood enhancers, bought from local dealers on the streets. Her purchases found their way into Shirley's lungs, down her throat, up her nose, and occasionally, in her veins.

No. While Stella's grandchildren had to be disciplined from time to time, she couldn't, wouldn't, deprive them of food.

"I'll stick your plate in the oven and keep it warm till you've had a good, long think about what you said in there and how unsuitin' it was for you to utter such things in front of the little 'uns."

"They're gonna know about it sooner or later," Marietta protested as Stella turned to leave the room.

"Yes, they will. But later's better than sooner, when it comes to matters like that. Let 'em be young'uns as long as they can. They'll have plenty of time once they're grown to fret about grown-up stuff."

"Like whether or not, after y'all get your hamburgers ate, Sheriff Gilford's gonna ask you to go to the motel and do nasty stuff with him?"

Stella caught her breath and whirled back around to face her granddaughter.

In the next few seconds, she prayed the fastest prayer she'd ever offered up to heaven, asking for the fruits of the spirit: love, wisdom, patience . . . and the strength not to jerk a knot in the kid's tail then and there.

She walked over to the bed, reached up, and took her grandchild's hand in hers. Looking deeply into the girl's eyes, Stella could see a bit of fear and was grateful for it. A child who harbored absolutely no fear at all in their hearts was in for a lifetime of troubles and woes. A little old-fashioned trepidation made a body more careful. She was relieved to see Mari had a tad.

Not enough.

But a little.

"My darlin' girl," she said, keeping her voice softer than the feelings coursing through her. "I love you to pieces. You know that I do. You are one of the seven bright stars in my crown and always will be—in this life and when I'm walkin' the streets of heaven, good Lord willin' and I make it there. But when you just said what you did, my heart hurt somethin' fierce. I'd a'thought you'd have more respect for me and for Sheriff Gilford, too, for that matter, to say such a thing. Neither one of us has ever given you any reason to think we'd behave in such a way. It was most unkind of you to suggest that we would, child."

To Stella's surprise, Marietta didn't reply with one of her ever-ready smart-aleck retorts. Instead, she stared down at her own hand and her grandmother's that was closed tightly around it.

When she didn't answer, Stella added gently, "I do believe that if you apologize to me, you and me both'll feel a heap better."

Marietta drew a deep breath, then looked up at her grandmother. When their eyes met, Stella saw the girl's tears of remorse.

Marietta Reid was feeling remorse! Enough of it to actually make her cry. A little.

Stella's heart soared, borne on the wings of hope for the future! Miracles *did* happen, after all!

"I'm sorry, Granny," she said. "I didn't really think much about what I was gonna say before I spit it out. I was just tryin' to make a funny. I didn't mean to hurt your feelings or make you think I thought you was a wanton woman."

Stella suppressed a chuckle. "*Wanton woman?* Where did you hear the likes of that?"

"Savannah."

"Savannah?"

Marietta shrugged. "She reads too many blamed books."

Laughing, Stella reached up, pulled her granddaughter down from the bunk, gave her a hug and a kiss on the top of her head.

"I reckon you've demonstrated genuine repentance for your transgressions. All's forgiven. Just don't do it again."

"I won't." Marietta grinned up at her, the same mischievous smirk that had gotten her in trouble before. "But you talk funny, too, like Savannah. I reckon it's from readin' the Bible too much."

As Marietta stepped in front of her, Stella reached down and gave her a swat on her rear. "You better be glad I do, turkey butt. Sometimes, that's all that keeps me from cleanin' your plow!"

"What's cleanin' my plow mean?"

"Let's just say—you aggravate me like you did, before I've done my daily readin', and you might find out, sweetcheeks."

Chapter 2

Not for the first time, when eating at McGill's premier dining establishment, it occurred to Stella that the tables in the Burger Igloo were pretty much the same as the one in her own kitchen. But the café's red and chrome, mother-of-pearl "retro" furnishings had been purchased new only a few years ago. They were far less scratched and scuffed than hers, which had been bought shortly after she and Art had been married, back in the fifties, when the dining set had been her pride and joy, the latest in fashionable breakfast sets.

The Burger Igloo's chairs were boring, lacking the character of hers. They weren't split, faded, and stained.

They were "less loved."

Sadly, the restaurant's tables lacked the one unique feature that greatly enhanced the appearance of her "worn to a frazzle" table—the raw plywood extender leaf that enabled a passel of kids to dine at one setting without anybody having to stand at the counter to eat.

Stella had learned that children take a dim view of kitchen

counter dining. Any suggestion they should do so produced grumblings of discontent, even among the most well-behaved young'uns.

Yes, the Burger Igloo's tables and chairs were boring, compared to Stella's. But otherwise, the restaurant was nicely furnished with charming décor that was reminiscent of the 1950s: old movie posters on the walls, black-and-white tiles on the floor, the jukebox near the window which, these days, played mostly music by Michael Jackson, Bruce Springsteen, Whitney Houston, and Madonna.

But tonight, Stella was hardly aware of the ambiance of the charming burger joint. She had scarcely even tasted her deluxe burger.

All she could think about was the fellow sitting across from her in the booth.

Although neither Stella nor the sheriff could be considered "youthful" these days, Manny Gilford was a "fine specimen of a man," as Stella's best friend, Elsie, often observed.

"Mighty easy on the eyes, that fella . . . even when he's walkin' away from ya," her neighbor, Florence, had said more than once.

Elsie and Flo weren't the only ones.

Long ago, Stella had noticed that when the sheriff entered a room every citizen of McGill took notice. Mostly, women gazed longingly at him, taking in his thick silver hair and powerful physique, which was complemented by his freshly pressed uniform, and his face, still as handsome as when he had been in his teens, twenties, thirties, and forties. The women of McGill, Georgia, might have grown up with him, but Manny had always maintained a certain mystique, which garnered adoration from females, appreciation from law-abiding citizens, and grudging respect from lawbreakers.

Stella was proud to be seen with him under any circumstances, let alone one that might, or might not, be considered semi-romantic.

Like the children in her home, Stella wasn't quite sure about the significance of this invitation. Often, he would ask her to accompany him while he was on duty and performing some task for McGillians. But when he had phoned the day before and invited her to have dinner with him, she'd heard a more serious tone in his voice. Maybe even a bit of nervousness, which was completely out of character for an otherwise self-confident man.

Even more confusing was the fact that they had been served ten minutes before, and Manny hadn't eaten more than a bite of his food yet.

Stella was starting to think that, for a man with a ravenous appetite, this was a possible cause for alarm.

As he stared down at his plate, she cleared her throat and said, "Manny, you feelin' all right tonight? You seem like you might be a bit off your feed there."

He looked up at her, his pale gray eyes filled with a level of concern that upset her even further. "No, Stella," he said. "Thank you for asking, but I'm not exactly all right."

Stella's mind raced. So many possibilities occurred to her. With a sheriff, his problem could be almost anything. Heaven only knew what evil might be afoot in the town. Over the years, she'd learned that living in a small town didn't guarantee that everyone inside its borders lived safe, peaceful lives.

He could be troubled about anything from an unpatched pothole to skullduggery of a serious nature.

Maybe somebody had said or done something disrespectful to him. Representing truth, justice, and the American way, as he did, he was often the target of mischief and sometimes genuinely foul play.

Only one week ago, she'd seen him scrubbing the remains of some rotten eggs off the hood of his cruiser.

Or maybe it was she who had done something to offend him. She certainly hoped not.

Sheriff Manny Gilford and his wife, Lucy, had always been close friends of Stella's and her late husband, Arthur. The four of them had made many lovely memories together, having attended high school together and later, as married couples, swimming, boating, and fishing at the Gilfords' lakeside cottage in the summers.

Come winter, they had enjoyed many gentle evenings, playing Monopoly or sitting on the couch, watching the fire blaze, their laps covered with cozy afghans Lucy had crocheted, and listening to oldies from the fifties and the newer hits from the Beatles, Elton John, and Creedence Clearwater Revival on Manny's enormous stereo system.

But all good things come to an end. Manny had lost his beloved Lucy. Then, six years ago, Art had been taken in an accident, working their small farm.

Both widower and widow grieved their losses together, bonding even more closely as friends.

But no more than friends.

Stella knew that Manny wanted to make it more. He had always been so kind to her and hers. He had even been instrumental in helping her gain custody of her grandchildren, when her daughter-in-law had gone to jail on drunk driving and child endangerment charges.

From that moment on, Stella's life was no longer her own. Taking care of seven kids was a twenty-four-hour-a-day job with no weekends off or vacation time.

Certainly, there was no time for something as distracting and time-consuming as a new man in her life.

Manny understood.

That's why Stella was confused when he asked if he could take her out for dinner. But she had heard a note of urgency in his voice, and she couldn't refuse. He'd sounded strange, like he had something important on his mind.

"Can you share what it is that's botherin' you?" she asked. "If it ain't a private matter of a confidential nature, of course."

He hesitated, and the silence was long and awkward. Finally, he said, still staring down at his plate, "I just can't figure out exactly what this is."

Stella studied the pile of food for quite a while, then shrugged and said, "As I recall, you ordered the meat loaf special." She glanced over at Jean Marie, the short-skirted, big-haired waitress, who was keeping a close and jealous eye on them.

As were most of the ladies in the establishment at that moment.

The townsfolk weren't accustomed to seeing their sheriff engaging in what might be a genuine social interaction with an unattached female. Stella was sure everyone in McGill would be discussing this highly suspicious "tryst" over breakfast tomorrow and expounding an opinion on it.

She returned her attention to Manny and his mystery plate. "I think you got the meat loaf you asked for," she said, "though Jean Marie pert near drowned the poor thing in gravy. Probably meant to impress you. She's carried a torch for you since she was eleven, you know."

Manny didn't seem impressed to hear he was the object of Jean Marie's or anyone else's affections. He looked up at her, and she was concerned to see the worried expression on his face.

"I wasn't talking about the meat loaf, Stella May," he said softly. "I'm talking about this. . . ."

"This *what*?" She tried to understand but had no idea what he meant. "I'm sorry, Manny, but—"

"This, Stella. This . . . us . . . going out to dinner together. Alone."

Stella swallowed, took a quick glance around the room at all the eavesdroppers, and whispered, "Alone, except for the quarter of the town's population that's eatin' in here with us tonight?"

He paused, perused the room, then shrugged. "I don't give a hoot about them right now, and I don't care what's on my plate. I just wish I could figure out. . . . Is this a real 'date' we're on now? Or is this just two old friends having a meal together?"

She sat, flabbergasted and unable to formulate one solitary sentence in her head to answer him.

Finally, she just started to giggle. Far too hard. Much too loudly.

She was further mortified when she realized that she sounded like Marietta after a knuckleheaded boy in her class had asked if he could kiss her behind the bookshelves at recess.

Manny wasn't helping, sitting there, studying her with his gray, piercing policeman's eyes. He missed nothing, and she was wondering what her ridiculous reaction was telling him.

At last, she gained control of herself, other than the occasional, nervous hiccup. "I'm sorry, Manny," she said. "I'm not laughing at you. Truly. It's just that my grandkids were bickering about the same thing as I was going out the door today. Some said I was leaving to have a date with you and others said it wasn't no big deal. Just a burger."

Again, his gaze never wavered as he said, "Well? What did you tell them?"

"I don't recall for sure, but I think I mentioned that Miss Marietta should mind her own business."

"That sounds like your Mari."

She laughed. He chuckled.

Both sounded tense, and Stella didn't like it that they were uneasy in each other's presence. That was unusual for them and most unpleasant.

She decided to be honest with him. Maybe even admit that, although the thought scared her, she had been hoping, deep inside, that it was more than just friends getting together for a burger.

She took a deep breath, and in as soft a voice as she could manage, she said, "To be honest, Manny, I was sorta wonderin' myself. I'm not sure, because I don't know exactly what you had in mind when you asked me."

She watched him start to answer, swallow his words, and then try them once again.

"Since you put it that way," he began, "I'll confess. I was thinking it was more of a date than just a burger between friends. But I wasn't assuming anything. I would've been happy with either—as long as I was with you."

She gave him a shy smile and ducked her head. "I reckon I might as well admit it. I was hopin' you'd say that."

"You were?"

She nodded.

He laughed, loudly enough for the deep sound of it to fill the room and draw even more attention to their table.

"Really?" He leaned closer to her.

"Yes. I think the world of Elsie but . . ." She pointed to her mouth. ". . . I wouldn't wear red lipstick just to eat a hamburger with her."

"I was thinking that!" he said. "When I picked you up, that was the first thing I noticed. I was hoping it was a sign."

She nudged him gently under the table with the pointed toe of her high heel. Actually, Flo's high heels, as she didn't personally own a pair of fancy shoes, high heeled or otherwise.

She continued, "I sure as shootin' wouldn't've borrowed these dadgum shoes that pinch my toes and make my back ache somethin' fierce, just to have breakfast pancakes with Flo."

"Oh, I noticed those, too. Believe me."

"And, hopefully, appreciated them, considering my sacrifice."

"I assure you, they *and you* are much appreciated."

She saw a glimmer in his eye that she had seen before, but not quite so pronounced. She glanced down at her burger to avoid the intensity of his gaze, as well as the way it made her feel.

"Thank you, Manny," she said softly. "I appreciate you, too."

To her surprise, he reached across the table and patted the back of her hand. Just lightly. Only for a second. But it was enough to cause her to draw a quick, sharp breath and feel her knees turn the consistency of a gelatin salad that had been left out on a picnic table, one hot, sunny Fourth of July.

She snuck a quick glance around the restaurant and saw at least ten of her fellow dinners suddenly pretend to be fascinated by their dinners instead of their sheriff and whose hand he was patting.

"I'll tell you what," he said. "Since I saw those fancy high heels tonight and how nice you look in them, I'll just hold that memory in my mind, and you don't need to wear them ever again. You don't need to be in pain or even uncomfortable to impress me, Stella May."

"I appreciate that," she said, slipping the heels off under the table. "You have no idea how much. They just ain't me."

She looked up at him and saw he was staring at her lips.

"Wearing lipstick isn't uncomfortable though, is it?" he asked with a grin.

"No. Not a bit."

"Then if you don't mind, and it isn't too much trouble, maybe you could keep wearing that. I must admit, I find it most . . . um . . . appealing."

Despite her best efforts not to, Stella couldn't help recalling what Marietta had said about her getting that red lipstick all over the sheriff's face, and she blushed. Hopefully, not as scarlet as Revlon's shade of Fireball Red on her mouth.

"It's a new stick," she said, when she'd somewhat recovered herself. "I'll only wear it for you, and it'll last forever."

"Maybe not forever," he quickly added.

"We'll see." She nodded toward his plate. "You better eat your supper 'fore it gets cold."

He laughed and picked up his fork, but no sooner had he and she dug into their meals than the bell on the front door rang and an elderly woman rushed in.

"Oh, no," Manny groaned when he saw her. "I already had one run-in with her this morning. I'd hoped I'd be off the hook for a day or two, at least."

As the woman entered the dining area, she looked around the room, her eyes wide with excitement that bordered on hysteria, until she saw Manny.

"It appears Miss Dolly Browning's got herself another emergency of some sort," Stella said under her breath as the woman scurried over to them.

"What else is new? One of those imaginary enemies of hers probably stole her car keys again or got into her refrigerator and drank the last of her milk or cracked one of her eggs."

Stella watched Dolly navigate a crooked path between the tables to get to them. Although Stella had heard she was in her late seventies, she couldn't help thinking Miss Browning appeared older. There was just something about her that suggested she had a lot of mileage on her, more than her years warranted.

Stella could tell that Manny was pretending to be totally focused on his dinner plate, but the newcomer wasn't to be deterred by common courtesy. In her haste to reach him, Dolly lost her balance and stumbled.

No doubt, she would have fallen to the floor if Manny hadn't jumped out of his seat and grabbed her in mid-tumble.

Stella rose, too, snatched an empty chair from a table nearby, and together, she and Manny eased the woman onto it.

Dropping to one knee beside her, Manny put his hand on the older woman's shoulder. "You gotta settle down there, Miss Dolly," he said, patting her. "Whatever's the matter this time, it's not worth taking a bad fall."

"It's bad, Sheriff," she said, panting. "Very bad, and it took me a long time to find you. I went to your office first, but—"

"That's okay. You found me now," he said. "Just take a deep breath and then you can tell me all about it."

As Dolly struggled to do as he'd suggested and collect herself, Stella looked her over and was surprised to see her so disheveled. Usually, in spite of her infirmities, Dolly Browning was impeccably groomed. But not at the moment. Stella couldn't recall ever seeing her silver hair mussed, her fair complexion so ghastly pale, or her eyes so wild with fear.

Yes, Dolly was prone to having paranoid fantasies, imagining all sorts of persecutions—usually of a minor sort—by unseen ruffians. These "enemies" of hers liked to torment her by moving items in her house around and leaving them in unexpected and inconvenient spots. Sometimes they caused her kitchen sink to leak and her toilet to run. On windy nights, they would bang tree limbs against her windows to frighten her. Worst of all, they frequently stole envelopes containing large sums of money out of her mailbox—cash sent to her from wealthy relatives living abroad.

Or so Dolly believed.

With all her heart.

Every "crime" she promptly reported to the sheriff and heartily expressed her determination that he would find these heinous criminals, arrest them, bring them to justice, and administer a punishment commensurate with their misdeeds.

They deserved capital punishment, she insisted, because who but the worst of the worst would do such things to a poor old woman living alone?

"What's the matter now, darlin'?" Manny asked. "Did they change the channels on your television again?"

"No! No! No!" she shouted. Instantly, the conversation in the restaurant stopped. The room was silent, as everyone turned to stare at her.

But she seemed unaware of them as she grabbed Manny's sleeve and shook his arm. "You have to listen to me, Sheriff," she said. "This is important. Something awful has happened. Not to me. To someone else!"

Stella knew Dolly Browning and her usual rants. This wasn't one of them. Kneeling beside Manny, Stella reached for Dolly's hand and pressed it between her own. It was shaking. Badly. And terribly cold.

"What is it, Dolly?" Manny asked. "Who's in trouble?"

"At the service station."

"Which one?" Stella asked, fearing it was the larger of the two in town, the one belonging to her neighbor. Florence wasn't good at handling bad news.

"The little station at the end of town," Dolly said. "Something terrible happened there. An attack. On Ortez."

"Raul Ortez?" Manny looked surprised.

So did Stella.

Raul was one of the more popular, easygoing citizens of McGill. A gentle, hardworking farmer with a failing farm on the outskirts of town, who managed to keep his head high in spite of his bent back. She couldn't imagine anyone wanting to harm him.

"Someone attacked Raul there at the service station?" Manny asked Dolly again, a bit louder and more insistent than before.

"No!" Dolly said. "Not Raul. His daughter. I can't remember her first name, but—"

"Yolanda?" Stella said, her heart sinking.

"Yes. That's it. The friendly, pretty one with the long black hair."

As industrious as her father, Yolanda Ortez had managed the garage for its absentee owner for the past three years, since she had turned sixteen. She had done a good job of it, too, considering how little she'd had to work with.

Manny looked at Stella, a sick expression on his face. "Long black hair. That's Yolanda all right." Turning back to Dolly, he said, "What's happened to Yolanda?"

"I don't know for sure. But I stopped at the gas station to ask that nitwit who works there with that girl—can't remember his name either, but I hate him—if he'd put some air in my tires for me. But I didn't see him anywhere. So, I walked around to the back, where they work on cars, thinking they might be back there. . . ."

"Yes," Manny prompted her, "and what did you see?"

Dolly shuddered and closed her eyes. "At first I heard them. Shouting. And then their footsteps when they were running away. Then I saw her, that sweet girl, lying on the ground back there, between one of those broken-down cars and a pile of tires. She's hurt, Sheriff. Badly hurt. She isn't dead. I know, because I checked. She has a pulse, and she's breathing. But she has a bad head injury, and I think someone . . . hurt her . . . or tried to. You must go help her! Now!"

But Manny needed no prompting. He had already grabbed Stella's hand, and they were racing toward the door.

Meat loaf specials and burgers deluxe, date or dinner with a friend . . . completely forgotten.

Chapter 3

Usually, it required less than a minute, maybe fifty-five seconds during "rush hour," to get from one place to another in a town that was three blocks long and had only one traffic light, which simply blinked red for a four-way stop.

But Sheriff Gilford took only fifteen seconds to drive his new 1986 patrol car—a Special Service Package Mustang—himself, and Stella to the opposite side of town and McGill's "other" service station. On the way, he even managed to call the police station and request that an ambulance and the town doctor meet him at the scene.

Upon arriving, he drove the cruiser around to the rear of the garage and came to a stop with his headlights illuminating an area that looked like a small junkyard.

"There's a pile of tires right there," Stella said, pointing to the haphazard mountain of decaying rubber.

"With a broken-down Buick next to it," Manny replied as he turned off the ignition and grabbed an oversized flashlight from his console area. He started to get out of the vehicle, then paused.

Turning to Stella, he said, "Stay in the car, till I see what's what. The perpetrator could still be here."

Stella fixed him with a determined eye, yanked her door open, and said, "If he is, then you're gonna need somebody to tend the girl whilst you beat the puddin' outta him. Unless you wanna do the tendin' and let me do the beatin'."

Manny didn't reply. He just groaned, got out of the car, and began to shine his light's beam into the darkness all around them.

The smell of an old garage—gasoline, dirty oil, and rotting rubber and vehicles—nearly choked Stella. She thought of the station owned by Flo, located in the center of town. Flo's establishment looked like a persnickety woman owned it. The restrooms were spotless. Stella swore they were clean enough for a body to cook their supper in.

Some folks even claimed that Florence had the garage floor scrubbed regularly with lavender-scented bleach.

The second station might have been only a short distance from Florence's, situated just outside the town limits. But it was a world away in character. Dark, dirty, and depressing.

The garage had been there for as long as Stella could remember, and that whole time it had been a run-down mess. The owner had long since left McGill and moved to Orlando. He visited the place once a year and was contented to see that Yolanda Ortez had managed to keep the doors open and the roof from caving in.

A nineteen-year-old girl could only do so much, and Yolanda had done all she could.

Stella couldn't bear the thought of the industrious young woman hurt. Or worse.

"Heaven forbid," she whispered.

They both peered into the areas that the headlights and

Manny's flashlight illuminated, looking for Yolanda. Or her attacker.

They listened, straining to hear any movement. Anything at all.

A bit of wind rustling the trees.

A dog barking in the yard that was adjacent to the station's property.

Then, a low moan.

Suddenly, a traumatic, painful memory dragged Stella back to another time, another dark and dirty area where a young woman had been injured.

Far worse than injured.

"Let this one turn out better'n that one," she whispered. "Please, please, please!"

Manny heard her. He reached out, grabbed her arm, and pulled her toward him. "Go back to the car, Stella. Please, let me take care of this," he said. Then, as though reading her mind, he added, "It's too much like before. Like Prissy, in the alley behind the tavern."

"I know. But—"

At that moment they heard another low moan. This time they could tell it was coming from a particularly dark area to their right.

The sound was almost more than Stella could bear. She shivered and mumbled, "I'm comin', Prissy. Hang on, sweetie."

She yanked her arm free of Manny's grasp and ran in the direction of the darkness and the groan. "I'm comin', darlin'. Help's here," she called out. "We're comin'."

In spite of Stella's head start, Manny got to the victim first. His flashlight cast an eerie white light on the ashen face of the young woman lying on the ground.

"Yolanda?" Stella heard him ask as he dropped to his knees next to her and leaned over her.

Stella could understand why he was questioning what he was seeing.

The female on the ground didn't look like Yolanda, the charming teenager whom Stella had known since she had been born. The black-haired, dark-eyed beauty was a town favorite. The citizens of McGill loved the Ortez family, small as it was now that Raul's wife, Maria, had passed.

Stella couldn't recall ever hearing a rude word said about any of them. Mostly, when people referred to Yolanda, they called her "that friendly young lady who runs the old gas station on the edge of town—the girl with all that long, pretty, black hair."

But as Stella knelt next to Manny and looked down at Yolanda, she realized there were terrible differences in the girl's appearance. Not only was her lovely face bruised, her left cheek swollen, but her long hair was gone. It had been chopped off. Considering how ragged the cuts were, Stella suspected a very sharp knife had been used.

The shorn hair lay on the ground around its former owner.

The sight made Stella sick with sadness and fury.

For a terrible moment, she feared the same instrument might have been used on the victim's body, as well. Manny seemed to be thinking the same thing, because he was running his flashlight beam up and down her form.

Thankfully, while there were bruises on her arms, they saw no blood anywhere other than on the top of her scalp.

But Stella's relief was short-lived when she realized that the girl's blouse had been torn and was hanging on her in tatters.

Yolanda made a slight whining sound, like a wounded puppy, as she attempted in vain to cover her exposed skin with her hands and arms. Immediately, Stella ripped off her own sweater and laid it gently across her.

In a halting, raspy voice, Yolanda said, "Th-thank . . . you."

"There, there, sugar," Stella said softly. "Don't you worry. Not a bit. The worst part's all over with. You're safe and sound now. The sheriff here done called an ambulance to come get you. They'll be showin' up here any minute."

Manny reached down and laid his hand on her cheek. "She's right, Yolanda. Doc Hynson's on his way, too. He'll ride with you in the ambulance to the hospital. Okay?"

Yolanda seemed to comprehend what they were saying, because she nodded slightly, and a bit of the fear seemed to leave her eyes.

"Somebody worked you over pretty bad, didn't they, sweetie?" he continued.

"Ye-yes, sir," was the mumbled reply.

"Who was it? Who did this to you?"

Instead of answering, she shook her head and started to cry.

Stella patted her arm. "There, there. Just calm down now. Was it somebody you know?" Stella asked, thinking she should probably stay out of it and let Manny do his job.

Yet, if the girl had been attacked by a male, Stella thought Yolanda might find it easier to speak to a woman. Manny seemed to think the same, because when she shot him a quick, questioning glance, silently asking for permission, he nodded and gave her a grateful look.

Stella sat down on the ground, right next to Yolanda's side, took her hand in hers, and began to stroke it. She glanced down again at the girl's body and saw that her jeans snuggly fitted, as was the fashion, were still in place, zipped, and buttoned.

She took that as a good sign. As good as it got under the circumstances anyway.

Thank heavens, she thought. *Coulda been worse.*

"Do you know who it was?" she asked again.

An expression of fear passed over the girl's face. She shook her head slightly and said, "Don't."

"Don't what, honey?"

"Don't ask me."

Manny leaned over her. "Yolanda, if you don't want to talk to us about it now, that's okay. The most important thing to me at the moment is that we get you taken care of. We'll talk later, when—"

"No. Never," Yolanda said. "Can't say. Never."

Manny's face hardened. "The man who hurt you, honey, he won't ever do it again. I promise you. I don't care what he said to you, how he might've threatened you. Where I'll be putting him, he's not going to get the chance to hurt anyone ever again."

She shook her head and looked frustrated, as well as terrified. "Not that. Not him. My . . . my dad."

Manny looked confused. He bent closer to her to hear her better, then said, "Yolanda, you aren't telling me that your father hurt you, are you?"

"No! He would never. Not me. Never hurt me, but . . ."

Stella understood and reached out to gently cup the girl's swollen cheek in her palm. "You're afraid your father will go after the mangy skunk that did this. Right?"

She nodded, then winced at the pain it cost her.

"Oh, okay," Manny grumbled. "You don't want your father to do anything that'll get him in trouble."

Again, she nodded, but ever so slightly.

Manny continued, his voice low and even, "Then you know the guy, and so does your dad, and your father knows where to find him."

Rising and dusting the dirt off his knees, Manny glanced around the garage with its open door and a car inside that was on the lift in mid-repair. He gave Stella a knowing, angry look.

"You don't have to tell me who it was, Yolanda. I've got a pretty good idea myself. There's only one yahoo peckerwood in this town that I can think of who's capable of doing something like this, and he works, off and on, part-time, right here in this garage. When he's sober enough to pump gas and twist a wrench. Right, sweetie?"

Stella looked down at Yolanda, and the fear in the girl's eyes told her that the sheriff was exactly right.

Billy Ray Sonner.

Even his name was enough to make Stella feel the need to wash her mind out with some bleach and a stiff toilet brush.

As deeply loved as the Ortez family was by their fellow McGillians, Billy Ray and his miscreant buddies were just as fiercely hated.

The odious threesome—Billy Ray Sonner, Deacon Murray, and Earle Campbell—had proudly dubbed themselves the Lone White Wolf Pack.

No one had been able to convince them that their club's name was a contradiction in terms, as lone wolves didn't hang out in packs. But their stupid name was the least of their offenses.

The Lone White Wolf Pack seemed to think that Adolph Hitler was a pretty cool guy with a lot of good ideas about how to make the world a better place.

That alone was reason enough for Stella and the rest of the town to think that the world would be much improved if the LWWP were to fall off the end of it and straight into the fiery furnace of hell.

Some folks had even expressed a desire to lead them to the edge, apply a stiff boot to their back ends, and send them on their way.

Until recently, their despicable attitudes aside, their crimes had been more mischievous than felonious. But some disturbing events had occurred lately that upset the town, and it was widely believed they were behind the trouble.

Sheriff Gilford had his eye on them.

Now more than ever.

At that moment, they heard a most welcome sound, the ambulance siren. Stella jumped to her feet and ran to the side of the garage, then around to the front, to direct them toward the rear of the building and their patient.

As they were pulling past her, heading in the direction she was pointing, Dr. Hynson drove in behind them, parked, got out of his car, and ran toward her.

"Who is it?" he shouted, moving quickly and easily for a man pushing seventy. Being the town's only physician kept him busy, mentally and physically fit. His once red hair was now mostly silver, but his face still flushed crimson when he was excited. As he was at that moment.

"It's Yolanda Ortez," Stella told him. "She's been assaulted. Head injury, I'm afraid."

"Is she conscious?"

"Yes. But she was down on the ground when we found her. We didn't try to move her."

"Good."

He rushed around the building, following the ambulance, with Stella only a couple of paces behind him.

Within less than a minute, Yolanda was being gently and efficiently attended by the two paramedics and the doctor. Stella and Manny stood aside and let them work as Doc Hynson checked her vital signs, calming her all the while, his blue-green eyes kind and his words reassuring. Once he had stabilized her neck with a cervical collar, he and the paramedics placed her on a gurney, and carefully loaded her into the ambulance.

As the doctor settled onto the seat next to her, Stella and Manny leaned into the vehicle for one last exchange with Yolanda. Both of them promised her that they'd be seeing her at the hospital soon.

"Please don't tell my father, Sheriff," she pleaded as the doors began to close. "Please!"

"I have to tell him you're hurt," Manny told her, "but I'll

make sure he doesn't do anything stupid. You've got nothing to worry about now but getting well."

As Manny and Stella watched the ambulance pull away, its lights flashing and siren sounding, Stella instinctively reached for his hand.

He clasped hers tightly and the strength and warmth that the gesture communicated gave her a sense of peace.

Manny would make everything all right. In the end.

Or at least, he'd make things better than they were at the moment.

"That was quite a promise you made the girl just now," she told Manny. "Her daddy's as kindhearted as any man I've ever known. He's slow to rage. A true gentleman. But when he finds out some guy hurt his little girl . . . and hurt her in that particular way . . ." Stella felt a tightening in her throat that cut off her words.

Manny supplied them. "He's gonna have a strong opinion about it, just like I do."

"Raul thinks the world of that child. Since losing his Maria to cancer and his farm failin' like it is, his daughter's all that poor man's got left in the world. He's gonna at least be tempted to do something fierce."

"Most any father would."

"Who're we gonna look for first? Them ignoramus Loner guys or Raul?"

"*We?* Before I do anything, I'm taking you home. This sorry so-called 'date' of ours has to be one of the worst first dates in history, darlin'."

"I'll give you a rain check, but I don't wanna go home just yet."

"That was a serious crime, Stella, and whoever did it has shown how dangerous they can be. I won't put you in danger by dragging you along while I hunt them down."

Again she asked, "Who are you lookin' to find first? Raul or the Loners?"

"Raul. He's got a right to know his daughter's been hurt, and those fools aren't going anywhere."

"They're too dumb to pull their heads in before shuttin' a window, let alone engineer an escape."

"Exactly."

"You're not afraid that Raul's dangerous, are you?" she asked, giving him a sly grin.

He sniffed and shook his head, obviously seeing through her ploy. "Only to Billy Ray and his boys, I reckon."

She slipped her arm companionably through his as they continued on toward the cruiser. "Then you ain't gittin' rid of me, boy. Not yet anyway. This 'Worst First Date Ever' we're sufferin' through, it ain't over till both parties agree it is."

He chuckled and grinned down at her. "Yes, ma'am."

Chapter 4

No sooner had Stella and Manny settled into the cruiser than the radio crackled, and an unpleasantly nasal voice filled the car. "Sheriff! Sheriff! You there?"

Manny sighed, picked up the microphone, and answered, "Yes, Mervin. What's up?"

"A ruckus and a half over at the grocery store. Miss Violet called it in. Said Raul Ortez was there, buyin' his girl's favorite cereal and the next thing you know, he went plumb crazy, makin' a big ol' stink over somethin'. Threatenin' to stomp a mudhole in them Lone White Wolf fellers' backsides, he was. One of 'em, that little one called Earle, works there, ya know."

Manny turned to Stella, sighed, and said, "So much for me needing to inform Raul." Into the microphone, he said, "Okay, Merv. I'm on my way over there now. And Deputy, I've had it up to here with bad news for one night. If you hear anything else amiss, just keep it to yourself, all right?"

"Yeah, sure. Gotcha, Sheriff. Ten-four," Deputy Mervin Jarvis replied with a suspiciously grave tone.

Manny sat silently for a moment, his brow furrowed. Stella

could tell he was mulling over that last exchange. Finally, he once again pressed down on the microphone button and said, "Deputy Jarvis."

"Yes, sir?"

"That thing I said about not bothering me with any more bad news . . . you know I was joking. Right?"

"Huh? Oh. Right, sir."

They heard a nervous chuckle, then Mervin clicking off.

Manny groaned. "That boy's one nut short of a pecan pie."

Stella giggled. "He ain't handsome, God love 'im, but he sure is dumb."

"Somebody done blew out his pilot light."

"His cornbread ain't quite baked in the middle."

"Yes, but he means well. . . ."

"Bless his heart."

Stella had been shopping at the Bagley's Grocery Store for most of her life. As a child Stella had seen Flo's father-in-law, Bud Bagley Sr., working hard behind the counter. He was a kind man in spite of the fact that his son, Bud Jr., had turned out to be one of the town's meanest ruffians. Unlike his no-good offspring, Bud the father understood poverty and, therefore, extended credit for groceries to families who would have otherwise gone hungry.

Stella's mother had been one of those.

If it hadn't been for the Ol' Man Bagley, as the town had dubbed him, Stella would have been one of those children sent to bed with a piece of stale bread, instead of a proper evening meal of fried potatoes and milk gravy.

Stella had never forgotten Mr. Bagley's kindnesses, even after he and his worthless son had passed on, leaving the store to Florence.

Having spent forty years working in that store, Flo had decided to retire after her husband's passing. She had sold the store to Violet Wakefield. Though Stella couldn't get used to the new sign over the front door, she continued to patronize the establishment.

Unlike many of her fellow townsmen, Stella flatly refused to drive to a bigger, nearby town to shop at one of those large chain stores who wouldn't even notice she had been there, whose giant budgets would devour her meager grocery money and never know the difference.

Violet Wakefield appreciated Stella's loyal patronage and never missed an opportunity to express her gratitude with every shopping trip Stella made to the humble, little store.

Until today.

The usually peaceful and gracious Violet met Stella and Manny at the front door. Her clothes—which were violet, as she took her name very seriously when it came to grooming, and her hair, which was also tinted with a slight purple dye—were as disheveled as Dolly's.

Her voice was high and shaky when she said, "Oh, Sheriff! I'm so glad you're here! You missed a fight and a half! Right back there in my produce section. They turned over all my oranges and smashed so many tomatoes that it looks like somebody bled to death there on my floor."

She turned to Stella, looked puzzled, and added, "Oh, hey there, Stella May." Violet glanced back and forth between Stella and Manny. "You . . . um . . . with him?"

"I was standin' beside him when he got the call from the station, so I came along," Stella said quickly. She could hear the almost apologetic tone in her own voice, and she felt something like indignation rising inside her.

Since when did she have to apologize to anybody in this town for being in the company of a fine man like Sheriff Gilford?

They were both unattached. Except deep in their hearts where the memories of their long-gone spouses were ever present.

As widow and widower, they were certainly free to see others if they chose to. Except deep in their still-mourning souls.

For some time Stella had been wondering why she felt the need to deny the ever-growing feelings she had for Manny. From the town. From him. Even from herself.

But now wasn't the time to fret about such things. Not with blood and tomato juice spilling right and left.

"It sounded serious," she told Violet. "I decided to tag along. Wanted to make sure you were all right."

"Thank you, Stella," Violet said. "You're a good friend."

Her curiosity seemingly satisfied for the moment, Violet turned back to Manny and the business at hand. "Come along, the both of you," she said. "Y'all gotta see this."

She ushered them inside the store and over to a quiet corner, away from the crowd that had gathered near the cash register—a tight knot of folks who were whispering excitedly among themselves.

"It was the strangest thing, Sheriff," she said. "First, Raul came into the store and was looking around, all friendly and jolly, like he always is. He grabbed him a buggy and was loading it up with Yolanda's favorite cereal, some little chocolate cream-filled cakes she likes, and some corn that I've got on sale. Four cans for a dollar if you're interested."

Stella smiled. Violet was quite the business lady. Long ago, Stella had decided she needed to stick close to her grocery list when shopping at Wakefield's Grocery Store. Sweet-talking Violet could sell ketchup Popsicles to a woman wearing white gloves.

"And then what happened?" Manny prompted Violet a bit curtly.

"Well, Earle works here, as you're probably aware. Earle Campbell. You know him."

"Ever'body knows Earle. Unfortunately," Stella muttered under her breath.

Earle Campbell was the flunky in the Lone White Wolf Pack, the "omega" wolf, the wimp pup, Billy Ray's lackey.

Several years ago, when Sheriff Gilford had pulled the threesome over for speeding, Earle had been foolish enough to shove an enormous bag of pot down the front of his jeans at Billy Ray's bidding.

Of course, Manny became suspicious about little Earle suddenly being so amply endowed and had searched and arrested him.

Since it was such a generous amount and Earle had been convicted of drug trafficking before, he had served several years in the state penitentiary for what had been Billy Ray's crime and his own ignorance.

Word on the streets of McGill—and in the tavern, pool hall, laundromat, and Wednesday night prayer meeting at church—was that Billy Ray had offered to pay Earle a thousand dollars when he got out of jail, if he kept his mouth shut about whose dope that was.

Deciding that a thousand dollars was a lot better than a poke in the eye with a sharp stick, or worse, from Billy Ray, Earle did as he was told and said nothing to anybody.

Unfortunately for Earle, the day he was released, not only did Billy Ray forget about the promised thousand dollars, but he even forgot to pick him up at the prison gate.

Earle had to hitchhike home, and since there were signs for miles and miles around the prison warning travelers to be wary of anyone seeking a ride, he'd worn out his shoes getting back to McGill.

Although Earle claimed he'd had some sort of spiritual awakening on his journey and decided to "forgive and forget," the town doubted he had done either. Billy Ray had behaved badly toward his loyal pack member, and Ol' Earle was known for holding a grudge.

They had all been waiting to see what revenge, Earle Campbell–style, might look like. So far, nothing had been forthcoming. The consensus was: Earle was nursing that grudge for all it was worth, and when he decided to cash in his chips, it'd be a doozy.

Stella wondered if this might be the moment.

Knowing Billy Ray as she did, she could only hope.

"Yes, ma'am. I know Earle," Manny was telling Violet. "Having fished a ton of pot out of the front of his jeans, I'm sorry to say I know him better than I ever wanted to. Frankly, Miss Violet, I'm surprised a fine lady such as yourself would hire him to work here in your store."

Violet shrugged and gave the sheriff a sheepish little grin. "I try to do the right thing," she said. "I figure everybody deserves a second chance."

Manny gave her an understanding smile, but Stella noticed his gray eyes were hard when he said, "Sometimes, giving somebody a second chance is like handing them a loaded gun because they missed when they shot at you the first time."

Violet lowered her voice, leaned closer to Manny, and said, "I'm afraid you're right, Sheriff. I can't have very many of these free-for-alls here in the store before folks'll be afraid to come and shop here."

Stella looked around the store, searching for the small, pasty-faced fellow in question. He wasn't difficult to spot, cowering in the far corner of the store, next to a display of stacked toilet paper rolls. His bald head caused him to stand out from the rest of the shoppers, who were huddled in tight groups, whispering excitedly to each other. Not a single can of corn was being purchased, sale or not.

Yes, Earle Campbell was easy to spot with that shiny noggin of his. While there were numerous older men with no hair in town, they had become so naturally. Among the younger set, only the LWWP three actually shaved their heads.

Earle was watching Sheriff Gilford with a wary eye, while trying to make himself invisible among the toilet paper rolls.

Sorta appropriate, Stella thought. At least he knows his place.

She saw Manny's eyes scanning the store, too, and she knew the moment he spotted his quarry. She watched as a look went back and forth between the two men.

Stella felt uneasy and a bit afraid for Manny because of the intense hatred in the younger man's eyes. If looks could kill, she'd be giving her dear friend CPR at that moment.

Good thing Ol' Earle's nothin' but a blowhard, she thought.

"I see Earle's wearing his usual T-shirt with the swastika," Manny observed.

"He wanted to," Violet said. "I nearly fired him over that on his first day. He does wear it, every day. Insisted on it. But I make him put that apron on over it, so it doesn't show."

Stella looked again at Earle's shirt. It was, indeed, a black tee, and she could see the top of a white circle showing above the bib of a workman's canvas apron. She's seen him wearing the shirt in public often enough to know there was a large red swastika in the center of that white circle.

She patted Violet's shoulder, gave a tsk-tsk, and said, "Violet, you are way too nice. I wouldn't let a dadgum swastika within a mile of any establishment I owned. Some things are just too wicked to be covered up, even with a big apron."

"I know. I know," Violet said. "I'm just a softie. Earle's momma came by here, begged me to hire him, said she was just about starving to death. Promised me she'd keep him in line. Till today, he's been pretty good. Not exactly work-brickle or overly bright, but . . ."

Manny squinted at Earle. "Is that blood under his nose?"

"It is."

"Raul did that?" Stella asked, trying to picture the quiet, kind farmer she had known for so long making anybody even cranky, let alone making them bleed.

"He did."

"What brought it on?" Manny asked.

"Like I said, Raul was shopping, all nice and peaceful like. Then Deacon Murray, that other fool that's part of their stupid little club—"

"I know him, too," Manny told her. "Go on."

"Deacon came charging in here, all excited about something. He went back there in the rear of the store where Earle was stacking up those toilet paper rolls, and Deacon started telling Earle something."

Manny smiled grimly. "I'll bet he was."

Violet looked a bit confused but continued. "I overheard them say something about 'that Ortez girl.' Raul must've heard it, too, because the next thing I knew, he left his buggy half-full up front by the cash register and went charging back there like he was fixin' to clean somebody's clock. He even grabbed one of my toilet plungers off the rack on the wall there and took it with him."

"Is that how Earle got his bloody nose?" Stella asked.

"I can't even tell you. Some mighty hard words flew back and forth between the three of them, and then Raul laid into them with that toilet plunger! Deacon skedaddled out the back door, and in no time at all, Earle was yelping and begging Raul to stop waling on him."

Manny grinned and shook his head. "Shoot. I wish I'd been here to see that."

"Me too," Stella said with a wistful sigh. "I'd've brought popcorn, a soda pop, and a foldin' chair and paid a quarter to watch that."

"What else?" Manny asked Violet.

"Raul kept hitting him and yellin', 'Where's he at? Where is he right now?' Finally, seems Earle couldn't take it no more, and he hollers, 'The pool hall! He's at the fu—darned—pool hall.' Only Earle didn't say 'darn,' Sheriff, if you know what I mean."

"I know what you mean, Violet. Continue."

"Once Earle said that word he shouldn't've said, and the business about the pool hall, Raul marched outta here. He left his buggy full of groceries, but he took my plunger with him. It was the deluxe model, too. I hope he's not thinking he can return it. It's probably got drips and drabs of Earle all over it. I couldn't in good conscience put it out for sale again."

"I wouldn't worry too much about the plunger now, Violet," Manny said. "It might wind up in an evidence locker before the day's out anyway."

"That's okay. I don't want to press charges against Raul for shoplifting or anything like that. I don't think he was in his right mind when he left here with my merchandise in his hand. Plus, I don't want to add to your workload. You've got enough on your plate."

Stella stifled a grin when Manny said with great seriousness, "I appreciate that, Miss Violet. I wish all the citizens of McGill and the surrounding countryside were as cooperative as you."

He reached out and shook her hand. "I'm going to go talk to Earle right now, see what I can wring out of him. But I'll take him out the rear of the store and into the alley. That way you can get your store back to normal and your customers settled down."

"Thank you, Sheriff." Violet batted her eyelashes up at him

for a moment, then she stole a quick glance at Stella, as though to see if she minded.

Stella made sure her face showed nothing, not even mild annoyance or curiosity.

It wasn't difficult. Stella wasn't the least bit worried about Violet striking up anything of a romantic nature with the sheriff, no matter how much she might want to.

Something told Stella that Manny just wasn't *that* fond of the color purple.

Once Violet had walked away, Manny turned to Stella. "Looks like my buddy Earle back there's just aching to talk to me. I'm going to go have a chat with him, ask him for the benefit of his expert opinion about what happened."

Stella nodded. "I'll stay up here with Violet and let you chat away in private, Sheriff," she said a bit reluctantly. She'd enjoyed enough of Violet's company to last her for a while, and she was fiercely curious about what Earle might have to say.

Either Manny saw something on her face or he knew her well enough to understand that she was simply being courteous.

She blessed him silently when he said, "I'd prefer if you came with me, Mrs. Reid." He glanced over at the wide-eyed Violet, who was taking in every nuance of this exchange. Then he added, "If I get into trouble with him, roadkill skunk that he is, maybe you could have a go at him with one of Miss Violet's deluxe toilet plungers."

"That'd make my day, Sheriff," Stella replied, unable to hide a grin. "In fact, go outta your way to rile him up. I'd welcome the opportunity."

Manny turned to Violet, saw a look of alarm on her face, and promptly added, "Of course, if it should come to that, the city would be happy to reimburse you for both the plunger and any produce that might be damaged while Stella here makes use of it."

"Oh, okay," was all Violet was able to squeak out, as she watched them walk away and head toward the rear right corner of the store and Earle Campbell.

"Do you reckon she knows?" Manny whispered, bending his head down to Stella's.

"Knows what?"

"That this is more than just a dinner between two old friends."

She blushed but didn't reply, because it was a small store, and they had already reached Earle and his ineffective barrier of toilet paper rolls.

He looks like a basement rat with its mouth full of cheese, who's just heard the click of the trap spring, she thought.

"Evening, Earle," Manny said as he stepped well inside Earle's personal space. Eyeing the blood under Earle's nose he added, "Looks like you sprung a leak there, boy."

"I was assaulted!" Earle shot back, sounding like a kindergartener whose milk money had been stolen out of his sock. "That stupid spic took a toilet plunger to my head and—"

Manny held up one hand, like a traffic cop. It was only inches from Earle's bloodied nose. "For the rest of this conversation, Campbell, the gentleman in question will be referred to as Mr. Ortez."

"That's right!" Stella interjected. "And if he ain't, that nosebleed you've got under control just might resume, if you know what I mean. That gentleman is a friend of mine, not to be confused with the likes of you!"

Earle was taken aback. Something told Stella that he wasn't accustomed to having females speak up to him. She knew his momma, and Mrs. Campbell was a soft-spoken woman, who was known to have taken a lot of nonsense off her only son.

Turning to Manny, Earle said, "She just threatened me, Sheriff! You heard it! What're you gonna do about it?"

"I'm going to warn you to look out for her. Mrs. Reid has quite a reputation for backing up what she says."

"Just 'cause she took an iron skillet to ol' Bud Bagley back in the day . . ."

Stella gave him an evil grin. "A toilet plunger'll do just as well in a pinch," she told him, "or so I hear tell."

Earle pretended to ignore her and turned back to Manny. "Are you gonna arrest that bean—that Ortez bastard or not? He just attacked me for nothin'! Nothin' at all."

"People don't do that," Manny told him. "Leastwise, not good people. I understand it was something he overheard that set him off. Something you and Deacon were talking about back here. Something disturbing about his daughter, Yolanda."

A look came over Earle that Stella recognized instantly, and it surprised her.

Guilt, she thought. *Plain and simple. Not one doubt about it.*

She was raising seven grandchildren, and she knew that look all too well. But this wasn't one of those "I-Ate-the-Last-Piece-of-Pie-Without-Asking" kind of looks. This was a "I-Stole-Five-Dollars-Out-of-the-Teacher's-Purse-and-Got-a-Whoopin'-from-the-Principal-and-Suspended-for-a-Week" look.

She knew Manny had registered the expression, too, because his eyes narrowed, and he leaned even closer to Earle. He was literally breathing down the hoodlum's neck.

"Which one of you stupid Loners brutalized that poor girl? Was it you, Earle?"

"No! It wasn't me! I don't know anything about it! I wuddin there! I swear on my momma's eyes."

Manny reached over and grabbed a handful of Earle's shop apron and underlying T-shirt. He yanked him forward and up, until he was practically dancing on his tiptoes. "Then your momma just went blind, you stupid fartknocker."

To the delight and amazement of everyone in the store—other than Earle—the sheriff pushed him backward, still holding tightly to his clothing and keeping him on his toes, all the way to the back door and out into the dark alley.

As Stella followed them, she thought that Earle looked like a disgruntled ballerina wearing slippers five sizes too small and lined with cockleburs.

"I don't have time to mess with you, Earle," Manny told him, shoving him against the back wall of the store, then releasing him. "Either you did it or you know who did, so speak up. Otherwise, I'm off to find Billy Ray, and you know what he'll say. He'll tell me you're the one who hurt her, just like he swore that bushel of pot in your crotch was yours. Then you'll be back in the pen again, and this time, you'll be an old man by the time you get out."

When Earle hesitated, Manny added, "And you won't be serving a drug sentence. You'll be in there for assaulting a young lady named Ortez. How popular do you figure you'll be with the Latino gang inmates when they hear that?"

His words had quite an impact on Earle.

Stella watched, amazed, as Earle turned an even grayer shade of white in the light of the single bulb above the store's back door. He started to tremble like a dried-up oak leaf in a stiff, late-October windstorm.

"It wasn't me that hurt her," he said, on the verge of tears. "Deacon neither. It was Billy Ray. He got the idea in his head that she liked him—which she didn't. He told us he was gonna, you know, do her—soon as the garage closed."

"And you two knuckleheads did nothin'," Stella said. "You did nothin' at all to bring a terrible thing like that to a halt before it got started. What kinda men are you anyway?"

"We tried!" Earle protested. "We told him it was a stupid idea. That he'd get caught."

"Did you mention it was a horrible, cruel, immoral thing to do to a sweet girl?" Manny said.

"Sayin' something like that to Billy Ray woulda just got me in trouble, and it wouldn't have done a bit of good. Billy Ray don't see it that way. I mean, she's just a . . . it's not like she's a . . ."

"What you mean is, she's not a white girl," Stella supplied, resisting the urge to slap him.

He shrugged and looked down at his black combat boots that had bright white laces. "Yeah. Somethin' like that."

Stella glanced up at Manny and was surprised to see that his face was flushed a deep red, like she had never seen it before.

She could hear his breath coming hard and fast when he said in a low, ominous tone, "Every woman in my jurisdiction, young or old, Sunday school teachers or hookers, with skin that's white, brown, or black—they shouldn't even have to think about something like that happening to them. Let alone worry about it. Let alone suffer having it done to them!"

"I know. I know, Sheriff," Earle said, holding his hands in front of his face as though he was expecting to be struck at any moment. "I feel the same way. That's why, once Billy Ray had her out there in back and got out his knife, we told him he had to stop! He was all mad, 'cause she was tellin' him, 'No way!' We thought he was fixin' to kill her, and I think he would've if we hadn't hollered at him, told him not to."

Manny seemed unmoved by Earle's supposed "gallantry."

So was Stella. "So y'all figure you did the girl a good turn, standin' there and watchin' while he whacked off her pretty hair?" she asked, her voice as bitter as the taste in her mouth.

"And when he tore her blouse?" Manny added.

"He was intendin' to do more'n that!" Earle protested. "But we warned him. We heard somebody comin' around back, and we told him we'd all better make tracks. Coulda been you, makin' a nightly check like you do."

Stella thought of Dolly, a tiny, scarcely five-feet-tall woman, who wouldn't weigh a hundred pounds if she'd been dipped in lead paint. If the Loners had known it was her interrupting Billy Ray's party, instead of the sheriff, who knows what might have happened instead?

She shuddered to even think of it.

Thank goodness for Dolly Browning and her half-flat tires that needed inflation.

"What did Deacon come here to tell you?" Manny asked.

Earle looked back down at his shoelaces, and Stella knew he was deciding whether or not to tell the truth.

"Speak up!" Manny shouted. "Now, man. Time's a'wastin'! I got bigger fish to fry than you."

"He was all excited, 'cause you and . . ." He pointed to Stella. ". . . your friend was there at the station. The ambulance, too. He said that gal wasn't dead after all. He was watchin' across the street when they loaded her into the ambulance, and he said she was awake and talkin' to y'all."

"He thought she was telling on you three," Manny said.

Earle shrugged. "Yeah. Somethin' like that."

"And poor Raul heard what you said," Stella added.

"He did. That's when he grabbed that plunger and tore into us. Deacon ran off and left me to get the worst of it, and I hadn't even done nothin' wrong."

"Except stand by and watch while your jackass of a leader terrified and damaged a sweet, innocent girl," Stella said.

"Well, yeah. 'Cept that," Earle replied.

For a moment, Stella thought she saw the glimmer of some unspilled tears in his eyes. *Maybe there's a smidgeon of hope for Earle Campbell after all,* she thought.

Manny must have seen them, too, because his manner softened a bit. He backed away to a more natural distance and put his hands into his slacks pockets. "Mr. Ortez wanted to know where Billy Ray was, right?"

"Yes, sir. He was quite determined on that point."

"You told him?"

"I had to. He was fixin' to murder me with that plunger. I tell ya, he's stronger than he looks, that guy."

"You told him Billy Ray was at the pool hall?"

"I did. Like I said, he was madder than a frog in a sock and swingin' that thing like a baseball bat. He was shoutin' stuff like, 'That Billy Ray's got days to live! Maybe hours!' I thought I was a goner, too, 'cause he thought I hurt her, too, and—"

The back door of the store flew open, and Violet appeared, her eyes bright with even more excitement than she'd shown before.

This here's a banner day for Miss Violet Wakefield, Stella thought. *One she won't forget for a month of Sundays. Maybe a year of 'em. The rest of us either, for that matter.*

"Begging your pardon, Sheriff," she said breathlessly, "but your deputy—not the smart one, but the other one—just called me on my store phone. Said he figured you were here, since this's where he sent you last. Said you'd better get over to the pool hall right pronto. Apparently, it's World War Two and a Half over there right now."

"Gee," Manny said, as he took Stella's arm and led her back into the store. "I can't imagine why."

As they made their way through the building and out the front door, Stella was somewhat surprised that Manny wasn't rushing. He wasn't dawdling, but he certainly wasn't breaking into a run or anything remotely like it.

"Are you worried about what might happen to Mr. Ortez?" she asked, when he casually opened the passenger door of the cruiser and graciously seated her inside.

"Not particularly," was the nonchalant reply.

He walked around to the driver's side, opened the door, and got in. As he stuck the key into the ignition and started the powerful car, he mused, "Let's see now . . . A father, a hardworking farmer who performs hard labor every day of his life, versus a punk who sits on his rear end in a rented basement apartment, day after day, smoking dope and playing video games where he can deliberately quash frogs trying to cross busy streets just so he can hear them splat . . . No, my money's on the outraged, hale and hearty daddy every time."

Chapter 5

Manny and Stella arrived at the pool hall in less than thirty seconds, but by the time they did, the activity had spilled from inside the establishment out onto the street in front of it.

A crowd of at least a dozen of McGill's least law-abiding citizens were assembled and in the midst of them stood Raul Ortez. He had Violet's plunger in one hand and a pool cue in the other. Both were bloody. As he waved them in front of him, like a ninja wielding two swords, he was yelling obscenities that Stella had never thought she'd hear on Main Street in McGill, let alone from this gentle fellow.

Hell hath no fury like a man whose daughter's been messed with, she thought.

"See, I told you," Manny said. "We didn't have to worry about Raul getting the bad end of this."

"I reckon not. But Lord help us," Stella said, trying to make sense of what she was seeing but only able to register the copious amount of red that seemed to be smeared all over everyone present.

The streetlamp provided little light. Mostly, it was the red neon sign in the window, blinking the words POOL HALL that illuminated the scene, making the red appear even redder. The entire scene looked as though it had been washed in blood.

"Somebody's dipstick's gonna show them a quart down at least," Stella said.

"Yeah, the source of it's on the ground over there by the door," he said, pointing to something that looked like a heap of dirty, bloody laundry on the walkway, leading to the entrance.

"Billy Ray." She watched for movement and saw none. "Is he dead?"

"No such luck." Manny turned off the cruiser's ignition, then froze and stared straight ahead. "What in tarnation is my deputy doing here?" he said.

She turned her head to see what he was referring to and saw Mervin Jarvis standing near the now wriggling body of Billy Ray Sonner. Jarvis was holding wads of what looked like brown paper towels from a bathroom dispenser in each hand.

When he bent down and tried to press them to an apparent wound on Billy Ray's arm, the unhappy "patient" kicked him soundly on the shin.

Mervin promptly returned the kick and caught Billy Ray squarely on the backside.

A second later, Manny was out of the cruiser and heading toward his deputy, his stride determined and his face dark.

"What the hell's going on here!" he roared.

Following close behind him, Stella saw Mervin jump when he spotted his boss coming toward him.

In a hurried, mindless gesture, Mervin tossed the paper towels in his hand down onto Billy Ray and folded his arms over his ample tummy.

"Deputy, step away," Manny told him. When Mervin didn't comply fast enough, Manny repeated, "Step away, Deputy Jarvis. Now!"

Jarvis seemed to come to life. He jumped backward in what Stella decided was the liveliest movement she had ever seen the slow-motion lawman make.

Like Shirley Reid, in the town of McGill, Deputy Mervin Jarvis was known for three things: not wasting a bit of energy he didn't absolutely have to, sweating twenty-four hours a day and every day of the year including Christmas, and his Pac-Man addiction. If he was in a place where there was a Pac-Man machine, nobody got a chance to play until he left.

Rumor had it, his obsession had cost him his new Chevy truck.

Those quarters added up.

The M.P.D. had a third member, who was far more confidence-inspiring than Mervin, but Deputy Augustus Faber had recently gotten married and was on his honeymoon in Savannah.

So, Manny was stuck with Mervin and, apparently, not too happy about it.

"I told you to stay at the station house and man the phones," the sheriff was telling his deputy under his breath, so the bystanders wouldn't hear. "Who told you to come down here?"

Mervin shrugged. "I knew you were at the grocery store and there's nobody at the station but ol' Elmer, sleepin' it off. Figured I oughta . . ."

". . . oughta follow orders, maybe?"

"Yeah. I reckon. But looks like Billy Ray's about to bleed out."

Stella and Manny studied the wounds on the fallen man's arms. Three of them. Indeed, all three were bleeding, but none as bad as the one on Yolanda Ortez's head.

Manny bent down to look closer and Billy Ray raised his leg again as though to kick the sheriff, too.

"Don't even think about it, Sonner," Manny told him. "You already assaulted one officer of the law today, and that's all you get."

Billy Ray scowled up at Manny, and Stella thought, not for the first time, what an ugly fellow he was.

It wasn't the fact that he had numerous teeth missing and the ones he had were broken and yellowed. In a town as poor as McGill, a lot of folks had less than straight, white, movie-star smiles.

It wasn't that his clothes were dirty. People in McGill worked for a living and that often meant their clothes were destined for the washing machine.

It wasn't even that his head was shaved, and blue veins tended to pop out on his gray scalp when he got angry—which was most of the time.

"Your deputy done kicked me," he yelled, literally spitting mad. Though, since he was lying on his back, most of the saliva landed on his own face.

"Yeah, I saw that," Manny replied.

"I'm gonna sue this town for all it's worth!"

"This town's worth about a plug nickel," Manny replied. "Go ahead. But don't spend it all in one place and upset the economy."

Turning to Mervin, Manny said, "Deputy, this guy has to go to the hospital for some stitches, and the ambulance is tied up at the moment, taking his victim to the emergency room."

"My *victim*?" Billy Ray objected, wriggling around on the sidewalk. "What victim? I ain't got no damned victim."

"Oh, yes, you do, and we both know it." Manny glared down at him. "Billy Ray Sonner, you're under arrest for assaulting Miss Yolanda Ortez. You have the right to remain silent, and I strongly suggest you do so. If you can't afford an attorney, we'll get you a free one. Understand?"

"Yeah! I understand my rights! You got no reason to arrest me! I didn't do nothin'! I'm gonna sue you, too, Sheriff. See if I don't!"

"Yeah, yeah. Whatever." Manny turned back to his deputy. "Have some of these guys help you put the prisoner in the back of your vehicle. Take him to the hospital to be treated. Watch him every minute until I get there to relieve you. Got that, Deputy?"

"What!?" Deputy Mervin was outraged. "He's bleedin' like a stuck pig. I don't want him in my car!"

"That's exactly why he's going in yours instead of mine." Manny gave him an unpleasant grin. "Plus I have to interview our . . . um . . . perpetrator." He nodded toward Raul. "Go on, Mervin. Shake a leg. Git 'er done."

A markedly morose Mervin shuffled away and began to canvas the crowd for volunteers. By then, most had moseyed back inside, and the remaining lookie-loos seemed reluctant to offer assistance of any kind.

"I ain't touchin' him," one said. "Who knows what kinda diseases he's got."

Another added, "That's for sure! I hear he keeps his fee-on-say in his uncle's barn. She's a mighty wooly girl. Don't say nothin' but, 'Ba-a-a-a.'"

The crowd guffawed.

Billy Ray fixed the speaker with an evil eye and bellowed, "That's it, Calvin Ketchum! You're a dead man! Soon as I get outta that hospital, I'm comin' after you and by the time I get done with you, you'll—"

"Shut up, Sonner," Manny told him. "Believe me, you got bigger problems than somebody casting aspersions on your love life."

From the corner of her eye, Stella saw Raul coming their way. His weapons were lowered, but the look on his face showed her that his rage hadn't yet been spent.

Manny saw him, too. He leaned down, gathered up some of the paper towels that had fallen to the ground, and handed them to Billy Ray. "Hold those on that biggest cut there on your forearm, the one that's bleeding most."

Once Billy Ray had reluctantly done as he was told, Manny

left him and walked over to Raul. He took the older man by the arm and turned him around, so that the object of his rage was behind him and at least temporarily out of sight.

Stella walked behind the men as Manny led Raul over to his cruiser, took the plunger and pool stick out of his hands, and stuck them in his trunk.

"Collecting evidence, Sheriff?" Raul asked, a slight grin on his deeply lined, sun-damaged face.

"Not unless ol' Billy Ray croaks from those injuries," Manny told him. "I don't reckon there's much hope of that. He's got enough meanness in him to keep him going."

"Those cuts weren't from those weapons anyhow. They were from a broken beer bottle. It's inside. Probably on the floor, if you think you'll need it for the murder trial."

"There won't be any murder trial, Raul. He's not gonna kick any buckets, and I wouldn't waste my time and the court's charging you, even if he did. There's not a jury in this county who'd convict you of doing what any other man would do under the same circumstances."

Raul sighed and his shoulder sagged. He leaned back on the cruiser's fender, as though suddenly too tired to stand on his own.

Stella felt for him. Other than when he'd lost Maria, this had to be one of the worst days of an otherwise difficult life.

"Thank you, Sheriff," he said. "I appreciate it. More than you can imagine."

"You're welcome. But that said, Mr. Ortez, you're done now. Don't you even raise your hand, a pool cue, or a toilet plunger to another person in this town. Let alone a broken beer bottle."

"Oh, I didn't go after him with that. He was the one who broke it and tried to use it on me. I took it away from him."

"And cut him with it."

"He ran into it! I swear."

Manny glanced toward the other cruiser, where his deputy was trying, single-handedly, to get Billy Ray into the back seat. "Ran into it several times, I see."

Raul smirked. "He did. Billy Ray's always been the determined sort. Determined to repeat his mistakes, that is."

"True," Stella said under her breath. "He's a fool, and you know the old saying, 'A fool's born ever' minute and ever' darned one of 'em lives.' "

She stepped over to Raul and put her hand on his shoulder. "You've had a busy day, sir," she told him. "You must be worn to a frazzle."

"Now that I stop to think about it, I am, Mrs. Reid. But I'm not done yet. I gotta get to the hospital and see how my daughter's doing."

"We saw her," Manny told him, "and I'd say she's going to be all right. Of course, you want to see her for yourself."

"I do, Sheriff. I truly do."

"Your girl was far more worried about you than she was herself," Stella said. "Afraid you'd get the awful news and, well, take it bad."

For a second, Raul looked a bit sheepish. He stole a glance over at Billy Ray, whom Mervin had just managed to get into the vehicle. Merv was studying the blood on his uniform and scowling.

"I guess I did . . . take it bad, that is," Raul said. "I'm sorry, Sheriff. I wasn't thinking. If I'd been thinking straight, I'd have gone to the hospital first, taken care of my girl, and then asked you to take care of that sonuvabitch that hurt her."

To Stella he added, "Sorry, Mrs. Reid, but I picked the best of a bunch of hard words I could've used there."

"I know you did, Mr. Ortez. No offense taken. That 'un's a lot better than the one I would've picked out."

Raul looked up at Manny, his eyes sad, more like a defeated

man than the one who had just beaten up the town bully. "Can I go now, Sheriff? Please. I've got to get to my girl. I know she's wondering where I've been, and I'm not too proud of it."

Manny gave him an encouraging pat on the back and said, "I'll do you one better than that, Mr. Ortez. Get in the back of my vehicle. Miss Stella and I, we'll take you to her."

Chapter 6

Stella had never liked hospitals. Of course, she was more than grateful for the folks who worked in them. She considered them saints with sacred callings and divine strength that enabled them to do the backbreaking work and perform the heartbreaking tasks their various jobs entailed.

Those were things she was quite sure she couldn't have done herself.

Like police officers, firefighters, soldiers, and teachers, health-care workers did society's heavy lifting. Usually, they did so for little money, praise, or even appreciation.

Stella sincerely hoped there would be a special place inside the Pearly Gates for the likes of them. As far as she was concerned, they sure deserved it, after spending most of their waking hours inside buildings with drab, pale blue walls, worn linoleum floors, and the smell of disinfectant that did little to compete with the less pleasant odors it fought to disguise.

To be sure, hospitals were necessary and precious babies entered the world inside their walls. So, they weren't all bad. But every time Stella walked through the automated, sliding doors of one, she was thinking how glad she'd be to pass through those doors again—on her way out.

Though she did admit, at least to herself, that this particular trip inside this place of sadness, misery, hope, and healing was better than most, simply because she had Manny Gilford walking beside her.

Manny had a way about him that set her mind at ease. It didn't seem likely that anything too terrible would happen when he was around. He just wouldn't let it.

Of course, she knew no human being possessed such powers. But even if something awful did occur, she believed deep in her soul that Sheriff Gilford would make it better somehow.

As though reading her mind, he placed his hand on her arm and pulled her a bit closer to him. "Are you hungry, Stella?" he asked. "I don't think you'd taken more than two bites of that hamburger before we got called away."

She thought it over for a moment, then said, "Not really. Can't say I got much of an appetite at the moment. You?"

"Naw. But I could sure use a coffee—one big enough to go swimming in. It's going to be a long night."

"Now you're talkin'." She glanced toward the cafeteria and noticed a phone booth to the right, over near the restrooms. "But first, if you don't mind, I wanna call home and make sure those little ruffians of mine haven't tied Elsie to a chair with her own hose, like they did the last time she sat 'em."

"They did?"

She laughed. "She gave them permission, thinkin' they'd be good about untyin' her once they'd had their fun."

"They did though. Eventually, right?"

"Once they'd polished off ever' crumb of the coconut cake she'd brought 'em."

Chuckling, he said, "Now that sounds like your brood, and having tasted Elsie's coconut cake, I can't blame them one bit." He released her arm, fished a quarter out of his pocket, gave it to her, then nudged her toward the phone booth. "You go call her and make sure she's still in once piece. I'll go get the coffees. Extra cream, one sugar, right?"

"You know me too well, Sheriff."

"Not as well as I'd like to."

He'd said it softly, under his breath, but she'd heard him.

Feeling her cheeks grow hot, she quickly turned her back on him and rushed to the booth.

Lord've mercy, she thought. *I swear, with his deep voice, that man could read a grocery list and make it sound sexy as Saturday night sin.*

She could have sworn she heard him laughing as she ducked into the booth and he went into the cafeteria.

When she dropped the quarter into the phone, she tried to ignore the fact that her hand was shaking.

Long night already, she told herself, *and it ain't even seven o'clock yet.*

Elsie picked up the phone at Stella's house before the second ring.

It's too early for her to have the young'uns in bed, Stella thought. *She ain't worried about me wakin' 'em up. She's heard the news and wants to hear more. That's why she pounced on that phone like a barnyard cat on a big, lazy rat.*

"I was hopin' you'd call!" Elsie exclaimed, sounding positively breathless with excitement. "Flo came by here, askin' all sorts of questions about the goings-on in town, and I had nothin' to tell her! Sounds like all tarnation's done broke loose!"

"There was trouble at the old service station and the pool hall," Stella said, glad that the telephone booth was the old-fashioned sort that had a seat in it. She groaned as she sat down on it. All of a sudden, she realized she was quite tired. Drama of the sort they'd experienced this evening took a lot out of a person.

Manny couldn't show up quite fast enough with that coffee to suit her.

"I heard Miss Yolanda got . . . oh . . . I hate to even say it, but—"

"Whoever told you, they probably exaggerated it."

"'Twas Flo."

"Then you know it was. She's got many good qualities, that Flo, but stickin' to the facts of a story ain't one of 'em."

"She does embroider the truth if she thinks it ain't juicy enough on its own," Elsie admitted.

Stella heard Elsie pause in her interrogation long enough to sit down. She could just imagine her friend sinking into her old, but comfortable, avocado-green recliner and taking a breather.

Like Stella, Elsie's fiftieth birthday had come and gone, and they were both feeling it.

Plus, Elsie's job was a tough one—the chief cook for Judge Patterson at his grand plantation just outside of town.

Many years ago, Elsie's ancestors had worked that plantation as slaves, picking cotton and performing other miserable, soul-and-body-crippling labor. But, thankfully, times had changed, and Elsie had worked her way up from washing dishes to head of the judge's kitchen. Everyone who was anybody in the area had tasted Elsie Dingle's cooking, and no one disputed her reputation as the finest chef in the county.

In spite of her illustrious career, Elsie had never married. As a woman with an independent spirit, she didn't mourn the fact that she had no husband. But she did grieve the fact that she had no children.

So, Stella was blessed with a best friend who was eager, almost desperate, to babysit for her, for free, any time of the day or night. And the children adored the tiny woman with her coffee-colored skin, silver halo of hair, and dark eyes that sparkled with humor. They loved her warm hugs that set the huggee's world right in an instant . . . almost as much as they loved her cakes and pies.

"Tell me all about it," Stella heard her say with a tired sigh. "The kids are all bathed, they're gettin' into their pajamas, and I'm in your chair. I wanna hear it all."

Stella glanced toward the cafeteria and saw through the glass partition that Manny was paying for the coffee. "I'm sorry, Elsie. I really am. A full rundown's the least I owe you for babysittin' for me all evenin', but—"

"Aw, that's nothin', and you know it. I'd rather be here any-time than sittin' on my fanny at home, watchin' television. Are you still in the midst of it? You and the sheriff workin' it all out?"

"He is. I'm just taggin' along for the ride. I just called to make sure everybody and everything there's okay."

"We're good. Little Alma complained of a tummy ache, but I chalk that up to her chowin' down a piece o' cake that was bigger than her. I gave her a spoonful of bakin' soda in warm water, and a few minutes later, she had herself a good burp. So I reckon she'll be feelin' better soon."

"Thank you, sugar. That's what I'd have done, too."

She saw Manny coming toward her, a cup in each hand and a smile on his face that she was pretty sure was meant for her.

"I gotta go now. I can't hold the sheriff up. Do you mind if I'm out a bit longer?"

"Not a'tall. You know that. How's about I just figure on spendin' the night?"

"Sure. Crawl into my bed and zonk on out."

"I'll be fine here on the couch. It's more comfortable than my own bed, and I got one of your quilts here to cover up with."

"Bless you, Elsie."

"You too, darlin'."

As Stella stepped out of the booth, Manny placed a large foam cup of coffee into her hand. She curled her fingers around it, gratefully absorbing its comforting warmth.

"Thank you, Sheriff," she said, giving him a playful grin. "I owe ya one."

"Just give me a piece of Elsie's cake tomorrow. The one she brought over for your grandkids."

"Sorry. You're outta luck. I hear tell Alma ate nearly all of it herself and has the tummy ache to prove it."

They both took long drinks from the cups, closing their eyes and savoring both the flavor and the fortification the beverage gave them.

"That ain't half bad . . . for hospital coffee," Stella pronounced.

"Not as good as the donut shop's, but a heck of a lot better than what you get at a service station," was Manny's review.

"Yolanda's is pretty good, but that stuff they serve at Flo's garage, I think they make that fresh ever' mornin'. Ever' Wednesday mornin', that is."

In a matter of seconds, Manny's was empty. As he tossed the cup into a nearby trash can, he said, "You take your time with yours, but I've gotta check on Billy Ray. I'm not comfortable leaving him with Merv."

"You afraid he'll lose him?"

"Lose him, accidently shoot him, take him to the school prom . . . you never know with Mervin."

Stella grinned. "That boy's 'bout as useful as a screen door in a submarine."

"As effective as a fart in a tornado."

"You just gotta overlook the likes of him. He ain't got no home trainin'."

"More dollars than sense, and he's flat broke."

After looking for Billy Ray in the emergency room, they located him in a space only slightly larger than a closet that the nurse at the desk had referred to as "the suture room."

The room was earning its name, as Billy Ray sat in a chair, grimacing and moaning as he had the twelfth stitch put into his arm. Unfortunately for him, it would take several more before the wound was closed.

Stella couldn't help noticing how salty Billy Ray's language was as he insulted the young nurse practitioner who was inserting his stitches.

He wasn't using any words that she hadn't heard before. But in a town where many people carried handguns on their persons at all time, such insults weren't uttered very often. For obvious reasons.

It was frequently observed, "A well-armed community is a courteous one."

Stella shook her head, wondering at the wisdom of Billy Ray's decision to verbally abuse his nurse.

Surely, there was some sort of life rule about not talking nasty to someone who was poking a sharp needle in and out of your flesh at that moment.

"Where'd you learn how to sew, girl? Your damned Home Ec class?" he shouted at her, after flinching at the precisely wrong moment and causing her to stick him in a nearby area that hadn't been anesthetized. "You poke me one more time like that and I'm gonna—"

"You won't do anything, Sonner, but sit there and shut up," Manny told him, walking up behind him, putting his big hands on Billy Ray's shoulders, and pressing down hard.

To the nurse, Manny said, "You're doing a good job there, Miss. Please continue and pay Mr. Sonner here no mind. He won't hurt you. Not in a well-lit room with witnesses around. Of course, if you're alone in the dark behind a garage . . ."

Stella saw Manny's hands squeeze Billy Ray's shoulders, probably tightly, she decided, because he flinched.

"I done told you, I didn't do that!" Billy Ray said, trying to whip around to face his accuser and getting stuck again in the process.

Manny's hands gripped him even harder, bearing down on him, forcing him to stay seated and still.

"I didn't!" Billy Ray insisted. "It was Earle that messed her up. Me and Deacon caught him foolin' around with her back there behind the station, and we told him to bring it to a screechin' halt, then and there, and he did. We saved her!"

"Sure you did, Billy Ray," Stella said, unable to resist jumping in. "You're one righteous crime-fightin' caped crusader and a half. That's you! Slayin' dragons and rescuin' fair damsels from fire-breathin' dragons like Earle Campbell."

"Are you intending to bribe ol' Earle like you did before?" Manny asked. "Reckon he'll believe the 'I'll give you a thousand dollars if you'll take my rap for me, Earle' story again?"

"Somethin' tells me he won't do another stretch for you," Stella told him. "You could've at least picked him up from the prison gate when they let him out. I've heard he's still pretty sore at you for that."

At that moment, Stella heard a movement behind her. She turned to see that yet another person was attempting to squeeze into the tiny room.

"Well, good evening, Deputy Jarvis," Manny drawled, his

tone heavy with sarcasm. "Fancy meeting you here. You know, *here* . . . in the same place as your *prisoner*."

Stella thought, *That boy looks as nervous as a fly in a glue pot*, and she couldn't blame him. Manny was glaring at him in a way that would have made anyone uneasy.

Manny was a nice guy, but he had his forty-five caliber "Sheriff glare" down pat.

"I had to go . . . um . . . I needed a bathroom break, Sheriff," he said. "I figured he was okay here for a minute while I ran down the hall to—"

Other than a few more seconds added on to the end of the glare, Manny said nothing. Instead, he turned to the nurse, who had just snipped the last thread and said, "If you please, Miss, would you get this patient a hospital gown to wear?"

"A hospital gown!?" Billy yelled, outraged at the very idea. "I ain't wearin' one of those things. They've got the whole back outta 'em!"

She smiled up at Manny sweetly. "Of course, Sheriff. Right away."

"And Nurse, Mr. Sonner here's not half as big a guy as he thinks he is. The gown you get him doesn't need to be a particularly large one, if you catch my drift."

"I understand. Right away, Sheriff."

She hurried out the door, the look on her face that of a woman with a mission.

"But I'm all done here now!" Billy Ray protested. "They told me I could go as soon as I got stitched up."

"You can," Manny told him. "As a matter of fact, I insist upon it. You're going to be enjoying the hospitality of the fine city of McGill, Georgia. We have a suite all prepared for you. I think you'll find the accommodations most comfortable."

Manny paused, thought a bit, then added, "Well, not exactly comfortable, but newly redecorated. We recently repainted the bars. A nice, neutral, dove gray. It's all the rage in the home décor magazines these days."

"But why're you takin' my clothes?" Billy Ray demanded.

"Because without even trying, I see evidence all over you. There's long black hair there on your shirt, dirty engine oil and mud on your knees—like back there on the ground behind the garage."

Billy Ray swallowed. Hard. He looked like he might be sick at any moment.

"Don't fret so," Manny told him. "You'll be getting a nice new orange outfit, and you can wear it for a good many years."

"I keep tellin' you, I didn't do nothin' to—"

"Of course you didn't."

Stella couldn't recall ever hearing Manny's voice sound so ominous as when he added, "How much do you want to bet that when we get you undressed, there'll be some fresh scratches on you? Your neck, your chest. Let's just say, Yolanda doesn't strike me as a young lady who'd quietly allow that sort of savagery done to her without fighting back. Hard."

Turning to his deputy, Manny said, "Mervin, would you please make yourself useful. Go to my cruiser, look in the trunk, and get my camera and several large evidence bags. We'll be taking *all* of Mr. Sonner's clothing with us, including his white suspenders and his boots with those lovely white laces."

"My boots?!" Billy Ray was beside himself with rage. "You're gonna make me walk into the police station in my bare feet and sportin' a damned hospital gown?"

Manny smiled. It was a benevolent smile that would have terrified anyone who looked into his eyes, which were cold as a January morning on a north Georgia mountain slope.

"Oh, and Deputy," Manny continued, "there in my trunk, next to the toolbox you'll find a pair of flip-flops. As I recall, they're blue. They'll match Mr. Sonner's gown. We want him looking fashionable for the town paper reporter."

"What?" Billy Ray's eyes bugged. "The paper's gonna be there for my perp walk? How're they gonna know you're bringin' me in?"

"Because I'm going to call and tell them. With any luck, Mr. Sonner, you'll make tomorrow's front page."

Chapter 7

Once Stella and Manny had locked Billy Ray's bagged clothing into the cruiser's trunk, and Manny had assisted his deputy in putting the prisoner into the rear seat of Merv's patrol car, they headed back into the hospital. Both were eager to see how Yolanda was faring and to offer emotional support to Raul.

Stella couldn't help giggling as she and Manny reentered the building and made their way to the elevator door.

"If I live another fifty years," she told him, "I'm gonna laugh when I think of Billy Ray tryin' to keep that hospital gown of his from flappin' open and showin' the world his 'better' side."

"Yeah, I've gotta get me one of those gowns." He pushed the elevator button, and the door opened instantly. "I hear it's what the well-dressed gentleman is wearing to formal events this season."

"Can't forget the flip-flops and the sour puss," she added as they stepped inside, and the doors closed behind them.

"Hey, accessories make the outfit."

They laughed and the warm, companionable sound filled the small space.

Once again, Stella felt the closeness of him, as she did when sitting in a car with him or when he stood near her.

It was a comforting feeling that gave her an inexplicable sense of peace. One she had never felt before.

Not even with her beloved Arthur.

"Billy Ray Sonner's seen better days," she told Manny, in an effort to divert her own thoughts, as the elevator began its short journey to the second floor, where Yolanda was being attended.

"When you were talking to Yolanda back there behind the garage, I found his knife on the ground, not even five feet from her," Manny said. "I know it's his; I've seen it before. One of those counterfeit German World War Two knockoffs. It'll have her hair and blood on it, and with any luck, his fingerprints. I've got his clothes that also have her hair and blood all over them."

Stella looked down at the cuff of her white blouse—her best Sunday morning church shirt—at the red smears she'd collected when touching the wounded girl. There was more where that came from on the front of the blouse.

Manny's uniform shirt had similar stains.

"I'm sure there will be blood on his clothes," she said. "If we got some on us just helping her, think how much he got on him."

"Exactly. Plus, this time Deacon will testify against him, and I doubt Earle's going to be stupid enough to serve more time for him."

"Considerin' how richly rewarded he was for his former sacrifice."

"That's going to come back to haunt our boy, you wait and see."

The elevator door slid open with a groan, and they stepped out.

"I hope she's okay," Stella said as they hurried down the hall toward room 207, where the nurse practitioner had directed them.

"That head wound bled badly—as head wounds do," he observed, "but she's young and very healthy. It should heal up pretty quick."

"She'll never feel really safe again though," Stella said. "The body heals a lot faster than a wounded spirit."

"Unfortunately, that's true. I'll try to get her somebody to talk to about it. A counselor or maybe Connie O'Reilly. She's a smart, sweet woman. Helped out before in these cases."

Stella nodded, thinking of the kindhearted pastor's wife, who had herself suffered abuse, sexual and otherwise, in her youth. While performing her many duties as a minister's wife, Connie O'Reilly had also been a source of understanding and support to victims of violence and abuse from all around the county.

If anyone can help Yolanda, it would be Miss Connie, Stella told herself as they approached the door of the young woman's room and found it closed.

Manny gave it a gentle rapping. Far different, Stella observed, from his usual building-rattling cop-style pounding.

It took a while before they heard someone on the other side unlocking it. When it opened, Stella wasn't surprised to see Raul on the other side.

If her daughter had been attacked by someone or somebodies who were members of a notoriously ill-behaved gang, she would have kept her child behind a locked door, too. At least until every guilty party was identified and behind bars.

Raul seemed pleased to see them. As pleased as anyone could be who had suffered what he had in the past few hours.

"Sheriff. Mrs. Reid. Do come in."

He opened the door and stepped back, allowing them to enter.

Immediately, Stella saw Yolanda, lying on the bed, wrapped in white sheets and blankets. Her eyes were closed, and her breathing was deep and even.

"Is she asleep?" Stella whispered to Raul.

He nodded. "Just nodded off a few minutes ago. I figure she can use the rest."

"Lots of it," Manny added. "I'm sure you'll see to that."

"I will." Raul sighed, walked over to his child's bed, and gazed down at her with a look of love and great concern. "Doc Hynson saw to it that she was well taken care of. Her head's all sewed up now, and they gave her something to calm her down and something else for the pain."

Stella moved closer and peered down at the girl's scalp. Instead of the ugly, bleeding gash, there was a neat line of stitches.

"The doctor went to see if he could find out anything else from the emergency room folks," Raul continued. "They took care of her when she first got here. They said they'd have the results of the tests and head scans and all that stuff pretty soon. Then we'll know more."

"She's in good hands here," Stella told him. "They know what they're doin', and I don't have to tell you how loved your girl is in this town. If anybody in this hospital's gonna get top-notch treatment, it'll be your Yolanda."

Raul's eyes grew moist and shiny with tears. He started to reply, but he choked on the answer and simply nodded.

"Also," Manny said, "you'll probably be glad to know that those cuts Billy Ray got, hurling himself repeatedly against that broken beer bottle you were holding, are all stitched up, too. He's not gonna die."

"Except maybe of mortification," Stella mumbled.

Looking confused, Raul said, "What?"

"Be sure to look at your newspaper tomorrow morning," Manny told him. "You might even want to buy an extra copy or two for souvenirs."

They heard the door open, and all three spun around to see who had entered. They were ready to do battle if necessary.

But it was Dr. Hynson, and he was wearing a smile on his face and a sparkle in his eyes.

"She's going to be okay," he said, setting their minds at ease right away. "They said she lost a lot of blood, but that transfusion they gave her was enough to top her off."

"I'm grateful," Raul said. "I heard folks were lining up, volunteering to give her blood. Way more than they needed, that is."

"That's true," Dr. Hynson said. "People around here are like that. Especially for somebody as special as Yolanda."

"Thank you, sir," Raul said, wiping his knuckles across his eyes.

"The other good news," continued the doctor, "is that the brain scan was all clear. If she's doing this well by tomorrow, they might let her go home."

"Oh, that's wonderful." Raul's entire body seemed to sag with relief. "I'm so grateful."

Stella was happy for him. Getting his daughter back home, safe and sound, had to be what he was living for at the moment.

"It's a much better outcome than we were fearing," Dr. Hynson said. "I'm happy for you, Mr. Ortez, and for her." He nodded toward the sleeping Yolanda.

"Yes, thank heaven," Stella said.

"Thank heaven for Dolly Browning," Manny added.

"Who?" Raul looked confused. "You mean, the old woman who lives in that big haunted house with all those cats?"

Manny smiled. "That very lady." He lowered his voice. "It's important that you keep this to yourselves, but Miss Browning was the one who interrupted the attack. She stopped by the station to get her tires aired up and heard what was happening. Seems, when they realized someone else had arrived, they took off running."

"They were afraid of Dolly Browning?" Dr. Hynson asked.

"What is she, barely five feet tall? She's so skinny she'd have to run around in a rainstorm to get wet."

"I don't think they actually saw who it was," Manny told him. "That's why I want you to keep this to yourselves. I'm sure some folks know it was her, because there were plenty of eavesdroppers there in the Igloo when she reported it to me. But the fewer people who know that, the better. Billy Ray may be in custody, but I'm still not sure what part Deacon Murray and Earle Campbell might have played in it. They might think she saw more than she did and feel she's a threat."

"I won't say a word, Sheriff," Raul promised solemnly. "I wouldn't want the person who saved my daughter's life to get hurt because she helped her in her time of need."

"I won't breathe a word of it to anybody either," Dr. Hynson agreed. "Miss Browning's a hero and needs all the protection we can give her. We certainly don't want her punished for her good deed."

Manny nodded. "I'll make sure she's fully informed of the situation and provided for."

"You're spread pretty thin, Sheriff Gilford," the doctor said. "It's a bad time for you to have something as serious as this happening, and you missing one of your deputies."

"Unfortunately," Stella murmured, "it's the one who actually *is* sharper than a bowlin' ball."

Manny glanced at his watch. Stella wasn't wearing hers, but she assumed it must be close to eight o'clock.

"We should get going," he told Stella. "I want to go interview Miss Browning. Most older folks go to bed earlier than the rest of us. I don't want to disturb her once she's turned in."

Stella hesitated. She wasn't ready to say good-bye to Manny, but Raul looked exhausted. "Mr. Ortez," she said, "would you like to go home and get a few hours of sleep? I'd be honored to sit here by your girl. I could call you if she wakes up and asks for you."

Instantly, Raul shook his head. "No. I wasn't there for her earlier when she needed me. I'm going to be here for her tonight. And tomorrow night. And for as long as it takes for her to get over this. But I do thank you, Mrs. Reid. You're a nice lady, always been kind to me and mine. My Maria thought the world of you."

"As I did her, sir. Our church choir ain't been the same without her pretty voice. She could always hit them high notes the rest of us couldn't knock off the ceilin' with a long broom handle."

He smiled. "That was Maria all right. I miss her singing. She'd even sing when she was milking a cow. The cows enjoyed it, too." He reached over and patted his girl's hand. "Yolanda sings just as high and sweet as her mother. About lifts our roof off when she gets going."

"I didn't know that. I'll have to talk to Mrs. O'Reilly about inviting her to join the church choir."

"Then maybe some good can come out of this after all," Raul said.

The exchange between them was pleasant but brief.

A second later, the hospital room door flew open and an excited and distressed Mervin Jervis burst inside.

He was sweating profusely.

Of course, Stella thought. *He just wouldn't be Mervin with a dry brow and no sweat stains on his uniform shirt's armholes.*

Manny sized up the situation in seconds. "Deputy Jervis, where the hell is your prisoner?!"

"I don't know, sir!"

"Do *not* tell me that, Deputy!"

"Oh. Okay."

In two long strides, Manny was across the room and towering over the squirming deputy, glaring down at him with a look that could have melted cold steel. "Where is Sonner?"

Mervin looked confused. "But . . . but you just said not to tell—"

"He got away from you?"

"Yes, sir."

"He was in your custody a whole ten minutes, and you allowed him to escape?"

"No, sir, I did not! All I 'allowed' him to do was take a piss."

Jervis glanced over at Stella. "Beggin' your pardon, Mrs. Reid, for the bad word."

"A crude word here or there is the least of your problems, Deputy," she told him.

He turned back to Manny. "Billy Ray was sayin' he really, really needed to go bad. Was 'bustin' at the seams,' he said. I didn't want him to let it go there in my patrol car. So I pulled over to the side of the road there by the 'Welcome to McGill' sign and let him out, so's he could"—he shot a look at Stella—"so he could water a bush. That's all I allowed him to do! I swear! He took it upon hisself to hightail it into the bushes and disappear in them woods there."

"Did you uncuff your prisoner, Deputy?" Manny asked.

"Of course I did. He'd have piss-poor aim without use of his hands, now wuddin he?"

Manny stared at him for what seemed like months, then sighed and shook his head. "So, you're telling me that you removed the cuffs from a dangerous suspect. Then, you allowed a man in a hospital gown and a pair of flip-flops to outrun you. Is that what you're saying, Deputy?"

"No, sir. He shed them flip-flops right away. I found 'em in the woods. First one, then the other."

Mervin dropped his remorseful look, lifted his chin a notch, and grinned broadly. "I collected them flip-flops for evidence, Sheriff. Put 'em in brown bags, sealed, and signed them, and ever'thing. Them and a piece of that blue nightgown he was wearing that I found hangin' from a sticker bush. I couldn't find nothin' else though. Certainly not him. Them woods at night . . . you know they're darker than the inside of a cow."

"Deputy Jervis . . ."

"Yes, sir?"

"Get out of my sight before I inflict major harm upon your sorry ass."

"Yes, sir."

Mervin didn't wait to be told again. In only two seconds, his presence in the room was a distant memory. Except for the ever-present smell of his sweat.

That's gotta be an all-time personal record for Deputy Merv, Stella thought, unable to recall ever seeing him move so quickly from one place to another. Mervin Jervis was known as more of a sauntering kind of guy than a sprinter.

Finally, Manny seemed to collect himself and refocus. He looked from Raul to Dr. Hynson, to Stella, and said, "Have any one of you ever considered a career in law enforcement? I hear there's going to be an opening for a deputy here in McGill very soon. As you just witnessed, the job qualifications are a bar that's set very low."

The doctor and Stella chuckled, but Raul had more serious problems on his mind.

"So, the man who attacked my daughter is out there, running around loose," he said.

Manny nodded. "I'm afraid that's true. But if you're concerned for her safety, I assure you that I'll gladly stay right here with the two of you for the rest of the night."

"If you're in here, guarding us, who's going to catch that devil, who's now on the run?" Raul asked, stating the obvious.

"I'll stand guard for your daughter," Dr. Hynson said. "Sheriff, you go catch Sonner. I'll spend the night with you, Raul, right here, keeping an eye on Yolanda and the door."

"A closed door isn't a lot of protection, Doc," Manny said.

Dr. Hynson gave him a grim smile and opened his jacket, revealing a shoulder holster and a SIG Sauer. "I've got my new birthday present right here with me, and I know how to use it."

"I know you do," Manny said. "I've seen you at the shooting range."

"Then you know we'll be fine," the doctor assured him. "You go do your duty, and I'll take care of my special patient . . . and her father, who's already proved what he can do with a toilet plunger."

Manny nodded, satisfied. "I'll inform the hospital security staff of the situation, and I'll let you know the minute I've got him in custody."

"Please do," Raul said, looking down at his daughter. "When I got to the hospital and saw her, I told her you'd already caught the guy who hurt her. When she wakes up, the last thing I want to tell her is that he's still out there."

"I understand, Mr. Ortez. I'll get him. Please try not to worry about Billy Ray. He's my problem. You just take care of your girl there and trust me to do my job."

"I do trust you, Sheriff," Raul said. "That guy you've got working for you . . . ?"

"I understand." Manny turned to Stella and took her arm. "Let's go," he said. "We've got a lot to do before that coffee wears off."

Chapter 8

While Stella's best friend, Elsie, was 100 percent convinced that the Earth was practically chockablock with restless spirits who hadn't yet found their way to their eternal resting places, Stella wasn't convinced.

She liked to think that Art dropped by sometimes, especially at night, when she was lying there alone in bed, missing him, to whisper, "Good night, Honey Bunny. Sweet dreams."

But she wasn't completely sure it was an actual visitation she was experiencing, or just a case of strong "wishful thinking" on her part. Grief was a powerful emotion, manifesting itself in countless ways.

However, Stella had decided long ago that, if McGill harbored any friendly ghosts or angry "haints" as Elsie called the nasty ones, they lived in Judge Patterson's antebellum mansion or Miss Dolly Browning's house—a once-beautiful but now sadly run-down Victorian-era mansion on a hill overlooking the cemetery.

No one in town was old enough to remember when the Queen Anne home had been lovely. No doubt, at one time, the robin's-egg-blue paint had been fresh, not faded and peeling. Back then, every piece of the ornate gingerbread that gave the home a lacy, feminine appearance would have been in place, not hanging loose or lying, rotting, on the ground around it.

The steeply pitched, complex roof with its gables and turrets would have been missing no tiles or ornamental spindles, and the stained-glass windows would have had no broken panes.

After the original owner died in the 1930s, the old mansion sat empty for more than a decade, until one summer day in 1945. McGillians now in their eighties and nineties claimed that a most attractive and well-dressed young woman named Dolly Browning had suddenly stepped off a bus on Main Street, carrying nothing more than an oversized alligator suitcase.

Some claimed the exotic piece of luggage was stuffed with money. Their theories were given more credence when Dolly purchased the decrepit house by the graveyard and paid cash for it.

Over the years, Dolly had enjoyed a higher standard of living than her neighbors without any visible means of supporting that lifestyle.

But even the nosiest of McGillians could corral their curiosity when it was to their advantage to do so. The fact that Miss Dolly Browning frequently donated sizable sums to the town's many charity drives and causes kept any meaningful inquiries in check.

In recent years, as her paranoia and claims of being stalked and tormented by her "enemies" had increased, folks had chalked her complaints up to "ol' timers' dementia" and steered clear of her whenever possible.

Over the past forty years, Dolly Browning had gone from being known as "the pretty mystery lady with the alligator suitcase full of money" to being called "that crazy lady in the haunted house with all the cats."

"I'm going to warn you," Manny said as he pulled the cruiser in front of the house and turned off the engine. "This house is a mess and it stinks to high heaven. She's got more cats than you've ever seen in one place, and she doesn't feel the need to even provide them with litter boxes, let alone clean ones."

"I know," Stella said. "It's sad. When she caught colds or that crick in her back acted up, Elsie and I brought her some frozen casseroles, to tie her over till she was up to shopping and cooking again. Pies and cakes, too. Let's just say, we caught wind of it on more than one occasion."

"It *is* sad," Manny said, keeping his voice low as they walked up the broken walkway to the house. "I've called Adult Protective Services about her a time or two, but they claim there isn't anything they can do. Except for the cats and that business of thinking somebody's after her, she's as bright as she ever was and able to take care of herself."

"Nobody chooses to live in a giant, dirty litter box if they're all there mentally," Stella argued. "If she wasn't so well off, I expect some government agency would've stepped in a long time ago and hauled her outta there, kickin' and screamin' if necessary."

Manny gave a wry chuckle. "Yes, I reckon that's true. If you live with a zillion cats who aren't housebroken, and you're poor, then you're considered 'nuts.' But if you're rich, you're just 'eccentric,' and they leave you alone."

"Do you really think she's in danger here with Billy Ray on the loose?" she asked as they got out of the car and walked up the weed-choked sidewalk to the house.

"No. I don't. Billy's probably already hightailed it out of here. I figure he hooked up with Deacon as quick as he could, got some clothes and transportation, and is on the run. He knew I've got a tight case against him. He'd be stupid to hang around."

"Well, he *is* Billy Ray Sonner, and stupid is as stupid does."

"True, but even a mosquito's smart enough to move out of the way if he's about to get swatted." Manny knocked on the door, being careful to use his fist only on the wood and not on the cracked beveled glass oval in the center of the door. "I just want her to know what's going on, in case she wants to go stay in a motel out of town or whatever."

A moment later, they heard a shuffling of feet and the deep barking of a dog.

"That's gotta be Valentine," Stella said. "I forgot about him."

"How could you forget Valentine?" Manny said. "Biggest dog I ever saw in my life. He's the other reason I'm not all that worried about her safety."

The door opened a crack, and an enormous black muzzle pushed through the opening, followed by an equally impressive chestnut head.

Stella had been around dogs her entire life and, while she had respect for them, she had no fear of them. But she was very curious to see the rest of this particular canine.

"I didn't get a clear look at Mr. Valentine in all his glory before," she told Manny. "She always knew we were coming and put him away in the bedroom."

"Valentine, no!" they heard Dolly shout. "Down! Sit!"

To Stella's surprise, when the door was fully opened, she saw the dog, who was as tall as a Great Dane with the musculature of a mastiff and the face of a German shepherd sitting docilely at the elderly lady's feet.

He looked up at Dolly with large, soulful eyes filled with remorse when she said, "Bad dog! How many times have I told you not to stick your face out when I open the door? One of these days, you're going to give somebody a heart attack."

She waved a beckoning hand and stepped back so Stella and Manny could enter. "Come on in," she said. "Don't worry. He's all bark and no bite."

"That's a good thing," Stella said, astonished at the size of the animal—especially his mouth when he gave a big yawn. "'Cause he could open those jaws and swaller ya whole."

Dolly laid her hand on the dog's head, which was higher than her waist, and smiled at him affectionately. "Valentine's just a big puppy dog. Won't even chase a cat."

Stella and Manny looked around at the felines, who were everywhere. Like Valentine, they also seemed excited to be having visitors, as they darted in and out among the old furniture, boxes, and miscellaneous clutter, some peeking at them, others running around as though they had mousetraps attached to their tails.

"Are you sure you'd miss one if he decided to have it for lunch?" Manny asked.

His question was asked playfully, but the dark look that appeared instantly on Dolly's otherwise friendly face told Stella that the high number of kitties she housed was a topic best left undiscussed.

"Let's just say," she told Manny in a somber tone, "as long as you're nice to me, I can guarantee you that Valentine won't eat *you*."

"That's most reassuring," Manny said with a half chuckle.

Once they were standing in the entry hall, Manny held his hand out for the dog to sniff it. "I remember when you got this guy as a pup," he told Dolly. "I recall looking at his feet then and thinking he was going to be a big boy when he was grown. I had no idea *how* big though."

"I know! He surpassed my hopes for an impressive watchdog." She reached down and patted the massive head. "That's why I gave him a sweet name like Valentine. People are afraid enough of him already. I thought the name would help."

"I'm glad you've got him," Manny told her. "If I had my way, every lady who lives alone would have a Valentine in their house. It'd make my job much easier and I'd worry a lot less about them."

Dolly looked around at her house, the once elegant home that was now terribly cluttered with cardboard boxes, old magazines, books, and newspapers. "I wish he was better at catching those culprits who sneak in here and steal my stuff. If he can't hear them when they're taking it, he should be able to let me know when they're returning it."

Stella and Manny exchanged a quick, knowing look.

There it was again. Dolly's paranoia resurfacing.

Not for the first time, Stella wished Dolly would make an appointment with Dr. Hynson about her anxiety issues. He might be able to prescribe a pill that would calm her concerns or arrange some sort of counselling for her.

Stella hated to see a kindhearted person like Miss Browning suffering so.

"Would you like to sit down?" Dolly asked, leading them into what had once been the house's grand parlor, but was now little more than a crowded junk room with a few chairs and a sofa.

Stella saw that each piece of furniture was currently occupied by at least five cats. As in the entry hall, they were everywhere. In that small room alone, there were at least twenty.

The stench of feline urine and worse permeated the atmosphere. Stella tried to breathe shallowly, knowing she would be taking a bath, washing her hair, and laundering her clothing the moment she got home.

"We're not going to stay long, Miss Browning," Manny said, rescuing them from having to clear away the kitties and sit on surfaces covered with cat hair and heaven only knew what else. "I just want to fill you in on a couple of things before I call it a night."

"You mean, like how you arrested Billy Ray Sonner and that knucklehead you call a deputy let him go?"

Manny cleared his throat. "I see you're already informed."

"I went to the grocery store for some food for my friends here." She waved a hand, indicating the cats. "Violet told me all about it."

"I reckon she did," Stella said. "Violet always has the best gossip, and she ain't against sharin'."

"But what she didn't tell me," Dolly continued, "and what I most wanted to know, is how that young lady from the service station is doing. I've been so worried about her."

"Thanks to you, Miss Browning," Manny said, "she's doing much better than expected. Doc Hynson says she might even be able to go home tomorrow."

Dolly didn't appear as happy as Stella had expected her to be. In fact, she looked terribly concerned.

"But if that fellow who harmed her is still on the loose and if they release her, she might be in danger."

"Please don't worry," Manny told her. "I'll take measures to ensure her safety."

"I hope you do, Sheriff. Something has to be done about those boys. They're evil. We can't have that sort of wickedness here in our town. Don't allow it, Sheriff. Please! You have to do something!"

Stella watched, dismayed, as Dolly's mood deteriorated rapidly. One moment she was smiling, the next deeply upset, almost to the point of hysteria. She couldn't bear to see the elderly woman, who had been so generous and kind to so many in their town, suffering the effects of dementia.

Dolly Browning was under attack, and her enemy, who seemed intent upon destroying all that she was and ever had been, was within her own brain.

Stella reached out and put her arms around Dolly, holding her tightly, as she did when she comforted her own grandangels.

It seemed like the most natural thing in the world. Stella's eldest, Savannah, was taller and larger overall than Dolly. The older woman felt like a child in her arms, a frightened little girl in desperate need of comfort.

But although Dolly melted into the embrace and accepted it fully for a moment, she quickly pushed Stella away and turned back to Manny, her face as angry as it had been friendly and then distraught only moments before.

"You have to catch that Billy Ray. Again. And make sure he doesn't get loose this time. Those other two fools who run around after him, they've got a chance at being human beings, but they never will be if they're following a monster like him. There's only three of them now, but if he's not caught and put away, there'll be more."

"I'm going to catch him, Dolly. Lawmen all over this county are looking for him right now. But for the moment, I need you to answer a couple of questions for me. You've already helped me so much, by letting me know Yolanda was hurt and needed assistance. Now I need to know a couple more things."

Stella could see that Dolly was fighting to regain her composure. Her breath was ragged, her face flushed, but she finally calmed herself enough to say, "Ask away, Sheriff. I'll do my best to answer you truthfully and fully. I want so much to help."

"I know you do." Manny gave her one of his most charming "Sheriff Gilford's got this" smiles. Then he said, "You heard it was Billy Ray I'm after. But before you heard folks say that, did you have any idea who it was that you overheard shouting and then running away back there behind the garage?"

"Of course I did!"

"Okay. Did you see them?"

"No."

"Did you recognize their voices?"

"Not particularly."

"What exactly did you hear when you went back there? Please think hard and don't leave anything out."

"I don't have to think hard, Sheriff. I'll remember what I heard, every bit of it for the rest of my life. Whether I want to or not."

"What was it, Dolly?" Stella asked. "What is it that'll haunt you for the rest of your days?"

"That girl crying, begging him to stop. I heard the other two men telling him, 'You're gonna get us all in trouble! Stop it now! Leave her be!' "

Stella shot a quick look at Manny. She was sure they were thinking the same thing: Dolly's account matched Earle's perfectly.

Manny nodded and asked, "Miss Dolly, did you hear any names mentioned?"

"No."

"Then, how did you know it was the Lone White Wolf Pack back there in the darkness?"

"Because I heard the things that Billy Ray was saying to that poor girl, the names he was calling her."

Manny hesitated, waiting for her to continue. When she didn't, he said, "I'm sorry to have to ask you this in mixed company, but could you tell me what it was he said?"

"No. I won't repeat those awful words, Sheriff," Dolly said. "I'm sure, if you give a second's thought, you'll think of some, and that will be them. They're the words men, awful men, use to describe women. Words meant to hurt and demean females and injure their spirits."

"Yes, ma'am," Manny said. "I understand. But I'm sorry to say that more than one man in this town is low enough to use those words, especially if he was in a fit of rage. Some even if they weren't. So, how did you know it was Billy Ray Sonner?"

"Because he used other ones, too. He called her horrible names that are only used for brown-skinned people. People who are from south of the United States border—or their ancestors were."

"Oh. Okay." Manny nodded. "I understand."

Dolly turned to Stella, her eyes moist with tears. Her voice was soft with compassion when she said, "I know about your mother. She was a full-blooded Cherokee. I'm sure that when you were growing up, you heard the terrible words she was called."

"Yes, and the things I was called myself for being her daughter," Stella replied, fighting back the feelings that surfaced so quickly at the mention of those times. "Of course I did. But I knew my mother was none of those. She was beautiful and strong, intelligent and kind. I was blessed to have her for a mother . . . even if it wasn't for long."

"Not everyone is as fortunate as you," Dolly said. "You know who she was and who you are, no matter what others say. Some people don't have that unshakable knowledge of who they are. They can be permanently scarred by what others say, how others define them."

"That's true," Stella said, recalling how Elsie had described the pain of hearing herself called cruel names, by being told she was "less than" because her skin was black and her ancestors from Africa. Dear, gentle Elsie was among those who bore permanent scars from her woundings.

"Billy Ray Sonner and his fool followers are the only ones I've ever heard say those words in this town," Dolly continued. "Nobody else here would call that beautiful young woman such ugly things just because she's a woman and not a white one."

"You're probably right," Manny said. "They're getting more and more bold about their meanness by the day. Though I can't prove it, I'm ninety-nine percent sure it was them who lit that cross on the Tuckers' yard last week."

"I wouldn't be surprised," Stella said. "I heard Billy Ray ranting the other day outside the post office about how remiss Franklin Tucker was in his duties as a father, lettin' his girl marry a white boy and her bein' black. 'Muddyin' up the pure white race' was how he put it. I told him he was a jackass for sayin' such nonsense, but I could tell it went in his left ear and flew outta his right. Not enough brain matter in there to even slow it down."

"See? It's growing! This sort of evil starts like a little spark, but it explodes into a forest fire before you know it!" Dolly said. She stepped closer to Manny, placed her hands on his chest, and looked up at him with pleading eyes. "Stop it, Sheriff, please. For the people of this town and their children. For the children yet to be born. Stop it—while you still can!"

Chapter 9

As Manny drove Stella home, there was very little conversation between the two. Dolly Browning's words, the frightened look in her eyes, and the alarm in her voice had shaken them both, more than either wanted to admit.

Exhausted, Stella was happy when Manny turned off the main highway and onto the humble dirt road that led to her little shack of a house.

It might be small, its porch sagging, its roof leaking during an especially heavy rainstorm, but it was home. Tonight, even more than usual, the sight of it brought a measure of peace to Stella's troubled heart.

She and Arthur had bought that house a dozen lifetimes ago, when they were young and newly married. They had thought it a mansion! They couldn't have been more excited if they'd been moving into the White House.

But time changed things.

A terrible tractor accident had taken Art, and another accident—thankfully, less tragic—had given her a houseful of grandchildren to raise on her own.

But the dirt road and the humble house remained the same, and sometimes, Stella really needed to feel that some things never changed.

"Glad to be back home?" Manny asked, as though reading her mind.

For as long as she'd known him, it seemed he could do that. She wasn't sure if it was because he knew her that well, or if it was just a gift he had. An ability that made him an excellent sheriff. He seemed to know what everyone was up to at any time.

She wondered if he would ever catch Billy Ray, or if the flea-bitten weasel was going to get away with what he'd done to Yolanda Ortez.

"I am glad to be back," she admitted. Then she thought perhaps she'd been rude, suggesting the date he'd planned for them was lacking somehow. So she added, "Not that I didn't have fun on our—"

He laughed. Long and hard. His deep voice filling the interior of the cruiser. "That's okay, darlin'," he said when he'd finally recovered himself. "You don't have to pretend you had a good time tonight. Overall, I'd say our first date was a dismal failure. I'll make it up to you. I promise."

"I don't expect you to make nothin' up to me," she told him. Sliding him a flirty, sideways grin, she added, "Though, if you feel strongly about it, you're welcome to try."

"I'll try and I'll succeed. You'll see."

Halfway up her driveway, he stopped the car and turned in his seat to face her. "There's a bit of business I want to take care of here and now. Before we get up there to the house with the prying eyes . . . and that's just Elsie's, not to mention all your grandkids."

Stella could feel her heart miss a few beats, then make up for it with double time.

A good-night kiss?

Of course, it had occurred to her that he might want one. Several times in the first half hour of their "date" she had weighed her own mixed feelings about the prospect, back and forth, without coming to a final decision.

But from the moment Dolly had charged through the door of the café and shared her awful news, such romantic notions had been forgotten, eclipsed by far more urgent matters.

As Manny leaned closer to her, many thoughts flooded her mind and emotions. He had kissed her once before, and the simple memory of it filled her with a longing so strong it was almost overpowering.

Manny knew how to kiss, she had decided that Christmas Day, there in her kitchen. Boy, did he ever know how!

She had enjoyed every second of it, and she had enjoyed it many times since, recalling every detail, every nuance of the experience.

But she also recalled the guilt she had felt afterward. As though she had betrayed her husband and even Manny's wife, Lucy, who had been her best friend.

She tensed, unable to decide whether to lift her face and offer her lips. But Manny made the decision for her. He gave her the quickest peck on her cheek, then the other cheek, and then a final, slightly longer one on her forehead.

"Thank you for the joy of your company tonight, Stella," he said. His voice and tone were tender and loving, as though they had just shared a great intimacy.

Brushing a wayward curl out of her eyes, he added, "In spite of all that occurred, I wouldn't have wanted to experience one moment of what happened this evening without you beside me. You were a great help and comfort to me through it all."

Stella didn't know what to say. So, she sat quietly, nodded her head, and cleared her throat.

Finally, she recovered herself and was able to croak out a simple, "Me too."

She was both relieved and disappointed when he settled back into his seat and continued to drive toward the house.

When they pulled up in front and stopped, she saw her lace curtains pull aside for a moment, then quickly fall back into place.

"Elsie," she said.

"You're going to have a lot of explaining to do."

"Not because I'm late," Stella said, thinking of how patient her friend was, how generous with her time when it came to free babysitting. "But she's going to want to hear every detail of everything that transpired. Down to the color of Billy Ray Sonner's underwear."

They looked at each other and laughed.

"I'd like to be a fly on the wall when you tell him that the last time you saw him, he wasn't wearing any," Manny said.

"That'll be one of the best parts." Stella saw the curtain move again and realized that poor Elsie was probably dying by degrees. She had to say, "Good night," and get inside.

"She's about to burst at the seams in there with all that curiosity," she told him. "She'll have a hundred and one questions, and by the time we're done, she'll know more about what happened than I do."

"That's our Elsie," he said. "Second nosiest woman in the county."

Stella shot him a playfully indignant look. "I'm not gonna ask who you think is the nosiest."

"Good idea. We want this date-from-hell to end on a good note that doesn't involve bloodshed." He gave her a long, sweet smile and said, "Let me walk you to the door."

"You don't need to. You're tired, and I know where it's at."

"No. You sit right there and let me do my manly man duty."

"Oh, well, when you put it like that, heaven forbid I'd get in the way of such a display of audacious gallantry."

"Exactly. Sit still and don't touch that door handle."

With far more energy than she would have expected from a man who had endured the evening he had, he hopped out of the cruiser, hurried around, and opened her door for her.

Though she hardly needed the helping hand he offered as she climbed out, she gratefully took it anyway and held tightly to it, enjoying the friendly contact as they walked to the door.

"I'd invite you inside, but . . ." she said.

"But you have to regale Elsie with your tales and get some sleep. Tomorrow's another day. Once you've got the kids off to school, you could drop by the station house. If you've a mind to, that is."

"I will. What'll you be doin' now? You headin' home to catch some shut-eye?"

"No," he said, all levity leaving his face, to be replaced by solemn determination. "I've got a bad guy to catch. And when I do, I'm going to take him to the station and stick him in a cell. Then I'm gonna rip off his left arm and whack Mervin up one side and down the other with it."

Stella was right about Elsie pouncing on her with questions the moment she entered the house. But her inquiries were more personal in nature than Stella was expecting.

"What'd you two do . . . stop down the road a ways to get your good-night kissin' done?" was the first thing out of Elsie's mouth before Stella could even get her purse set down and Flo's miserably uncomfortable high heels off her aching feet.

Shocked, Stella gave a little gasp that was better than any affirmation to Elsie's overly inquisitive mind.

"You did!" Elsie clapped her hands and did a little wiggle-dance of glee. "I knew it!"

"How did you know it?" Stella shook her head, incredulous. "How on earth could you possibly know that? I do believe, Miss Elsie Jo Dingle, that you have the spiritual gift of knowledge—knowin' stuff you got no business knowin', that is."

Elsie shuffled over to the couch, where one of Stella's best quilts was spread, and stretched out on it. "I might never've gotten married," Elsie said with a grin, "but I was young once. I know all about gittin' that last good-night kiss done and over with before you show up on your doorstep where nosy family members might be peepin' out the window."

"Or nosy best friends."

"Eh, stop it. I was more excited about this date than you were, girl. I've been proppin' my eyelids open with toothpicks, tryin' to stay awake till you got back. I wanna hear all about it."

"*All* about it? It was a long evenin', Elsie. A lot happened."

"All. Ever' bit."

Stella plopped down in her recliner, lifted the footrest, took a deep breath, and said, "Okay. First of all, let it be said that Billy Ray Sonner's got the scrawniest, most pimple-pocked, and altogether least appealing rear end of any man in this here county, and I'm fixin' to tell you how I know that for a fact. . . ."

Two hours later, Stella was lying in bed, staring at the ceiling and listening to Elsie and her grandson, Waycross, snore. Elsie was winning the contest for sheer volume. Waycross's little boy noises were cuter. By far.

As Elsie frequently did after babysitting late hours for Stella, she slept over, rather than make the trip back to the Patterson plantation. As long as she made it back to work the next morning, in time to have Judge Patterson's and his wife's late morning breakfast on the table, Elsie was free to do as she pleased.

What pleased her most was spending time in the home of the people she loved most in the world.

They were happy to have her, except for Waycross, who loved Elsie dearly, but he also loved his bed—the living room couch.

Some time back he'd decided he was too old to continue sleeping in a bedroom filled with girls, and he'd demanded "couch rights."

Understanding his need for privacy and a giggle-free zone to "be a guy" without having to listen to squabbles over hair ribbons and such, Stella had granted his request.

Come bedtime, the couch was his.

Unless Elsie was visiting.

In which case, he had to sleep with Gran.

The prospect didn't please him overly, but he admitted it was better than sleeping in the same room with Marietta and Vidalia and being awakened in the middle of the night to Marietta hollering about how Vidalia had reached up from her own bottom bunk to Mari's top one and stuck her sister with a pin.

"Granny snores," Waycross had told his sisters, "but she smells better than y'all—like flowers and bath powder—and she's a whole heap less quarrelsome."

Lying next to her sleeping grandson, Stella reached over and gently touched one of his soft, copper curls. He was the only red-haired child in the family, the only one to inherit his Grandpa Art's auburn locks.

Like most gingers, he got teased about it in the small town, but Waycross wouldn't have traded his distinctive hair color for the world. He considered it a bond between himself and the grandfather he adored, but hardly knew.

Sadly, that relationship, which existed in the child's own mind, was the closest thing to a loving, attentive male that Waycross had ever known. Thanks to a wayward father who spent as little time as he could raising the children he so frequently brought into the world.

Stella had spent many nights lying in bed shedding tears and praying about that situation. So far, there hadn't been a measurable improvement, but that didn't keep her from asking for one.

Tonight, she had even more things to think about, worry about, and pray about.

Someday, she vowed she'd go straight from thinking to praying without that fretting stage in the middle that cost her so much joy and peace.

But it won't be tonight, she told herself. I ain't there yet. *I still got a lot of room for improvement in the "Vexation and Botheration Department."*

She heard a slight movement to her left, turned, and saw Savannah standing next to her bed.

By the dim glow of the nightlight, Stella could see the child had a troubled look on her face.

"I can't sleep," Stella told her, knowing what the girl wanted but couldn't bring herself to ask for. "Do you reckon you could cuddle in here and keep me company?"

She certainly didn't have to ask twice. Instantly, the girl hopped into the bed. Stella wriggled closer to Waycross to make room.

With one grandkid on each side of her, all warm and snuggly, Stella felt like a mother hound with puppies. It was a feeling she loved and wouldn't have traded for the largest, most luxurious but empty bed in a queen's palace.

"I keep thinking about Miss Yolanda and what happened to her," Savannah said, stroking the sleeve of Stella's flannel nightgown, her head against her grandmother's shoulder.

"How do you know about Miss Yolanda's situation?" Stella asked.

"Miss Florence heard something about a ruckus at her pool hall and the other gas station. I heard her and Miss Elsie talking about it. Sounded downright awful."

"It was, honey. But Miss Ortez is in the hospital now with her head mended, and she's gonna be fine, thank goodness."

"How can she be fine, when all that bad stuff happened to her?"

Stella hesitated. The thirteen-year-old might be precocious, but Stella felt strongly that there was no need to add to her already overly extensive education of the world and its ills.

"What bad stuff are you referrin' to, darlin'?" Stella asked tentatively.

"Her getting beaten and raped."

Stella sat up on one elbow and stared down at her granddaughter, a sick feeling in her soul. "Now hold your horses there," she told her. "I don't know what you overheard, but it sounds to me like somebody went and embroidered the truth there. I won't name names but—"

"Florence Bagley."

"Okay, Flo has a bad habit of exaggerating when she's passing along a bit of gossip. Somebody can spot a brown bear cub down in the woods by Hooter Holler and by the time Flo gets done tellin' it, they was ate and spit out in chunks by a rabid, two-ton grizzly."

To Stella's relief, she heard Savannah snicker.

"Miss Flo doesn't let the facts get in the way of a good story," the girl added.

"That's exactly right. But she's wrong to do that in a case like this. The bear cub who was spotted wouldn't mind bein' lied about, but that poor girl, Yolanda, she's got enough to deal with as it is, without the whole town thinking the worst about what happened to her."

"Then she wasn't raped?"

Stella fought down the revulsion she felt, just knowing her granddaughter knew of such an act and even what to call it. "No, she was not," Stella told her. "There's a good chance it might have led to that, if the feller who hurt her—"

"Billy Ray Sonner."

"Yes, him . . . if he hadn't gotten interrupted by Miss Dolly Browning—"

"The crazy lady with all the cats who lives in the haunted house."

"Yes, but let's call her, 'the brave lady who's now the hero of the day here 'bouts.' "

Savannah thought it over a moment. "That's kinder."

"A heap kinder."

"So, what exactly *did* happen to Miss Yolanda? Miss Florence said she had her clothes all torn off her."

"That isn't true either. Her blouse was ripped—maybe he did it on purpose, might've been done durin' the struggle—but it was still on her. So were her jeans, her socks, and shoes."

"Her head was bashed in though? Her brains showing?"

"Good Lord've mercy. That Florence should take up writin' horror novels for a pastime. Obviously, she needs an outlet for that overactive imagination of hers."

Stella wrapped her arm around her granddaughter and pulled her closer. "The truth is, and I should know 'cause I was there and saw the aftereffects, is that Miss Yolanda was attacked by somebody. We're pretty darned sure it was Billy Ray Weasel-Face Sonner. He attempted to get way too friendly with her, and when she refused his attentions, he hurt her. He cut off her hair and hit her so hard on the head that she needed quite a few stitches and—"

"Twenty-five pints of blood, Miss Flo said."

"Good grief! I'm gonna have to give that girl a serious talkin' to about her fibbin'. It's outta control! Twenty-five pints, my foot. That's more'n twice what a body's got in 'im in the first place. Miss Yolanda lost one pint, and one transfusion put 'er right as rain. Blood-wise anyhow."

"What do you mean?" Stella heard the concern in Savannah's voice. "How is it that she's not right?"

"She'll recover from her injuries real quick, 'cause she's young and healthy," Stella said, kissing the girl's forehead. "Her beautiful, long, black hair will grow back, you'll see, and it'll cover up the scar on her scalp, so's it won't show a bit."

"But . . . ?"

"She's got wounds inside now, not in her body, but in her mind and spirit. Those won't ever heal completely. She's never gonna feel quite as safe as she once did. She won't trust people, especially men, as much as before. She'll have to do a lot of soul-searching to handle the bad feelings she's bound to have after this."

Savannah was silent for a long time. When she finally spoke, Stella could hear the deep sadness in her voice. "I like Miss Yolanda," she said. "A lot."

"We all do. She's easy to like. She's kind."

"Last week, I took some empty soda bottles in to her, so's I could get the change and buy Alma a ginger ale. Her tummy was acting up."

"It was? Last week, too? Why didn't you tell me?"

"You've got enough to bother with, and the ginger ale sets her right most times."

"Oh. Okay. But next time tell me."

"I will. Anyway, Miss Yolanda asked me if I like ginger ale, I told her I do, but it was for my little sister, who was griping up a storm, because she had a bellyache. She laughed and handed me two bottles instead of one. Said I should have a soda, too, because I was a good big sister."

Stella chuckled and kissed the top of Savannah's hair. "You are, darlin'. The best ever. Miss Yolanda's kinda like a big sister herself, lookin' out for people the way she does."

"Then we have to look out for *her.*"

"We will, darlin'. We'll do all we can."

As Stella held her granddaughter tightly and stared up at the ceiling, she knew that even with her grandpuppies near, this was one night when sleep wasn't going to come quickly.

Even with a cessation of fretting and copious amounts of fervent prayer—considering all that had transpired in the past few hours—Stella knew that precious peace was going to prove elusive.

Chapter 10

The next morning, Stella felt a bit like a wet mop that had been used, wrung out, and tossed out onto the porch to dry. She felt stiff, dried out, and in spite of her nightly bath, a bit dirty.

"Bein' around scoundrels like Billy Ray Sonner can do that to ya," she muttered to herself as she dried her cast-iron skillet and placed it in the oven.

"You're talkin' to yourself again, Granny."

She turned and saw Waycross standing in the doorway, a smirk on his freckled face.

"Now I'm talking to you, young man. Do you think you can get your sisters corralled and into the car in two minutes? We piddled around this mornin' and y'all done missed that bus. If you don't get in the truck in the next couple of minutes, y'all are gonna be late for school. Think you can light a fire under them and get 'em goin'?"

"I sure can!" A second later, he was a red-haired streak, racing into the girls' bedroom and living room, yelling, "Get a move on, girls! Get the lead outta your britches and fill up that truck out there! Granny said so!"

"Granny didn't say nothing about lead in our bloomers, Waycross Reid," replied a sassy female voice.

"Yeah, that's something you'd think of, not her!"

"We don't gotta mind you, Waycross! You're just a dumb, pee-pee-headed boy!"

Stella rolled her eyes, dried her hands on the dish towel, and hung it neatly on the oven handle.

"Poor child," she whispered. "He gets no respect from those girls. Can't be easy, being the only male in an eight-person house."

She hurried into the living room, where Savannah, Waycross, and Alma stood, their books and lunch sack in their hands, patiently waiting for the rest of the brood.

Elsie had left an hour before, scurrying off to the plantation and her morning duties. Only the folded quilt and pillow on the end of the sofa marked her departure.

"Go on out to the truck," Stella told the three kids. "I'll round up the rest of 'em."

As the trio headed for the door, Stella reached out and nabbed nine-year-old Alma by the arm. "Hold on there a minute, sweet-cheeks," she said. "What's this about you having a bellyache for some time . . . one I ain't heard about till last night?"

Alma shrugged. "It comes and goes," she said. "No big deal."

"Is it in any way tied to an overabundance of eatin' sweets? Like Miss Elsie's coconut cakes or ginger ales your sister buys for you with empty bottle money?"

The girl grinned sheepishly and shrugged. "Might be."

Stella looked her up and down. Alma was small for her age.

She had never quite thrived like her siblings, who were larger than most of their classmates. Dark-haired and blue-eyed, she was a miniature version of Savannah with the same sweet disposition.

But she lacked Savannah's steel core, that deep inner confidence that helped the oldest of the siblings get through the hardest circumstances that life threw their way.

Stella didn't worry a lot about Savannah, but she was concerned about little Alma.

"Do you reckon you might need to stay home with that tummy ache?" Stella asked her, refastening the barrette that was holding her curls out of her eyes.

"No! No! I have to go to school today! My tummy's fine, and I've gotta be there!"

"What's so all-fired important that you can't take a day off, Miss Alma Joy?"

"The spellin' bee's today! I gotta go and win again. I've been studyin' to beat the band, and I'll betcha I'll beat that Kathy Beckerman again!"

"Ah, yes. The great annual Reid-Beckerman spelling bee showdown! How could I forget somethin' as earthshatterin' as that?"

"I know! I need another blue ribbon to go with them other two! They're lonesome on their own!"

"I understand. What's two when you can have *three?!*"

"That's it! Three would be way better! You understand."

"I do. So, you can go to school, but you promise me that if your belly starts actin' up again, you'll have your teacher get ahold of me. I'll either be here at home or with Sheriff Gilford. He's got a phone there in the station house and a radio in his car. He'll tell me if you need me to come get you. Okay?"

"Okay. But I won't call. I'll be busy beatin' the socks off that stuck-up Kathy Beckerman."

"You be a good sport about it!" Stella shouted as the girl raced out the door, legs and tummy apparently in fine working order. "We don't gloat in this family. It ain't fittin'."

But Alma was already out of earshot, on her way to beat the Beckerman girl sockless.

Marietta, Jesup, Cordele, and Vidalia came racing through on their way from the bedroom to the door and nearly knocking Stella off her feet.

"I got your red bow!" Marietta yelled, holding up a scarlet hair ribbon and waving it under Vidalia's nose as she raced past her. "I got it, and you don't! I'm gonna be pretty today, and you . . . you're gonna look like the south end of a north-goin' skunk! Nanny, nanny, boo-boo! Ha! Ha! Ha!"

Stella sighed and shook her head. "Well," she said, reaching for her purse, which was lying on her piecrust table behind the door. "We don't gloat in this family . . . all *that* much."

Once the children were dropped at school, Stella wasted no time heading for the sheriff's station. With all her heart, she hoped that she'd walk in, look over at the main desk, and find Manny sitting there with a self-satisfied smile on his face, signifying that his prisoner was once again in custody.

That might not be the cure for world hunger or bring about universal peace, but it'd sure make my day a sunny one, even if it rains, she told herself as she pulled her old, panel truck in front of the station, turned the engine off, grabbed her pocketbook, and climbed out.

But it wasn't Manny's smiling face she saw when she opened the rickety screen door and walked inside.

It was Deputy Mervin Jervis sitting at the desk, a deck of cards spread out before him. He was so deeply engrossed in his solitaire game that he didn't even notice when she entered.

She was almost to the desk before he spotted her.

He jumped, dropped the cards in his hand, and clutched his chest.

"Lord've mercy!" he said. "You liked to've scared the puddin' outta me, Mrs. Reid. Warn a body when you're fixin' to sneak up on 'em like that!"

"I didn't sneak. Just moseyed in like I owned the place, Deputy," she told him. "If I'd been a dangerous felon, you'd been facedown in cow doody right now."

He reached down to retrieve his dropped cards from the floor. Due to his ample and ever-expanding girth, he grunted a bit doing so.

Had it been anyone else, Stella would have helped him. But she thought of poor Manny out there, stumbling around in those thick woods, looking for the prisoner Merv had allowed to slip from custody.

She thought, *Good ol' Deputy Merv can pick up his own dad-gum cards off the floor, if he can find a way around that belly of his to do so.*

"Where's the sheriff at?" she asked, anticipating the reply.

"Him and that old Indian buddy of yours are out there in the woods, trying to track Billy Ray."

Stella fixed him with a cold stare as she said with a calm that would have bothered a more observant person than Mervin Jervis, "My dear Cherokee friend's name is Magi Red Crow, and we should all be so young when we've been around as long as he has."

"What?"

"Never mind. When do you expect Sheriff Gilford to return?"

"Don't know." He chuckled. "When he's got Billy Ray in tow, I expect."

The telephone rang, and Merv took his time answering it.

For a moment, Stella feared it was the school calling to say that Alma had tossed her cookies in the middle of the spelling bee. With any luck, it would have been in Kathy Beckerman's direction.

Stella had to admit that she agreed with Alma's assessment of Little Miss Beckerman. *Kathy's a snob, all right, but it ain't the child's fault,* Stella reminded herself. *It's her momma's. Myrtle Beckerman's done stuck up higher than the flag on the county courthouse, come the Fourth of July.*

But she put the Beckerman family and their uppity attitudes out of mind when she heard Deputy Merv say to the caller on the phone, "A threatening letter? What kind of threatening letter?"

Stella could feel her heart pounding as she listened to the rest of the conversation. "Yeah. I'll tell the sheriff when he comes in," Merv told the caller. "But he's out in the field right now. Well, the woods, actually, but—"

"Who is it?" Stella asked, unable to contain her curiosity any longer. "Who got a threatening letter?"

But Merv didn't answer her as he finished his call. "Yeah. Okay. Bye-bye."

"Who was that?" Stella demanded the moment he set the phone down.

He picked up his cards and began to shuffle them.

Her patience shot, Stella reached over, grabbed the cards out of his hand, and tossed them down on the desktop. "Dadgum it, Mervin! Would you stop actin' like a horse's rear end and at least *try* to do the job this city pays you to do?"

"You slapped them cards right outta my hands!" he shouted. "What'd you do that for?"

It occurred to Stella that Merv's face looked like Marietta's when she was tuning up to pitch one of her fits.

"I wanted to get your attention, Deputy, and now that I have, maybe you can tell me who that was on the phone. Who got a threatening letter?"

"Not that it's any of your business, Mrs. Reid, being as it's top secret, official police stuff and all that, but it was Harper Everson."

"Harper? The mailman?"

"Yep."

"The mailman got a threatening letter?"

"'Twasn't addressed to him. He found it in a mailbox when he was pokin' other mail in there."

"Whose mailbox?"

He gave her a catty grin and said, "Now, wouldn't you like to know?"

She leaned over the desk until they were nearly nose to nose. "Mervin, you are drivin' me, an otherwise peace-lovin' woman, to violence. I'm fixin' to do you serious bodily harm."

"You'll get arrested."

"The way the sheriff feels about you right now? I'll take my chances."

At that moment, a loud noise behind Stella made both of them jump. She whirled around to see Dolly Browning burst through the door and run into the station.

"I got a letter! Some horrible person left this awful thing in my mailbox and my mailman found it and brought it in to me!" Dolly was shouting, waving a piece of paper in her hands.

Her eyes looked wild with a mixture of fear and excitement. "Just wait till you see this! It's dreadful! They're threatening to do something terrible to me!"

"What?" Stella asked, her own heart pounding. Dolly's terror was contagious. "What do they say they're fixin' do to ya, darlin'?"

Dolly hesitated. "Well, I'm not sure. But it sounds absolutely awful! Just read it and you'll see what I mean. I think they might even mean to kill me!"

Chapter 11

"We already heard all about your nasty letter," Mervin told Dolly, looking so smug and condescending that Stella felt the need to smack him. "That mailman of yours already reported it to the police all proper like. So you got nothin' to worry about, little lady."

Stella turned to Mervin and made a face at him, not unlike the one she had seen earlier on Marietta's when she'd been taunting Vidalia. "That's what you refused to tell me, Deputy Smarty-Pants Jervis? So much for your so-called top-secret police information."

"I don't gotta tell you nothin', Stella Reid. You're just a civilian. You got no badge, no authority."

Stella's temper soared. "And you got no right to tell this poor, scared lady that she's got nothin' to worry 'bout. You haven't even read her letter, and you haven't done a blamed thing about that phone call you got neither. You haven't even informed the sheriff, so's he could do something 'bout it, if he chose to."

She paused and took a deep breath before launching into the second phase of her attack. "There's more to bein' a deputy than holdin' that chair down and makin' sure it don't float away, Mervin Jervis. From what I can tell that's all you're good at—that and pokin' quarters in them Pac-Man machines ever' chance you get."

Before Mervin could reply, the door burst open again, and this time it was Sheriff Manny Gilford who rushed inside.

He hurried over to Dolly, grabbed her by the shoulders, and turned her toward him. He gave her a quick look up and down, then apparently satisfied that she wasn't hurt, he said, "What's going on with you, woman? I saw you running down the middle of the street out there and thought your tail was on fire or something. Didn't you hear me yelling at you to get out of the road before you got hit by a car?"

"What?" Dolly looked genuinely confused. Finally, she said, "No, I didn't see you or hear you. I was just trying to get to the station here as fast as I could to show you this."

She shoved the paper into his hands, then stood with her arms crossed defensively over her chest, looking as indignant as she was upset.

"You ran all the way here from your house?" Stella asked her, as Manny read the letter.

"Yes. I guess I should've used my car, but I was all upset and not thinking right. I just read it and took off running here."

Manny looked up from the letter and said, "Miss Dolly, where did you get this?"

"I know that!" Merv piped up, excited and eager to contribute his bit. "I got a call from—"

"Oh, shut the hell up, Merv," Manny barked back. "I've got ticks and chiggers all over my legs from traipsing around in that woods trying to track the prisoner you lost, so I'd much prefer that you just keep quiet."

Manny turned back to Dolly. "As I was saying, Miss Dolly . . ."

"Harper, the mailman, brought it in. He told me he found it

when he stuck my other letters and bills into my box. It was in there already."

"You opened it right away?"

"Sure. I was curious."

"Of course you were, and when you read it . . . ?"

"I went from curious to worried. Very worried."

"I can see why."

Stella couldn't stand it. She moved closer to Manny. "What does it say?"

"May I read it to her, Miss Dolly?" Manny asked.

"Sure." Dolly thrust it into his hand as though it was something dirty she'd like to be rid of. "Stella's my friend. I'd trust her with my life."

"Okay then. Here goes." Manny held the letter up, touching it only on the edge with two fingertips, and began to read. "Dolly Browning, you are hereby warned. No more poking around in other people's business. If you continue, you could end up like that Sonner guy at Mabel's."

"That Sonner guy at Mabel's?" Stella repeated, running the phrase through her mind, trying to make sense of what she'd heard. "What's that supposed to mean? Who's Mabel? Do we have a Mabel in town?"

"Not that I know of," Manny said.

"That Sonner guy," Stella continued. "They must mean Billy Ray. He's the only Sonner left around these parts now. Does he have a girlfriend named Mabel that he could be holed up with somewhere?"

"I've never known a Mabel in McGill," Manny said. "Maybe in a neighboring town . . . ?"

"Wait a minute," Dolly said, scratching her head. "Isn't there an old, old motel way out there on the other side of the Patterson plantation, near the cotton gin? It's set off the road a way back. It's falling apart, always has been that I can remember. But I'm trying to picture the sign on the front. It's all faded, but I think it might say Mabel's Motel."

Manny's eyes went from dull and tired to bright and alert in one second. "I do believe you're right, Miss Dolly. That rings a bell. Maybe that's where Sonner's hiding."

He laid the letter on the desk and told Mervin, "Deputy, that is evidence. Could you please put it in an evidence envelope and—"

Instantly, Mervin's eyes began to glaze over, like a kindergartner being given a long division problem to solve.

"Never mind," Manny said. "I'll do it myself."

"Oh, good." Merv looked overly pleased and relieved. "Sounds complicated and I'd probably just do it wrong."

"You reckon?" Manny grumbled.

In seconds, he had pulled a brown envelope from the desk drawer, and using a pen from the desk, he eased the letter inside it. "It's bad enough that Harper and Miss Dolly and I have all handled it. We don't need any more prints added to it before we see if we can lift some others. If we're lucky, the person who typed it may have left one or two behind."

"*Typed* it?" Stella asked. "I figured it was handwritten."

"No," Manny replied, as he turned it toward her so she could see the portion that was still outside the envelope. "Typed. Looks like an old typewriter, too, whose ribbon needs adjusting."

Stella peered at the printing and noticed something she had seen before, but not often. The top parts of the letters were black, as she expected they would be, but the lower parts of the letters, especially the ones with tails like "y's" and "g's," were red.

She agreed with Manny. It looked like an old typewriter had been used, one with a ribbon that hadn't been properly inserted and aligned.

Once Manny had the letter safely inside the envelope, he hurried over to the office safe, opened it, and stuck his piece of evidence inside.

"Miss Dolly," he said, walking over to her and putting his arm around her shoulders. "I don't want you to worry about this too much. Okay? I'm going to head out there to that old motel right away to see if you're right about that sign. I'll give it a thorough going-over. With any luck, we'll have Billy Ray back in custody within the hour."

"That would be wonderful, Sheriff. Then we'd all breathe a bit better for sure."

"Would you feel safer if you stayed out of town for a few days? I could help you get into a hotel or motel if you'd like that."

"No. I need to take care of my animals, and I'm not worried about Billy Ray. You'll catch him. I know you will."

"All right then, I'll drop you off at your house on my way," he told her. "You go inside, lock the doors nice and tight, and stay there with Valentine at your side until I call you or come by with the good news. Okay?"

She nodded eagerly. "Thank you, Sheriff. I appreciate your concern."

"No problem." Manny looked over at Merv. "Man the desk. Don't bother me unless it's really important, got it?"

"Yes, sir."

Manny turned to Stella. She had a feeling he was going to tell her to go back home.

She decided to nip that particular weed in the bud before it even sprouted. "I'm going with you," she said.

He gave her a half grin. "Are you, now?"

"I am."

He stood there a long time, and she could tell he was debating the pros and cons of taking a civilian along on what might turn out to be the arrest of a suspect wanted for a violent felony.

"Come on," she said, heading toward the door. "Time's a-wastin'."

She figured, if he'd been distracted while chasing Dolly into the station, he might have left the cruiser unlocked, and she could get into the passenger seat before he could stop her. She couldn't picture him trying to throw her out right there on Main Street in broad daylight, in front of God and everybody.

Chapter 12

"Stella May, you know I have great affection and respect for you, as a woman and a wonderful human being," Manny said as he drove the cruiser down the highway that led out of town, toward the old Patterson plantation and beyond to the rundown motel in question.

"Why, thank you, Manny," Stella replied. She shot him a too-bright smile in hopes of warding off the second half of his statement. She could smell a big "but . . ." coming and the tone of his voice told her she wouldn't like it. "I've always thought the world of you, too. You are truly a man among men, Manny Gilford."

The sideways look he gave her told her that he wasn't falling for the flattery. "Yeah, yeah. Turn down the charm there, girl. You're about to blind me with it, and I left my sunglasses back at the station."

"You know I meant every word of it." She batted her eyelashes at him and wished she'd thought to put on some of that red lipstick he liked so much before she'd come out today.

"I meant every word I said, too. But that's not gonna stop me from saying my piece before we get to that old motel. You're going to hear what I've got to say, or I'm going to turn this vehicle around and take you back home right this very minute."

She dropped the playful, flirtatious routine and sighed. "Okay, okay. I can tell you feel mighty strong about it, so let me have it. Both barrels. Just remember that your birthday's coming up, and you're particularly fond of my apple pies."

"Oh, man. You don't play fair at all, Stella Reid. Holding an apple pie hostage? That's downright ruthless."

She shrugged. "Just as long as you remember, you might have a badge, but I do the cooking."

"I'll keep that in mind. What I've got to say is: Fine woman that you are, you've got a major flaw in your character. It's a failing that could get in our way today, and I need your reassurance that it won't."

"What's that?"

"You don't take orders worth a tinker's damn. Not even when it's important, maybe even life and limb being at stake. That's not going to do today."

"What's the matter, Manny? You're not comfortable with a woman using her own best judgment in a situation? I thought better of you, Sheriff Gilford. I thought you was one of them enlightened gentlemen who understands that womenfolk are just as smart as the men around them."

Manny groaned and shook his head. "This is not the time for a political discussion, Stella. My whole life, I've understood that females are considerably smarter than us knucklehead men. I'm pretty sure you know how 'enlightened' I am in that regard. But I'm not talking to you now as a man to a woman or even as a friend. I'm talking to you, a civilian, as your sheriff."

Again, she shot him a coquettish grin. "You gonna arrest me, Sheriff Gilford? You gonna put handcuffs on me and throw me into a jail cell and feed me burnt biscuits and water gravy?"

"I'll do worse than that. I'll stick you in a cell with the drunkest bum I've got in residence at the moment."

Stella looked down the road and realized they were fast approaching the driveway that led to her house. Farther down the highway was the plantation and then the motel. This was a critical moment when Manny could change his mind, and if he was aggravated enough, he could just dump her there on the highway and let her walk home.

She didn't really believe he would. He loved both her and her apple pies far too much to take the chance of losing her friendship forever.

But one couldn't be too careful, and he was wearing a particularly serious scowl at the moment, so . . .

"How do you suggest I correct this serious character flaw I've got, Sheriff Gilford? Feel free to offer whatever wisdom and guidance you feel you need to dump on me. Don't hold back. Let me have it all. I can take it."

He pulled over to the side of the road, shifted the cruiser into "Park," took a deep breath, and said, "As your sheriff, and more importantly, the one who's actually been trained for this job and has done it for years, and therefore knows what's best and safest for all concerned . . ."

"I've always respected your authority, Sheriff. You know that."

"Bullshit."

"Manny!"

"You never do what you're told, but if you wanna go out there with me to that motel, you promise me right now—and you mean it, too, like you've got your hand on a stack of Bibles—that you'll do what I say."

"I swear, as God is my witness, if you say, 'Jump,' I'll hop as high as a toad frog with a firecracker up his butt. Would that suit you, Sheriff?"

"I detect a note of sarcasm, Mrs. Reid."

"You do? What a smart feller you are. All that trainin', I presume."

They sat in silence a moment, then he reached over and took her hand in his. Squeezing it tightly, he said, "Stella, I'm sure you'd hop or run or clobber somebody good and proper, if I asked you to. Probably *before* I even asked you. You're very brave and smart and strong. The problem is—you're also headstrong and opinionated. You look to your own judgment in every circumstance and don't take 'No' for an answer."

Stella started to argue, but then she remembered all the times her mother, Florence, and even gentle Elsie had said the same thing. Even Pastor O'Reilly had chastised her a couple of times for not being as cooperative as she needed to be when serving on several church committees.

"Okay," she admitted. "I might've heard that once or twice in my lifetime. You could have a point there about this bein' a serious flaw in my character. I accept that."

He chuckled. "Thank you for that concession, Mrs. Reid. I can't imagine it was easy for you." He squeezed her hand again, then patted it. "Don't get me wrong. On a regular day I find bullheadedness most appealing in a woman. But on a day like today, independent thinking on your part could get one or both of us killed. I'm looking to arrest a man who's known for his violence and overall rotten attitude. Yesterday, he nearly killed a woman, and he knows if I take him in, he'll be spending a long stretch in prison. That makes him a desperate character. You understand?"

She nodded.

"Today, right now, I want you to promise me that you'll do what I say without any argument or hesitation. Even more importantly, if I tell you to do nothing and wait for me, or hide somewhere, or keep quiet and say absolutely nothing, you'll do that, too."

Stella thought it over but only for a few seconds. She turned in her seat to face him, looked directly into his eyes, and said with great solemnity, "I promise you, Manny, like as if I got my hand on a ton of Bibles right this very minute, that I'll do everythin' you say. I won't put you or myself in jeopardy."

He looked enormously relieved. "Thank you, Stella. I believe you, and I appreciate it. You've put my mind at ease."

He leaned over and kissed her quickly on the cheek, then pulled the cruiser back onto the highway and headed down the road toward the motel.

As they continued on their way, she was uncharacteristically silent. Finally, he reached over and nudged her elbow.

"Okay," he said. "What's up? You got something else you need to say?"

"As a matter of fact, I do."

"Oh no. I knew it couldn't have been that easy. What is it? Spit it out."

"That promise I just made you . . ."

"Yeah? What about?"

"It ain't an open-ended agreement. It's just for today. In fact, it might just be for this one trip out here to this old motel. Once that's over and done with, we go back to just being you and me, and me doing what I think is best in any given situation. Unless, of course, you're about to arrest some vicious felon with a bad attitude toward womenfolk. Okay?"

He laughed, hard and long. "I never thought for a moment it

was a permanent state of affairs, Stella May. I know you far too well for that."

"Okay, there it is," Manny said as they passed a copse of trees and saw the end of a long, ramshackle building, mostly hidden among a pervasive overgrowth from the nearby, encroaching woods.

"It probably never was the Taj Mahal, but I expect it looked better in its youth," Stella said, taking in the sagging roof, broken windows, and rotting walls that were almost completely bare of their former protective paint.

Even the sign that read MABEL'S MOTEL was almost unreadable and hung haphazardly from one corner, blocking the door to what had once been the office.

"It's youth . . . like maybe forty years ago," Manny said. "I'd forgotten all about this even being here until Dolly reminded us."

"Good thing she did, or we'd still be wondering who on earth 'Mabel' was."

Manny drove slowly, as he approached the motel. No true driveway remained intact, but there was something resembling a path—or at least, a disturbance in the vegetation—that led from the front and around the side of the building.

"Looks like a car came through here recently," Manny said.

"That's what I was thinking, too." Stella could feel her pulse rate quickening. One glance at Manny told her that he was on high alert, as well.

Now that they were at the motel and the situation was unfolding, she realized with a sense of gravity how important his former words and insistence on her cooperation had been.

She was a grandmother with seven grandchildren to raise.

He was, for all practical purposes, the provider of law and

order to a community that seemed to be increasingly in need of it.

Plus, he was Manny, her friend, one of the people nearest and dearest to her heart. She would never forgive herself if, through a moment of arrogant stubbornness, she allowed him to be hurt or worse.

Likewise, if anything happened to her, he would never forgive himself. Manny already carried a heavy burden of misplaced guilt on his soul over the death of his Lucy. Stella couldn't imagine him handling the tragic passing of yet another woman he cared for.

"What do you want me to do, Manny?" she asked him with all sincerity and humility.

"I'm going to drive just a little bit closer. Then I'm going to get out and walk up there. I don't want him to see or hear us or the cruiser. If he is in there, it's best he doesn't know I'm here until it's too late for him to run."

"He might not even be here. All we had to go on was that letter, and that didn't say anything about a motel."

"True. This could be nothing at all. Just a wild goose—"

Manny caught his breath, and so did she.

They had both seen it at the same moment. The battered old pickup that the Lone White Wolf Pack members were so proud of.

The truck itself was nothing to boast about. It was in much the same condition as Mabel's Motel. Rusty, rickety, and on its last legs.

It was the "decoration" that the LWWP had been positively giddy to display to their fellow McGillians when they had driven the truck so proudly down Main Street a couple of months ago.

The most "artistic" of the three, Billy Ray, had taken a can of spray paint to both doors and adorned them with swastikas.

The rendering was sloppy at best. The cross misshapen, with

curved corners and streaks of red paint running down, lacked sophistication, but it was disgusting and offensive, and the citizens of McGill figured that was exactly what Billy Ray had intended.

Sheriff Gilford had demanded that they paint over the symbols of hate, but Billy Ray, who had never managed to learn his multiplication tables, considered himself quite the expert on the United States Constitution. He had informed the sheriff and any other citizens who dared to object that his swastikas were protected under the freedom of speech afforded to him as an American citizen.

Manny had spoken to Judge Patterson about it. The judge had advised him that, if it went to court, Billy Ray would probably prevail. So, Manny had decided it wasn't worth the ruckus or running the risk of having Billy Ray's ugly mug on national TV, representing the fine city of McGill, Georgia.

"If his truck's here, he's here," Stella told Manny. "Since he painted that mess on the side of it, he ain't been drivin' anything else."

"True. He's in there. Which makes everything I said to you earlier all the more important, Stella."

"I know. Tell me what you want, and that's what I'll do."

Manny thought for a moment, then said, "I'm going to leave the car here. With all those weeds he can't see it from inside. I'm going to sneak over there and get a look-see through those windows. Hopefully, I'll spot him, go inside, and arrest him without incident."

"I'm afraid for you, Manny," she said. "You need backup. You need deputies—and not ones like Mervin the peckerhead."

Manny shrugged. "Sometimes you gotta make do with what you've got."

"Again, what can I do to help?"

"You can stay here in the cruiser with the windows closed and the doors locked. Do not get out of this car until I tell you it's okay."

"How's that gonna to help you though?"

"It will free me up to think about my job and not about whether somebody I love is about to get hurt."

"I understand. What else can I do? There's gotta be something."

"There is." He drew a deep breath and avoided her eyes when he said, "If you hear or see anything, anything at all, that suggests that maybe things haven't gone my way in there—I want you to drive this cruiser back onto the highway and hightail it outta here. Once you're well on your way, a good piece down the road, then stop, pull over to the side, and use that radio to call the station and tell Merv what's going on. Tell him to get hold of Doc Hynson, and as many other able-bodied men that he trusts, who have weapons and know how to use them, and get them out here on the double."

Stella gave him a solemn nod. "You got it, and what's more, I'll be prayin' for you the whole time."

"There you go. Better yet. The fervent prayer of a righteous woman avails much and all that good stuff."

"Exactly."

To her surprise, he leaned over and a gave her a quick but sweet kiss on the lips.

Then he pulled his sidearm from his holster, checked, and replaced it. Moment later, he had gotten out of the cruiser, locked its doors, and was making his way through the thick brush toward the derelict motel.

"Lord, watch over him and keep him from harm," Stella whispered. "I know you love him, good man that he is, and I don't know what this town and its people would do without him."

As she watched him creep up to the nearest filthy and broken window and peep in, she added, "I don't know what me and my grandbabies would do without him either, for that matter."

It was after the sheriff had checked the final window, turned, given her a thumbs-down, then disappeared, working his way around to the front of the building, that Stella realized . . . Manny Gilford had just told her that he loved her.

Chapter 13

"Somethin's wrong. Somethin's just gotta be wrong," Stella told herself as she squirmed on the seat of the cruiser and strained to hear any sounds or see anything moving through the tangle of weeds and overgrowth that surrounded the motel.

She glanced at the time on the dashboard clock, did some quick math, and figured that Manny had been gone for twelve minutes.

"It doesn't take that long to check ten rooms and come back," she said.

Her own pulse was the only sound she could hear as it pounded in her ears. That and a couple of crows quarreling in a nearby tree.

In all the time he'd been gone, not a single car had passed on the highway.

Is this it? she thought. *Is this what he meant when he said if I thought he might be in trouble, I should haul buns outta here and call for help?*

"He ain't in there, layin' on one of them ol' rotten beds, takin' hisself a nap," she muttered to herself. "He's gotta know I'm out here dyin' by degrees wonderin'. If he was all right, he would've—Oh! There he is!"

He had reappeared on the right side of the building, the same place he had disappeared, what felt to Stella like several lifetimes ago.

He seemed okay. No blood or even dirt on his clothes. He was moving fine, not like an injured man.

The only thing that seemed amiss was the look on his face.

He looked . . . perplexed. That was the only word she could think of to describe his expression.

To her delight, he waved an arm, beckoning her to join him.

She did, in record time.

"What is it?" she said softly when she reached him. "What did you find? Is he here? Did you—?"

"You don't need to whisper. Nobody's going to hear you."

"Oh." A wave of disappointment swept over her. It had all been for nothing. No Billy Ray. No arrest. They were back to square one.

"Come see this," he said, taking her hand and leading her back the way he had come, along the side of the building, then to the front.

"See what?" she asked. "There's something to see? This wasn't just a dry run after all?"

"Wasn't a dry run, darlin'," he said. "Not by a long shot."

"Oh, good." She looked up at his troubled face and added, "I reckon."

"Down here," he said. "In room five."

A moment later, he was opening the door with the faded symbol of a five on it. The metal numeral had long since fallen to the ground in front of it.

He took her hand and led her into the room.

"I apologize ahead of time for what you're about to see, Stella," he told her. "It's not pretty."

"Okay," she said. "Forewarned and all that."

Her eyes took several moments to adjust to the dim light. When they did, all she saw was a bed with a bare mattress. On it lay some bloody bandages, a blue, torn hospital gown, some jeans and a black T-shirt, a knife, a pistol, and six empty beer cans.

"He was here!" Stella said, excited.

"He still is."

She looked up at Manny in surprise. "Really?"

He nodded.

"Where?"

Pointing to a small door on the far wall, he said, "There."

The door was more than halfway open. She was vaguely aware of something ragged, torn, hanging down around the frame. She had to step around a cheap, metal chair to go inside.

The bathroom was small and even darker than the bedroom, as it had no window and the light was off.

Instantly, she was aware of an odor that seemed vaguely familiar. For some reason, it reminded Stella of baking, but she couldn't recall where she'd smelled it before.

Manny pulled the powerful penlight from his service belt, but before he turned it on, he said, "Are you sure you want to see this, Stella?"

Stella considered it for a moment, then nodded. "I want to know the truth, and there's no knowin' like seein' with your own eyes."

"Okay." He turned on the small flashlight and shined the beam into the darkness.

It took a while for Stella's brain to discern what she was seeing.

On the floor, just inside the door, was a pale, white body. It was lying on its side, the arms curled around and over its head and face, as through trying to protect itself from something that was attacking it.

But there was no sign of injury, other than some dried blood on the fingers and a bit more in the ear.

Even without seeing the face, Stella knew exactly who it was. She recognized the tattoos on the chest, arms, and shoulders.

The snarling skull with a swastika in the middle of its forehead on the body's torso, the black snakes that curled out of the top of that skull and down both arms, baring their long, blood-dripping fangs onto the owner's wrists—those and the lightning bolts that formed the words "Lone White Wolf Pack" across the belly could only belong to Billy Ray Sonner. Billy Ray was extremely proud of both his physique and his branding. In the summer, he was seldom seen wearing a shirt as he strutted around, showing off each new addition to his artwork. The more his neighbors expressed their distain and disapproval, the more he liked it.

Billy Ray lived by the motto, "Better to be noticed and hated than not to be noticed at all."

"But he ain't alive no more," Stella said, more to herself than to Manny. "He's definitely among the departed. Gone on to his eternal reward . . . or otherwise."

"I checked him, and he's got some pretty solid rigor mortis going on there. Herb would have a better idea, once he takes his temperature, but I'd say he died sometime during the night. Maybe not that long after he escaped."

"He had help then," Stella said, tearing her eyes away from the horrible sight on the bathroom floor and looking back at the room and the items on the floor. "He's got a change of clothes, a weapon, and then there's the truck outside."

"I'm thinking he managed to get hold of a phone and call Earle," Manny said.

"I heard Billy Ray and Deacon haven't been gettin' on so well lately. From what I understand, Deacon was thinkin' he might move up in the world, take over the top spot from Billy Ray."

"I heard that, too. Deacon's going to be at the top of my list."

"What list?"

"List of suspects."

"Like in a murder case?"

"Yes."

Stella studied his face. Even in the dim light she could see he was serious. He was wearing his grim and determined look.

"You think somebody killed him?"

"I do."

"But there aren't any injuries. I just figured he died of an overdose of drugs, or maybe he just expired from pure meanness. Lord knows he had enough of that in him to kill him, if anybody ever did."

"If pure meanness killed people, I wouldn't have a job," he said. "Besides, you didn't find the place undisturbed the way I did. If you had, I'm sure you'd feel differently."

"Why's that?"

She looked around, then paid closer attention to the stuff hanging down from the window frame.

"Can I have use of that flashlight for a second?" she asked, holding out her hand.

"You may." He gave it to her and pointed to the door. "Check it out and tell me what you see."

As soon as the bright light shone on the frame, she could see that it was covered with tape—heavy, wide duct tape—hanging like a tattered band around the door's frame. "It looks like it was stuck around the door and somebody cut it," she said.

"I did. I had to in order to get inside."

"It was stuck all around the door?"

"Good and tight," he replied. "Like . . . airtight."

"Wow."

"Yeah." He nodded toward the nearby chair. "That was jammed against the door, the top of it under the doorknob."

"Tape and a chair. Somebody wanted to make sure he didn't get out."

"They succeeded."

She aimed the flashlight's beam at the back of the door, the side that had been in the bathroom. "That's blood," she said, pointing to the dark red streaks and smears all over it, then to the dead man's bloody fingertips. "Oh, Lord have mercy, he was trying to claw his way outta there!"

"Looks like it, for sure," Manny concurred.

"That's sad." She shook her head. "Even for a toad's butt wart like Billy Ray Sonner, that's a frightful way to leave this world. Such desperation! I wouldn't've wished that on anybody. Not even him."

"Me either. But what I'm not sure of was why he was so frantic to get out, or why he even died," Manny said. "I can understand wanting to get out, trying, yelling maybe, getting mad and kicking till you hurt your feet, but to tear your fingers up like that . . ."

"Maybe he was claustrophobic."

"Never seemed to be when I locked him up in my smallest jail cell. Or when I was driving him around in the back seat of my cruiser. That's enough to set off most folks who're claustrophobic."

"I'm sure if he'd been, he would've mentioned it. Billy Ray wasn't exactly the sort to suffer in silence."

"That's for sure."

Stella looked down at the body on the floor once again. "You've gotta call Herb. Get him over here to take a look."

Manny gave her a kind smile. "You're a generous lady, Stella, assuming that old Herb's going to see anything that's not obvious to you and me."

She shrugged. "He's gotta earn that big coroner's paycheck he gets somehow."

"True. Make sure the city of McGill gets their thirty-eight dollars a month out of him."

Stella looked one more time down at the body, then the rest of the bathroom that contained nothing but Billy Ray and one ragged, dingy bath towel.

"At least nobody's gotta worry about this ol' boy anymore. His bullyin' and insultin' and hurtin' good folks who don't deserve it—that's come to a screechin' halt."

"Thankfully, it has. In spite of Deacon's great ambitions, I'd say the Lone White Wolf Pack's days of 'glory' are behind them now. I heard Billy there cussing them out in a downtown alley one night because neither one of them could remember to bring beer to their weekly meetings."

"Yolanda's gonna be relieved that he's dead, like the rest of the town. She doesn't have to worry that he'll hurt her again. Dolly won't have to fret none either."

They both looked at each other and their smiles turned somber.

"Except . . ." Manny began.

Stella finished it for him. "Except for the polecat that put that threatening letter in her mailbox."

"We've got to find out who wrote that thing," Manny said, "as well as who put this ol' boy out of his misery."

"Outta *our* misery is more like it." She handed Manny back his flashlight. She had seen about as much as she could stand. "Maybe, if we're lucky, they'll be one and the same."

"We can always hope."

Chapter 14

Sitting in the cruiser's passenger seat, Stella watched as Herbert Jameson's hearse pulled away from the motel and headed down the highway toward his funeral home.

Next to her, behind the wheel, Manny watched, too. His face looked pale beneath his tan and his eyes seemed red and irritated.

"When's the last time your head made acquaintance with a pillow, Sheriff Gilford?" she asked, her words playful but her tone serious.

He had to stop and think about it.

Never a good sign, she thought.

"Night before last, I guess," he said. "Though I think I was half-asleep on my feet when I was trudging around in those woods last night with your buddy Magi Red Crow."

"I don't reckon that counts as restorative slumber."

"I suppose you're right. Maybe I can catch a few winks in one of the cells later."

"Charming."

"The second cell on the left's not so bad. The mattress doesn't sag."

"I'll keep that in mind if I get incarcerated in your jail someday, like you keep threatenin' me with."

He laughed, reached over, and tousled her curls, the way she frequently did Waycross's hair, only not as hard.

"How are the kids these days?"

"Okay. Energetic as ever. Alma's had a tummy ache off and on, but she just had to go to school anyway. The spelling bee's today, and she wouldn't miss that for the world."

"She's our little champion when it comes to spelling. Two years in a row now, right?"

Stella nodded. "Determined to make it three." Stella glanced at her watch. It was already past noon. "I told her to have the school call me if she got to feelin' poorly again. I hope they didn't try while we was inside. I'd hate to think she needed me, and I was outta reach."

He nodded toward the radio microphone. "Give Merv a call. Tell him to ring the school secretary and patch you in."

"He can do that?"

Manny hesitated. "Most folks could. Second graders. Most anybody who's even semiconscious. A trained monkey."

Stella rolled her eyes and reached for the microphone. "I'm not especially optimistic, but . . ."

"Try to keep your expectations low. That way you won't fall too far, too hard."

Stella reached for the microphone. "I learned long ago, a girl just can't trust her heart to the likes of Mervin Jervis." She pushed the button, as she had seen Manny do so many times, and said, "Sheriff's station—come in please."

It took a while, but eventually, an annoyed voice replied. "Who's this?"

"Stella Reid. I'm at the old motel and—"

"What the hell's happenin' out there? I heard ol' Herb's done run out there and picked up a dead body. Why hasn't anybody told me what's going on?"

Stella looked over at Manny, who shook his head "no" vigorously.

"You'll have to speak to the sheriff about it later, Merv," she said. "I'm sure he'll fill you in on all the nasty details."

"There's nasty details? What kinda details? How nasty?"

Stella could tell this was going nowhere fast. "I need you to do me a favor, Merv, if you aren't too busy, and you don't mind too much."

"Well, I *am* busy, and I *do* mind. I ain't your servant. Just because you and the sheriff's been keepin' company lately, that don't mean you can boss me around."

Stella reached inside her tired spirit and managed to find a bit of patience that she didn't know she had. Though she didn't feel particularly self-righteous about it. She knew that if Merv was within arm's reach and Manny wasn't around, chances are he would've gotten his left ear boxed.

"I beg your pardon, Deputy Jervis," she said. "I didn't mean to come across bossy. I just wondered if you could—"

Before she knew what was happening, Manny had snatched the microphone out of her hand. He pushed the transmit button and said, "Dammit, Mervin, put down those playing cards this minute, and do whatever this lady asks you to do. It's either that or, I swear, when I get back to the station, I'll put you to scrubbing out the cells with the toothbrush, bleach, and ammonia. Got it?"

In record time, Stella was speaking to the secretary of the school, who reassured her that little Alma was not only feeling just fine but would have good news to report when she returned home that afternoon.

Stella thanked her profusely, feeling a weight lifting from her spirit. She hadn't realized how worried she was about the child until she heard she was okay.

"Feel better now?" Manny asked her when the call was finished.

"So much better. Thank you."

"Then let's head back to the station. I've gotta get this evidence sorted out, looked over, and locked away." He pointed to the brown paper bags that covered the cruiser's rear seat.

"I'd like to help you with that, if I could," Stella said eagerly. "I've still got a few hours before the kids get out of school."

"I'd be glad to have you. Believe me, these tired eyes of mine would much rather look at you than Mervin's sourpuss."

"Only if you promise to make me a fresh pot of coffee. My head's a little achy. I hope I'm not coming down with anything."

"I don't feel that great either. I could use a mug of it myself. One fresh pot of coffee within minutes of you walking through the station door—how does that sound, Mrs. Reid?"

"Pure dee divine!"

"How's about we make a quick pit stop and get some donuts to go with that coffee?"

"Ah, boy . . . you'll spoil me rotten, treatin' me like that."

"It's high time somebody did. A good woman like you, Stella, you deserve a break once in a while, bless your heart."

There was a sad tone in his voice that Stella didn't quite understand. It was as though he had something on his mind that he wasn't saying, and she wasn't quite sure what it might be.

But after the morning she'd had, dealing with Mervin and the terrified Dolly Browning, then seeing that body lying there on the bathroom floor, she decided not to worry about it.

Fresh coffee and donuts were on the way. Little Alma was feeling okay and had good news to share when she got home from school. No doubt the evening would be spent celebrating with the grandkiddos.

A body's gotta take full advantage of the good times when they pop up, she told herself, *'cause, heaven knows, there's plenty of not-so-good times to suck the energy clean outta you. You just gotta recharge them batteries . . . and sometimes, sharing a cup of strong coffee and a fresh donut with a good-lookin' fella like Manny Gilford . . . that's just the thing.*

Unfortunately, Stella's "rest and restore" interlude was short-lived.

No sooner had Manny made the coffee and sent Mervin on an errand to buy tweezers and a magnifying glass than the station door opened and half of the population of McGill poured over the threshold.

But after taking a second look, Stella realized that it was only the Tucker family: Franklin Tucker and his wife, Gertrude; their daughter, Daisy; and Daisy's fiancé, Donald Barton.

Stella decided that the reason the "crowd" had seemed so large at first glance had more to do with their mood than their numbers.

Four angry, upset people seemed to take up a lot more room than the same number of happy, peaceful folks.

Franklin led the group, followed by his wife, with the young, engaged couple bringing up the rear.

Franklin Tucker was one of the tallest and overall largest men in town. When he marched up to Manny, the two of them were eye to eye, a rare occurrence for either of them on the streets of McGill.

"Good morning, Frank," Manny said, but his eyes were less friendly than his words. No one in the room was under the impression this was a casual, social visit.

Gertrude Tucker glanced over at Stella, who was sitting in the chair next to the desk, a mug of coffee in her hand. Stella gave the woman, her daughter, and her future son-in-law a warm smile each. They acknowledged her with curt nods, then turned their attention back to Manny and Franklin and the showdown that appeared to be imminent.

Besides being exceptionally tall, Franklin Tucker presented a striking figure with perfect posture and a highly developed physique. He radiated dignity and a high degree of confidence that prevented most people from doing anything that might put them on his bad side.

As president of the town's only bank, he was usually dressed in a smartly tailored suit, a crisp white shirt, and a navy tie. Though today he wore slacks with sharp creases and an elegant, pale blue sweater that complemented his skin, which was so deeply black as to have a bluish tint.

The ladies were as feminine as he was male in their starched pastel cotton dresses, accessorized by white, patent leather pumps and strands of pearls.

Stella couldn't help thinking that the Tucker family always looked like they were going to Sunday morning church services—even when attending a Fourth of July town picnic or strolling through the livestock displays at the county fair.

As she looked them over, Stella thought, not for the first time, *The Tuckers look more like a family from the nineteen fifties than the eighties. Now days, folks'll wear any ol' thing any ol' where and think nothin' of it.*

The other male in their group was less impressive. Daisy's intended, Donald, was as white as her daddy was black, slouching in his worn T-shirt and faded jeans.

Donald worked at the bank as a teller, his future father-in-law having hired him. But no one thought for a moment that Don would ever be the bank's president.

Following in Franklin's wake, poor Donald looked as though he would have preferred to be anywhere on earth than in a police station.

Stella had heard a few snide remarks, as well as the outright rude ones that Billy Ray had made, about the young, black Daisy marrying a white-bread boy like Donald.

Stella didn't give a hoot about their colors, but she did think they were setting themselves up for a lifetime of trouble, forming a married couple named Daisy and Donald. She figured, if they didn't mind hearing the occasional quack when they walked down the street together or up and down the aisles of the grocery store, then God bless them.

"We've come by this morning to see if you've made any progress on our complaint," Franklin said, his deep voice booming in the small office.

"I figured that's why you were here," Manny said. "Would you like to sit down? I can get some extra chairs from—"

"We won't be staying long," Franklin continued. "It's been nearly seventy-two hours since we were terrorized in our home, each member of my family threatened, our property defaced in the most hideous way."

"I know, Mr. Tucker," Manny said. "I saw the menacing graffiti on your garage doors, the burned cross on your front lawn. As I told you then, I'm furious that you and yours had to endure something like that, and here in my town."

"But what have you done about it?"

"I did what I could, sir."

"Have you arrested anyone yet?"

"No, sir. Unfortunately, there wasn't any conclusive physical evidence at the scene. Plus, no one actually witnessed the acts of burning that cross or painting your doors, so we don't have much to go on, sir. I'm very sorry. I wish we did."

"You know who it was!" Gertrude shouted, surprising everyone in the room. They all turned to stare at the otherwise quiet, dignified lady, who was known in the town as the very picture of gracious restraint. "What proof do you need? There are only three . . . individuals . . . in this town who are hateful and racist, who would do something like that."

"They don't even try to hide it," Daisy chimed in, as angry as her mother. "They cornered my fiancé and me the other night when we were coming out of the library—not even two hours before our home was vandalized—and called us awful names and told us we had no business getting married."

"That's true," Donald piped up, stepping forward, his hands thrust deep into the pockets of his baggy jeans. "I would have hit them for what they called Daisy, but there were three of them and I . . ."

His voice trailed away, and his face turned pink as he glanced up at Franklin, who seemed less than impressed with his narrative.

Stella couldn't help thinking that the Lone White Wolf Pack wouldn't have shot off their mouths to that degree if the older and larger of the two men had been present.

Donald Barton had a way about him that suggested he wore a permanent KICK ME sign on his rear, and Stella couldn't imagine that an overtly masculine fellow like Franklin Tucker was as impressed with his daughter's choice as the young lady was.

That made Stella respect the father all the more, that he would suffer racist attacks with dignity and stand behind his daughter and future son-in-law, whether he approved of their union or not.

"I didn't know about you being harassed, Miss Daisy, Donald," Manny told them. "Only about the cross burning. I'm glad you've brought this to my attention."

"Will it help you build a case against those criminals?" Franklin asked. "This town has suffered quite enough from them in the past, and now we hear Yolanda Ortez has been attacked, probably by Billy Ray Sonner. What can be done about him?"

Manny shot a quick look at Stella, then cleared his throat and said, "Actually, Mr. Tucker, we haven't officially announced this just yet, so I would appreciate you folks keeping it to yourself until we get a chance to make a public statement."

Franklin Tucker's dark eyes searched Manny's. "Okay, Sheriff," he said. "You can trust my family and myself to be discreet. We'll keep anything you tell us strictly among ourselves until you've made your announcement. What is it, Sheriff?"

"I have every reason to believe," Manny began, "that it was, indeed, Billy Ray Sonner who attacked Yolanda Ortez. But he's no longer a danger to her, your daughter, Mr. Barton here, or anyone else."

"Why is that?" Gertrude Tucker asked. She shot a sideways look at her husband, then another at her daughter's fiancé. "Has something happened to Billy Ray?"

"It has," Manny replied. "His body was discovered this morning."

"His body?" Daisy asked. "You mean, he's dead?"

Stella couldn't help noticing the note of almost desperate hopefulness in the young woman's voice when she spoke those two words.

For a moment, Stella thought how horrible it was that anyone would feel relief, even joy, at another human being's passing. What a dreadful legacy Billy Ray Sonner was leaving behind.

It could be said that the best thing he had done in his entire life for his neighbors was to die and leave them in peace.

"Yes, Billy Ray's quite dead," Manny assured her. "The coroner is examining his corpse even as we speak. And since he was the leader of his so-called pack and the others are nothing but brainless followers, I think the trouble you experienced is over now."

"I'm very happy to hear that," Gertrude said. "I wish I wasn't, because it sounds cruel, but I was very worried for my family. We've never had any problem here in McGill. Franklin and I have lived here twenty years and always felt welcome."

"That's true," Daisy added. "This was the first trouble, of a racist sort, that we've ever experienced. It was awful. Really scary. I'm glad he's dead, too, as terrible as that sounds."

"I understand completely," Manny told her. "I'm sure most of the people in this town, if they were really honest, would admit they feel the same way. Don't feel guilty. It's a sad situation, but it's to be laid at Billy Ray's door, not yours or your family's. You have good reason for feeling the way you do."

Stella said nothing, as she studied the family members one by one. The women appeared to be extremely relieved. Donald still looked concerned and ill at ease.

Franklin Tucker's expression was enigmatic, and it puzzled Stella. Though he struck her as a stoic man, she would have expected a different and more animated reaction from him at hearing the news that the man who he suspected of tormenting his family was dead.

However, she did notice that for a brief moment, he turned and gave his daughter's sweetheart an intense, searching look.

What's he lookin' for? she asked herself. *A sign of guilt maybe?*

Was Franklin Tucker thinking the same thing she was? That

maybe the seemingly timid, passive young man, who had chosen not to defend his fiancée when outnumbered three to one, might have found revenge on a man who was alone in a deserted motel?

She stole a glance at Manny and saw he was wearing his "extremely alert" policeman's expression.

Apparently, he, too, had seen the look Franklin had given Donald, and his suspicions were also aroused.

As Stella watched, Manny donned what she liked to call his "Saturday night in the back room of the barbershop poker face." He walked over to his desk, casually sat down, picked up a pencil, and began to scribble something on a notepad.

"Just for the record," he said in a tone as nonchalant as his expression, "may I ask where you were and what you were doing this past evening, Miss Daisy?"

"Why does it matter where my daughter was last night or any other night?" Franklin asked in a tone that would have intimidated a lesser man than the sheriff.

Manny stopped his writing; looked up at Franklin, who was far too close for comfort; and said, "It's just a routine question, Mr. Tucker. Certainly no disrespect to your lovely daughter. I'll be asking everyone I meet the same question for days. Please don't take it personally." Manny turned back to Daisy and repeated himself. "Where were you last night, Daisy? As I said, just for the record."

"She was with me," Donald blurted out.

Manny gave him a long look that suggested he might not believe him. "Oh?" he said.

"Yeah. We went for a drive down by the river. Then we went to my house and watched some television." He turned to Daisy and nodded vigorously. "Isn't that right, sweetie?"

"Don't answer that," Franklin said, putting his arm around his daughter's shoulders and drawing her close to his side. "You don't have to answer any questions at all about anything, Daisy. None of us do. We've done nothing wrong. We're the victims here."

He turned to Manny and, with a stoic, inscrutable face, said, "I'm sorry we can't help you with your investigation, Sheriff, but considering what we had done to us, you'd be remiss in your duties if you didn't consider us suspects in this hoodlum's murder. Given that fact, I think we should postpone this conversation until we have our attorney, Mr. Joshua Glasser, present."

Manny studied him, saying nothing, for a long and uncomfortable time. Finally, he laid his pencil down, pushed the notepad away from him, and stood. Holding out his hand to Franklin, he said, "I understand. You certainly have that right. If I feel I need to question you or any of your family members further, I'll speak to Mr. Glasser and set up an appointment."

At first, Franklin just stared at Manny and didn't acknowledge what he had said or his outstretched hand. Then, to Stella's surprise and relief, he grasped it, gave it a firm shake, and said, "Thank you, Sheriff. I appreciate your cooperation."

With that, Franklin Tucker and his family filed out of the station, leaving Stella and Manny to sit and stare at each other in bewilderment.

"Can you believe that?" Stella said, once she was sure the station house door was closed behind them, and they were out of earshot. "That was just plain ol' weird."

"It was," Manny said with a thoughtful nod. "Not what I would have expected out of them at all. They've always been some of the nicest, most law-abiding, and peaceful folks in this town."

"Well, I wouldn't hold their behavior today against them. Getting a cross burned on your lawn and having your daughter and her intended harassed and threatened, that'd get the sweetest guy in the world riled up. The whole family, too."

"I agree with you, darlin', and I don't hold anything against them for marching in here and speaking their mind, calling me on the carpet, and such. That's not what I'm referring to."

"Whadda ya mean then?"

"I'm talking about the way they acted once I told them about Billy Ray."

"Like maybe they had somethin' to hide?"

"Exactly. Did you see the way that boy jumped in and gave himself and Daisy both alibis and how surprised she was to hear she'd spent the evening with him?"

"Yes, I did notice that, and I also saw the way Franklin looked at him, all suspicious, like he didn't trust him."

"If he doesn't trust his own future son-in-law, why should I?"

"I hear ya."

"Then there's the other thing." Manny paused to take a long drink from his coffee mug. "I told them Billy Ray was dead, that his body had been found. Not a single one of them was curious enough to ask how or why he died."

"That's true, Manny! You never said he was murdered. They just seemed to know it." She shivered to think that someone, or maybe even several someones, in that fine family might have done something to end Billy Ray Sonner. Not for Billy's sake, but because she'd hate to see any of them go to prison for the rest of their lives.

She looked at Manny and could see his own mental wheels were spinning. "What does this mean, Manny? What're you gonna do?"

"I'm going to bump them right to the top of my suspect list, even higher than Deacon Murray, Earle Campbell, or even Raul Ortez."

"If I had my druthers, it'd be one of those first two. Someone from that stupid wolf pack of his and not good folks who never did nothin' wrong in their lives."

"Me too, Stella," Manny said. "Me too. But one of the worst parts of working in law enforcements is, we don't always get to choose who we have to lock up."

Chapter 15

"Granny! Granny, look! I won again!" Little Alma exclaimed as she bounded off the bus and into Stella's outstretched arms. "They gave me another blue ribbon! That means I'm the best speller in the whole wide world!"

Stella and her ecstatic granddaughter's hug was interrupted when Marietta stomped down the bus's three steps and bumped into them so hard that she nearly knocked her grandmother and sister off their feet.

"She ain't the best speller in the whole wide world!" Marietta shouted, displaying an unusual degree of agitation, even for her. "Miss Prissy Pants Alma ain't even the best speller in the school. She's the principal's pet, and Miss Richardson gave her the easiest words. That's the only reason why she won!"

"Marietta Reid!" Stella reached out and grabbed the girl as she flounced past, her chin in the air and the ugliest look Stella had seen in a long time on her young face. "You apologize to your sister this minute, young lady, for those unkind words."

"I will not! It's the truth, and everyone there who saw that spelling bee knows it. After it was over, they were all whispering,

'Alma Reid's a cheater. She don't deserve that ribbon. She deserves an ice cream sundae with poop on the top instead a hot fudge."

Savannah had exited the bus and was standing nearby, listening to the exchange. Calmly, she stepped up to Alma, put her hands on her little sister's shoulders, and knelt so she could be eye to eye with her.

"Alma, sugar," the older girl said, "I was there during that contest and afterwards, too. I know exactly what happened. They gave you hard words to spell, and you spelled every single one of them perfectly and you won, fair and square. And afterwards nobody said anything about you cheating. Marietta is lying through her teeth, because she's jealous of you."

"That's right," Vidalia agreed, as she, too, climbed down from the bus and joined the gathering.

"Marietta don't like studyin'," Cordele added. "She won't apply herself like you do, Alma, but she gets all in a dither when she sees somebody else getting a reward for their hard work."

Waycross nodded solemnly, like a judge about to deliver his verdict on a federal case. "Yep, that's the truth of it. She's just jealous of you, Alma, and all the good things everybody said about you winning, and especially that blue ribbon of yours. She wishes it was hers."

"I don't want that stupid ribbon, and I ain't jealous of the likes of her," Marietta protested. "Alma's dumb and ugly, too. Her front teeth stick out so bad she could eat corn off a cob through a fence post."

In the next three seconds, Stella had removed Marietta from the area and was marching her around the house to the backyard.

She wasn't exactly sure yet what she was going to do when she got to wherever she was taking her. But this was above and beyond even Marietta's usual unpleasantness.

"This just can't be abided," she said more to herself than the child who was dragging her feet and trying to pull away from her by twisting her arm.

"You're hurting me!" the girl screamed. "You lemme go, or I'll tell the sheriff you was mean to me, and he'll arrest your butt!"

Stella knew how hard she was squeezing the child's wrist, and while it might not be comfortable, she certainly wasn't inflicting pain.

Besides, Stella knew the difference in a child who was hurting and one who was furious.

"The next time you see Sheriff Gilford, you go right ahead and tell him all about what I done to you. How bad I mistreated you."

"I'm gonna! You just watch me!"

"Marietta Reid, I could pull the switch off one of these trees and make you dance a jig with it, and he'd tell me it was high time I done it and put a shiny gold-star sticker in the middle of my forehead."

The mention of the switch seemed to make an impression on Marietta. She stopped struggling and looked up at Stella with frightened eyes.

"Are you going to switch me, Granny? I don't want you to do that, okay? It burns real bad, and the marks don't go away for a long time. I'd have to wear knee socks to cover 'em, and it's too hot for knee socks right now."

Stella stopped, looked down at her granddaughter, and her heart melted.

As a child, Stella herself had been in the care of a cruel man, who had readily employed switches when she had misbehaved, or when she was being good but he was angry and wanted to improve his mood by hurting someone incapable of fighting back.

She knew, firsthand, about the terrible, stinging pain and the red welts that remained for days afterward. She knew about wearing knee socks on hot Georgia days.

She pulled her granddaughter over to a bench next to her flower garden, gently pushed her down onto it, and sat beside her.

"I'm not gonna switch you, Mari, 'cause I know how awful bad it hurts, and I don't think I could find it in my heart to hurt you that bad, 'cause I love you dearly."

Marietta stared down at her folded hands in her lap and began to pick at a hangnail on her thumb. She said nothing, but Stella saw her lower lip was trembling a bit.

"But what you did back there, what you said to your sister, was ever' bit as mean and hurtful as pullin' the biggest, heaviest switch you can find off a tree and hitting her with it, all over her back and legs with all of your might."

Marietta gasped and looked up at her grandmother. "It was not! I wouldn't hit nobody with a switch. Not never. Not even stupid, weasel-face Alma! One time, Momma was beatin' the tar outta Alma with a switch, and I took up for her. I told Momma to stop it, and so Momma whupped me, too."

The girl's face had turned bright red, and she was gasping for air as she added, "I wouldn't ever hurt nobody with a switch. I don't care what anybody says, I'm not *that* mean!"

With her final words, she started to sob. For the first time ever, Stella realized that Marietta was aware of her reputation, and she hated it.

In spite of her granddaughter's momentary angst, Stella was somewhat relieved. There might be hope for her second grandchild, after all.

But for the sake of the others—at the moment, little Alma—Stella had to make the most of the learning opportunity.

"I know you don't mean to be cruel, darlin'," she told her. "I know that in your heart of hearts you're a good girl. But we all have to learn lessons. All through our lives we're learnin'. And one of the lessons you need real bad to learn is that the words that come out of your mouth are very important."

Marietta shrugged. "They're just words. Words ain't nothin'. You can't even see them."

"Words are some of the most powerful things in the world. Sweet ones can heal bad, bad hurts. And bitter ones can injure a heart worse than any switch could ever hurt a leg. If you'd beaten your sister with a switch, it would've hurt somethin' fierce, she would've cried, and in a week or so, the marks would be gone, all healed up. But the words you spoke to her just now, those names you call her almost every day that you think are funny, they are leaving switch marks on her heart that are never gonna go away. She'll remember them till her dying day."

"But she calls me 'Contrary Mari.' They all do. Even the kids at school."

"That's not nice. That's mean, and they shouldn't do it. But which would you rather be called, 'Contrary Mari' or 'skunk butt face'? Or would you rather be accused of cheatin' in a contest, one that you won fair and square and worked hard to do so?"

Again, there was no answer. Marietta just continued to stare down at her hands and pick at the hangnail on her thumb. But Stella saw a tear roll down each cheek, which gave her a bit of hope the seed she had just attempted to plant had fallen on soft, fertile ground.

"I'm going to give you a choice," she told the girl, slipping her arm around her waist. "You can either sit out here and think for the rest of the evening, look at the flowers and figure out what you should do to make this situation right . . ."

"That sounds boring as watching weeds grow. What's my other choice?"

"You could go back to your sister, tell her you're sorry for what you said and congratulate her on her new blue ribbon, and help us eat the brownies I'm going to bake to celebrate her victory."

Marietta debated for a while. "Is there a third choice that involves eatin' brownies, but leaves out that Alma part?"

"Nope. Just those two options. What's it gonna be?"

With a deep sigh that was normally reserved for those with the weight of the world bearing down on them, Marietta rose and began to trudge back to the house.

About halfway there, she looked back at Stella, who was following close behind. With a mischievous twinkle in her eye, the girl said, "Them brownies you're fixin' to bake—you're gonna be throwin' in some extra pecans, right?"

Stella reached down and smacked her playfully on the rear. "Good try, kiddo. You know darned well your little sister despises nuts."

To her shame, Stella had to admit that she had been absorbed lately and hadn't been concentrating on her grandmother role as she much as she usually did. Between the pleasure of Manny's company and the dramas of Yolanda's attack and Billy Ray's murder, she had found plenty to distract her from her duties.

Of course, the laundry could wait a day or two, the floors could skip a daily scrubbing, and a stack of hamburgers was quicker to throw together than a dinner of fried chicken, mashed potatoes, and cream gravy.

Washing clothes and cooking weren't the neglected duties she felt bad about.

She regretted the fact that she hadn't been as attentive to the children themselves as she liked to be.

Their parents had neglected them shamefully, and she was determined to show them a completely different experience inside the walls of her home than what they had endured before.

As she sat at the head of the kitchen table with its plywood extension and looked down the sides of it at the little heads, intently bent over their plates, she reminded herself that this was what it was all about.

Raisin' these young'uns, she told herself, *is why I'm here on this earth. It's my sacred callin', as sure as if I was President Reagan or Pope John Paul hisself.*

As she watched the children devouring the fried chicken with all the "fixin's" dinner she had prepared with such love and care, she decided she wouldn't have traded places with either of those fellows . . . or anyone else she could think of, for that matter.

The blessings around her table were the reason why she had to hold even as fine a man as Sheriff Gilford at a distance. At her age, with limited energy and resources, she had to avoid any distraction. Even one who set her heart pitter-patting with a flirty grin or who caused her heart to ache with longing when he held her hand or gave her even the most chaste of kisses.

No more men, Stella May, she told herself, *and certainly not a lawman whose work you find positively fascinatin'. You just ain't got the time or the energy.*

As though materializing out of her thoughts, Manny appeared at the kitchen door. Through the screen, she could see his face clearly, and she thought he looked especially tired. Maybe worried.

Her promise to herself instantly forgotten, she jumped up from her chair and hurried to the door. Unhooking it, she said, "Evenin', Sheriff. Your timin' is perfect. Come on in and have a bite of supper with us."

Even the kids perked up as the large man walked into the already crowded kitchen with its extended table and throngs of children, filling it with his presence.

Manny was a family favorite, and it took only seconds before Waycross had dragged a chair from the living room up to the table and the others had scooted their chairs around to make room for him to sit.

Stella couldn't help noticing that Savannah, who was directing the rearrangement, had managed for the new, empty chair to be placed between hers and Stella's.

Shortly afterward, Manny had a plate of his own in front of him, laden with as generous a helping as the carefully meted out supply could afford.

If it had been anyone else dropping in on them unexpectedly, Stella was sure Waycross would have resented having to give up his extra wing. But Manny was a great favorite, especially with the boy, who was perpetually surrounded by females, so Waycross didn't seem to mind sharing one bit.

Sweet tea glasses were refilled, and Manny offered a rather long-winded toast to their in-house celebrity. Alma glowed, soaking in the attention. Marietta pouted, but kept her mouth shut, except when stuffing it with mashed potatoes.

Even Manny seemed to enjoy the break, a bit of levity in what had otherwise been a stressful few days.

But from time to time, when the group was quiet, intent upon their eating, Stella thought she saw a kind of sadness on the sheriff's face that she hadn't seen earlier in the day. Not even when they had found Billy Ray's body had he seemed so weighed down.

She wondered why he had dropped by unannounced. It wasn't like him. Usually, he called first to make sure it was a good time.

Yes, Stella thought, *somethin's buggin' him. Somethin' bad. No doubt about it.*

As soon as they were finished eating, and the brownies had been enjoyed, as well, Stella began the nightly routine of assigning the chores. "Savannah, please clear the table. Marietta, you wash the dishes. Vidalia dries and puts 'em away. Jesup, wash off the counters when they're done, sugar. You're tall enough to reach all the way to the back of 'em now. Waycross, please take the paper trash out to the barrel and burn it. Cordele, I'd appreciate it if you'd feed the chickens and make sure you rinse out their water bucket real good, while you're at it."

Marietta propped her hands on her hips and said, "What's Alma gonna do?"

Stella reached over, ran one of Alma's silky black curls through her fingers, and gave it a little tug. "Alma is going to go take a nice, long, hot bath and relax. She had a stressful day. Since it's a special occasion, she can even use some of my fancy lilac bath soap that y'all gave me for Christmas."

Marietta opened her mouth to object, Stella gave her "the look," and the child seemed to think better of it. Instead, she spun on her heel, marched over to the kitchen sink, and began to fill it with hot water and suds.

"What would you like me to do, Granny?" Manny asked, leaning over her shoulder, so closely that she could feel his warm breath on her neck.

She glanced over and saw Savannah watching them. She could tell her granddaughter, who wanted nothing more than to grow up and be a police officer herself, was as curious as Stella was about why the sheriff had paid them an evening visit.

Stella turned to Manny and said, "I'd like you to join me in the living room for a cup of coffee, Sheriff, if it ain't too much of a hardship."

"It is," he replied with a chuckle. "A terrible burden. But I'll bear up."

Chapter 16

When Stella and Manny had finished about half their coffee, she decided to just ask him outright what was going on. She could tell he had something on his mind, something he appeared reluctant to tell her.

That, of course, made her all the more curious.

"Spit it out, boy," she said, keeping her voice low, in case it was information of a sensitive nature that he didn't want the children to overhear. "You didn't come by here tonight just to snag a fried chicken supper and a brownie."

"Actually, I was cruising down the highway tonight with my windows open. When I passed your driveway and smelled the heavenly aroma of—"

"Oh, bullpucky. You can't smell what I cook from the highway. You came by to tell me somethin'."

"Yeah, okay."

He hesitated for a moment, then reached into his shirt pocket and pulled out a brown envelope.

She recognized it as one of the type that he'd been using at the motel earlier in the day. "I've got something here I'd like you to look at. I was staring at it all afternoon, and I'm still not sure what I'm looking at."

She reached for her reading glasses, the ones she used when she did fine needlepoint, because the magnification was the highest the drugstore carried.

For extra assistance, she pulled a gooseneck lamp closer and turned it on the brightest of its three settings.

"Okey-dokey," she told him. "I'm ready as I'll ever be. Let's see whatcha got."

"Here, put these on first," he said, handing her a pair of surgical gloves, also like the ones they had been wearing when handling objects at the motel that might be considered evidence.

"Oh, we're gonna be all official now, are we?"

"We are. Technically, I shouldn't be letting a civilian touch it, but I won't tell if you won't."

"My lips are sealed," she said, then added with a grin, "now that I've finished that brownie."

Just as Manny was handing Stella the envelope, Savannah poked her head around the corner and said, "I've finished clearing the dishes now, Granny. Is there anything else I can do for you?"

There was no mistaking the wistful tone in the girl's voice or the pleading expression on her face as she looked down at the envelope that was now in Stella's hand.

Stella laughed. "You mean, like take a look at this here evidence with me?"

"Something like that," she replied with a giggle.

Stella turned to Manny. "If she doesn't touch it, can she look, too?"

"Of course she can," Manny answered right away. "I've got a spare set of gloves, so she can even touch if she wants."

No one had to ask Savannah again. In record time she had crossed the living room, grabbed the gloves out of the sheriff's hand, put them on, and was waiting, hands up, with the expectant look of a surgical nurse eager to assist with a complicated operation.

"I assume your grandmother told you what we found this morning," Manny said, while Stella opened the envelope and looked inside.

"Yes," Savannah replied. "I guess I should feel bad, and I do, if somebody murdered him, because that's just plain wrong if they did. But I'm not sorry he's gone. I don't think he'll be missed much, and poor Yolanda's going to feel a lot safer."

"I'm sure a lot of folks feel that way, sugar," Manny told her. "We'd be lying if we said we were all choked up about his passing. But you're right. If somebody killed him, that's even worse than what he's done. Nobody deserves that."

"Did you inform Yolanda and her dad yet?" Stella asked Manny.

"As soon as you left the station, I went over to the hospital and did it in person. She's conscious now and doing really well. Raul was especially relieved. Doc Hynson, too. He hadn't left their side and was happy to go home and get some sleep."

"You got any yet?"

Manny didn't reply but nodded at the envelope. "Can you get it out of there okay? It being sticky, it doesn't . . ."

"Here it comes," Stella said as she tugged to get the contents of the envelope to release and slide out. When it did, and she got a look at it, she said, "Tape. It's part of the duct tape that was stuck all around the frame of that bathroom door."

"There was tape around the door of the room where you found the body?" Savannah asked, her eyes bright with curiosity as she bent over Stella's shoulder and stared at the gray wad of duct tape that was lying in her grandmother's gloved palm.

"There was," Manny told her.

"On the inside of the door?" the girl wanted to know.

"No. On the outside."

"Was there a window in the room?"

"No window."

"Then Billy Ray couldn't have put tape around the door, gone outside, and climbed in through the window. Not that he would have, because that would've been stupid, but even a ding-a-ling with no good reason couldn't have done it even if he'd wanted to."

Stella and Manny stared at the girl blankly.

"I know," Savannah said, "that didn't come out right. I was just thinking out loud." Then she added in a most authoritative tone, "But the bottom line is: The homicide victim couldn't have put the tape on the door himself. It must have been the perpetrator."

Both Stella and Manny grinned, amused by Savannah's logic that, for all its meanderings, was sound, as well as her use of what she obviously considered official police terminology.

"She gets that lingo from the detective books she reads," Stella told Manny.

"I assumed so. Hey, she has to learn all she can. She's going to be a cop someday, I hear."

But Savannah was too absorbed in studying the evidence at hand to absorb his words or the supportive encouragement he was offering.

"I'm confused," she said. "Why would anybody put tape around a door? Even duct tape's not strong enough to keep a grown man inside, if he was determined to get out. Is it?"

"It's strong, and it might. They used a lot of it," Manny replied. "But what was keeping the door closed for sure was a chair.

The top of it was shoved beneath the door handle nice and tight."

"Wow! Whoever did it *really* wanted to make sure that Billy Ray didn't get out! Sounds to me like it was somebody who was afraid of him."

Both Stella and Manny gave her another long, searching look.

Then Stella said, "You might be right there, Savannah girl. We just assumed he was killed by somebody who was mad at him. Someone he'd done wrong. Heaven knows, there's enough of them folks walkin' the streets of McGill. But the murderer might've been somebody who was afraid of him, not mad at him."

"Actually, the killer could've been both," Manny suggested. "Fear and rage aren't mutually exclusive. Quite the contrary, in fact."

Stella held the tape closer and peered at it under the strong light. "What is that?" she asked, pointing to a fuzzy substance around some of the edges of the tape.

"To be honest, that's why I brought it to you. I was wondering myself." Manny reached into his other shirt pocket and pulled out a magnifying glass with a glittery, hot pink, plastic frame. "No comments on the equipment here, girls," he said. "This is what Merv brought back when I sent him out to buy one. Either he meant it as a joke, or he's dumber than he looks."

Savannah grinned. "They aren't mutually exclusive." She took the magnifier from his hand and gave it to her grandmother.

Stella squinted through it for a long time, then let Savannah have a look.

"It appears to me to be some sort of cloth fibers," Stella said. "Blue ones."

"That's what I thought," Manny agreed. "But what kind?"

"Ain't cotton," Stella replied. "I know what those look like, and they're too fluffy to be silk."

"Looks like fur to me," Savannah suggested.

"Fur?" Manny scowled. "Blue fur? I don't think I've ever seen a blue animal, other than a blue jay or parakeet."

"But it looks like bunny fur," Savannah told Stella. "Like those big, fluffy bunnies that Farmer Dixon and his wife, Miss Peggy, used to raise. Remember how soft and fluffy their coats were? She used to clip their fur off them like they were woolly little sheep and then she'd sell it."

"That's true, Manny," Stella told him. "Them was angora rabbits. Their fur's real fancy. Peggy Dixon told me that angora's used for expensive sweaters."

"Expensive blue sweaters, huh?" Manny nodded thoughtfully. "You mean like the one Franklin Tucker was wearing today."

"Yes," Stella said. Although, thinking the world of the Tuckers as she did, she could hardly bear to admit it. "Exactly like what he was wearing."

"There are a lot of blue sweaters in this town," Savannah said. "I've got one myself. You've got one, Gran. I'll bet you do, too, Sheriff."

"Two actually," he admitted, "but last time I checked they were plain old wool from sheep, not fancy angora rabbits."

"Can't be too many of those in town," Stella said sadly. "Folks can't afford them . . . unless maybe they're president of a bank."

Stella stuck the tape back into the envelope and handed it to Manny.

When he took it from her, he noticed the sad expression on her face. "I'm sorry, Stella," he told her. "Believe me, I'd much rather think Earle or Deacon did this killing. But I have to go where the evidence takes me. I don't believe for a moment that either of those knuckleheads own a sweater like that."

"Unless they stole it from Mr. Tucker," Savanah added. "But since they wouldn't wanna wear it and couldn't sell it for drugs, I can't imagine they'd bother taking it. Besides, you just saw him wearing it."

"I'm afraid she's right, Stella." Manny tucked the envelope and the magnifier back into his pockets.

"She usually is," Stella said, proud as always of her oldest grandangel, but wishing, at least this once, that her remarkable Savannah had been wrong.

Chapter 17

Later, when the chores had all been accomplished, Alma thoroughly celebrated, and there wasn't a brownie left on Stella's best company platter, the children went to bed. Even Savannah retired, though she was loath to do so with Sheriff Gilford still around. She lived for his visits, hung on his every word, and gazed at him with goo-goo eyes every moment she was in his presence.

Manny has that effect on females, Stella had told herself many times, mostly to justify her own infatuation. *A handsome man in a uniform . . . us gals just can't help ourselves.*

But when she walked him to the doorway to tell him goodbye, and he asked her if she would step outside with him for a moment, she knew it had nothing to do with his uniform or his good looks.

Manny Gilford was one of those men who made a woman feel safe. Even a strong woman, who took pride in the fact that she was self-reliant, found it reassuring to know that a man would place himself between her and danger without the slightest hesitation.

It was a trait she found most endearing.

So, when she walked out with him onto the porch, and he reached down to take her hand in his, she was enjoying the feeling that all was right in the world—at least, in her world at that moment.

Until she looked up into his eyes.

What she saw shocked and troubled her. Something *was* wrong. *Badly* wrong.

She had seen Manny angry, troubled, and when Lucy had passed, he had been beside himself with grief for months. But even in his darkest times, he had always been able to look her in the eye. Now, for some reason she couldn't even imagine, he wouldn't meet her gaze.

"Manny, what on earth's wrong with you?" she asked, squeezing his hand. "Come on, darlin', you can tell me."

To her surprise, he reached out, pulled her into his arms, and held her tightly against him. She felt him kiss the top of her hair before he finally released her.

"Okay," he said. "I've put this off as long I can. I have to tell you, before somebody else does." He looked around, then nodded toward the porch swing. "Let's have a seat. You'd best hear this sitting down."

Suddenly, she was afraid. What news could he have that was so bad she couldn't be told when standing on her feet?

"Manny, you're scaring me to death," she said, allowing him to lead her to the swing and ease her down onto it.

"Don't be afraid, Stella." He sat beside her and eased his arm around her shoulders. Pulling her close, he added, "I have something to tell you. Actually, that's why I asked you out for dinner the other night. I was going to take you for a walk along the river and tell you then, but, well, Dolly came running in, and you know the rest."

A walk along the river? she thought. The river that bordered to the south end of town was the prettiest and most romantic area in McGill. Most fellows took their ladies there to propose marriage, and considering how many dark, secluded areas there were along the river's edge, it was commonly known that a sizable portion of the town's population had been conceived along that stretch.

He had wanted to walk along the river with her. Why?

Was he going to propose the other night? she wondered.

He certainly didn't look like a man who was about to declare his love, let alone ask a woman to be his wife. He looked more like a sheriff who was about to inform someone that their loved one had passed away.

She couldn't stand the suspense any longer. "Manny, tell me. The suspense is killin' me here."

"Okay." He drew a deep breath. "I don't know if you're going to consider this good news or bad news. I suspect a bit of both. But a few people in town have found out, so it's just a matter of time until you hear it. I wanted you to hear it from me."

"Go on then. Lemme have it."

"I got a call from a guy I know, a corrections officer, who works there at the prison where Shirley's at."

Stella gasped. "Oh, no! She hasn't gotten herself killed, has she? Those kids couldn't bear it, if she did."

"No. She's started some pretty bad fights, which will go against her when she comes up for parole, but she's healthy enough."

"Then what?"

"Seems they've allowed her some visits with your son." He paused, then added, "Alone."

A light came on in Stella's brain. "No. No, no, no!" she said, trying to keep her voice low and not shout. "They should know better than that. Those two are worse than jackrabbits and—"

"I know."

"Don't tell me that she's—"

"Yes. She sure is. Five months along."

"Heaven help us. Another young'un's the last thing they need."

Stella pictured Shirley in her jail cell, her tummy swelling with yet another baby inside her. What a horrible situation to bring an innocent child into.

A wave of nausea swept through Stella, and for a moment, she thought she might be sick.

"I know the Lord loves little ones," she said as tears clouded her vision. "But why would He allow such a thing to happen under those circumstances?"

Manny chuckled, but there wasn't a lot of humor in the sound. "I don't suppose Shirley and Macon asked for heaven's blessing once that cell door was closed. I don't believe 'forethought' has been high on their list of priorities over the years."

"That's for sure. But then again, if they'd been more sensible, I wouldn't have had some of those precious faces that you saw around my table tonight, and what a loss that would've been."

"True. I know you wouldn't take a million dollars for any of them."

Stella laughed. "Actually, this afternoon I would've taken a wooden nickel for Marietta, but I do have faith she'll come around. One of these days. Maybe after I'm long gone."

"You're not going anywhere soon, Stella May," he said, giving her a tight hug. "Not if I have anything to do with it."

"Thank you, Manny, I appreciate that. And thank you for being the one to tell me about this. You were right. It ain't news I'd wanna hear from anybody else."

"Well, prepare yourself, because a couple of her old drinking buddies from the Bulldog know about it. So it'll probably be all over town by tomorrow morning."

"Oh, goody. Something to look forward to. I can just hear them now. 'Hey there, Miss Stella. I hear you're fixin' to be a granny all over again. Too bad that daughter-in-law of yours is a jailbird.' "

He nodded. "That sounds about right. The more polite among them will say, 'Congratulations, Stella. Another rose to add to your bouquet.' "

"Then they'll walk away snickerin'."

"Probably."

Suddenly, Stella thought of something, and the very idea of it filled her with a powerful mixture of emotions: joy, dread, excitement, and terror.

"Oh, Manny!" she said, her pulse racing. "They won't let her keep that baby. Sure as shootin', they'll take it away from her as soon as it's born."

Manny looked down at her, his eyes filled with kindness and sympathy.

Stella realized this was why he had been so reluctant to tell her. The fact that Shirley was pregnant, once again, was only half of the story.

"They *will* take it from her, darlin'," he said. "Obviously, she can't raise a baby in a place as dangerous as a prison. Plus, some of the charges that put her in there in the first place were felony child endangerment, neglect, and abuse."

"Then what's going to happen?" Stella asked. "What'll they do with that sweet little baby?"

Manny cleared his throat, then said, "I reckon they could put it into foster care, if—"

"No! That ain't gonna happen, Sheriff Manny Gilford. That little one belongs here with its brother and sisters. If somebody besides its mama's gonna raise it, then that's gonna be its grandma."

She turned toward him on the swing and placed her hands on either side of his face. She could feel the scruff of his beard on her palms. The usually meticulously clean-shaven sheriff hadn't shaved or slept for days.

He was obviously exhausted, and yet he had taken the time to come out here to her home and tell her this difficult news, just so that she could hear it from a friend rather than a casual neighbor on the street, someone who would have no idea what this turn of events would mean to her personally.

The last thing she wanted to do was ask him for yet another favor, but she had to.

"Manny, you helped me get custody of my grandbabies. Without you and your influence with Judge Patterson, it never woulda happened. Do you think you can help me this time? I can't let that little grandbaby get put into the system. You know I can't. I'd never have a moment's rest, wondering what's happening to it."

He pulled her close until her head was resting on his shoulder. Stroking her hair, he said, "You know I will, Stella. I'd do anything for you, for those children that were around your table tonight, for the one who's on its way into the world. You know that."

She nestled into his warmth, his comfort, his strength, taking it all in and making it her own. "I know you would, Manny. God bless you."

"He does. He blesses me all the time. He gave me you."

Chapter 18

The next morning, the instant that Stella reentered the house after seeing all the grandchildren onto their school bus, her telephone rang. Even before she picked it up she knew who it was or at least had a strong suspicion.

It's bound to be Manny, she thought. *He's gotta be wonderin' how I feel about the news he gave me last night. He wants to know what I'm thinking now that I've had a chance to "sleep on it."*

Not that she had done a lot of sleeping.

"Good morning, kiddo," he said with a voice that didn't sound as exhausted as he had last night.

Seems at least one of us got a little sleep, she thought. *That's good. Heaven knows, he needed it more than I did.*

"Good mornin', Sheriff," she replied, trying to sound as cheery as she could.

"Did you get any sleep at all last night?" he asked.

"There's no point in tryin' to fool a lawman, is there?"

"Depends on the man, I'd say. I just sent Mervin out to buy some neon lightbulbs for the desk lamp here."

"But that desk lamp don't take neon bulbs. Just regular ones."

"I know. But I needed some peace and quiet, and I didn't want to look at his face for a little while. So he's the hardware store's problem at the moment."

"You ever think of firin' that boy?"

"Only every day and twice on Sunday."

"When's Augustus gonna be back from his honeymoon?"

"Next Wednesday. Or in other words, not soon enough to suit me."

"Buck up, darlin'. Could be worse."

"How? In two days I've had an attack on a young lady and the murder of a guy that everybody in town hated and wanted to see dead."

"But you had me to help you out and add a bit of sunshine to your rainy days." She laughed. "Nothing like tootin' my own horn, huh?"

"It ain't braggin' if it's true. You been a lot of help to me, and while we're on the subject . . ."

"Yes?" she asked, trying not to sound too eager.

"What are you intending to accomplish this morning there at home?"

"Laundry. These kids go through a lot of clothes."

"Oh, well . . . I don't want your grandkids running around dirty on my account. I couldn't bear to have that on my conscience."

"Then your conscience is way too sensitive, boy. Whatcha got to offer as alternative entertainment?"

"Billy Ray's autopsy results? Herb just called me and said he's finished. You wanna go with me?"

"I'll be there in eight minutes. Five if you promise not to gimme a speedin' ticket."

"Make it four, and I'll pin a deputy's badge on you."

* * *

It took Stella ten minutes to arrive at the sheriff's station, because her old truck didn't start right away. Most days she considered it ancient and herself not even close to ancient. Unlike her vehicle, she was just a tad weathered, with a six-figure mileage reading, but a lot of good miles ahead.

After hearing Manny's news and a sleepless night, she felt every bit as old as her truck.

On the way to the station, it occurred to her that with a newborn baby in the house she wouldn't have these hours of the day free any longer, while the children were in school.

"There's a reason why the good Lord doesn't give babies to women my age," she whispered to herself as she pulled in front of the station and parked. "But, then again, it seems sometimes He does. One way or the other."

As she climbed out of the truck and walked up to the station's door, she looked heavenward and whispered, "I consider it an honor that you think I'm up to the task. But I'm afraid you have more faith in me than I have. You're gonna have to help me, Lord. How are you at changin' diapers and two a.m. feedings?"

It occurred to her that some people in her church would've considered her prayer blasphemous. But they were the same folks who claimed it was a sin to wear sandals to church on a hot summer day, so she didn't worry too much about whether or not she rose to their highfalutin standards.

If the Lord above was half as loving and wise as she'd always thought He was, she figured He'd understand that she wasn't gung-ho with the idea of signing up for several more years of dirty diapers and forgive her for it.

She'd done far worse than that over the years, and she and He were still on speaking terms.

When she entered the station, she overheard a snippet of conversation between Manny and his deputy that made her chuckle.

Mervin Jarvis was holding the desk lamp in one hand and trying to screw an odd-shaped bulb into its socket. "Are you sure, Sheriff, that this is supposed to fit in here, 'cause it don't seem to."

"How am I supposed to know, Deputy?" Manny said. "You're the one who bought it."

Manny was gathering some papers off the top of the desk and putting them into a large manila folder.

Stella recognized it as the sort he used to store the documents relating to a case. No doubt, that was Billy Ray's file, and it was bound to get thicker before the day was over.

Manny looked up, saw that she had entered, and gave her a smile. "There you are. Let me guess, that truck of yours wouldn't start again."

"I had to talk to it nice and promise to fill it up with gas later."

"Whatever works." Manny grabbed his jacket off the back of the desk chair and told Mervin, "I'm off to the funeral home. I want to hear if anything important comes up. Right away. Got it?"

"Yes, sir." Mervin glanced at the clock on the wall. "It's about time for Zach Walters to take his garbage out. He'll be calling to complain about his neighbor's dog barkin' at him."

Manny gave him a long, annoyed stare. Then he said, "Deputy Jervis, if you call me away from a murder investigation to bother me about a barking dog—one that we hear about every dadgum morning—I will beat you with your own billy club. Do you understand?"

Mervin didn't look particularly terrified, as he continued to work on getting the tiny bulb base to stay in the much larger socket. "Gotcha, Sheriff. Ten-four."

With his hand on her back, Manny hurried Stella out of the station. Once they were outside and walking down the sidewalk toward his cruiser, Stella said, "He wasn't exactly shaking in his boots over that billy club threat of yours."

"Deputy Mervin Jervis is a seasoned lawman. He hides his terror well. He was petrified."

"Hm. Reckon he'll get over it?"

"Naw. He's scarred for life."

At that moment they heard Mervin whistling a merry tune, no doubt still working on replacing that lightbulb.

Stella giggled. "Brave little soldier."

"I know. I hope to be just like him when I grow up someday."

Stella didn't like having to go inside Herb Jameson's funeral home.

In particular she didn't like going in with Manny. Between the two of them having lost their mates at early ages and under tragic circumstances, they both had more than their share of bad memories of the place.

So, when they went in together, she felt as though her grief was doubled. It was almost more than she could bear.

But then, she supposed most people felt that way about funeral homes.

Herb had done his best to make the place cheerful and comfortable with the flower beds brimming with nasturtiums and petunias beside the door. The colonial columns that supported the Southern antebellum façade were always freshly painted. The circular brick driveway in front was always swept clean, thanks to Herb's daughters, whom he was having to raise alone, since their mother's passing.

As Manny parked in front of the establishment and the two of them exited the cruiser, Manny said, "Hey, isn't that Raul's truck over there behind the hearse?"

Stella looked where he was pointing and saw that it was, indeed, Raul's old red pickup, the one he used to haul feed for his livestock, parked in a rather snug place, between the hearse and the building. It was almost as though the vehicle had been stashed there, so as not to be visible to traffic going up and down the street.

"What's Raul doin' here?" she asked. "I'd think he'd be at the hospital with his girl or at home if they released her."

"I'm wondering the same thing myself. I'm certainly going to find out."

They hurried up the stairs to the double doors. Manny opened the one on the right and held it as Stella entered.

Once they were inside, Stella braced herself, expecting the rush of melancholy that usually accompanied a walk down that hallway with its dark, mahogany-wainscoted walls and thick, navy-blue carpet.

But today, her anxiety seemed less than usual, which she attributed to the mission at hand. Not only were they both interested in hearing anything Herb had to say about Billy Ray's passing, but she was also curious to see what Raul was doing here.

The serious look on Manny's face told her that he felt the same.

They didn't have long to wonder. They passed Herb's office and peeked inside but saw no one.

As they continued on toward the rear of the building, where Herb prepared bodies and, on rare occasions, conducted autopsies, they heard a door open and close, then footsteps, and male voices coming toward them.

Stella soon recognized them as Herb and Raul. Although she couldn't distinguish their words, she thought their tones sounded cordial enough. Liking both men, she was relieved.

Stella knew the instant that Raul spotted her and, more importantly, the sheriff, coming toward him.

She didn't like the guilty look that flashed across his face, along with the sort of apprehension she usually saw her grandchildren display when they had been caught doing wrong.

Very wrong. Not just nabbing the last brownie without asking permission or tracking a bit of mud onto her freshly mopped kitchen floor.

"Good morning, Mrs. Reid, Sheriff," Raul said, far too loudly and much too brightly.

"A good morning to you, too, Mr. Ortez. Fancy meeting you here," Manny said with equally fake-sounding cheerfulness, as he approached the two men and stood close to Raul.

In an instant, Raul seemed to melt in front of them. The false nonchalance disappeared from his face, and his entire body seemed to sag with fatigue and submission in the face of authority.

Stella looked at Herb and saw that he, too, looked sheepish, as though he'd been caught in the act of something he knew wasn't going to go over well with the sheriff.

"I'm sorry, Manny," Herb began. "I knew I shouldn't, but—"

"But I asked him to," Raul interjected. "I begged him to. It's on me, Sheriff Gilford. I take full responsibility."

Manny studied first one man, then the other, his own face inscrutable. Finally, he said in a soft, kind voice, "Before we decide who it is that I'm going to tar and feather, why don't we figure out if anything's amiss. Why are you here, Raul? Got a funeral you need to arrange?"

"No sir. Thanks to you and Mrs. Reid here taking care of my little girl, I'm *not* planning a funeral today, and I'll be forever grateful to you for that."

"We're happy about that, too, Mr. Ortez," Manny told him. "But again . . . why are you here?"

There was a long, tense silence, which Herb interrupted by saying, "He just wanted to look at the body, Sheriff, and that's all he did. I made sure there was no form of contact. He was never closer than five feet from it, and he only stood there for a few seconds."

Manny mulled it over for a while, then nodded to Herb and turned to Raul.

The farmer was staring down at his hands, which were clasped in front of him. As she watched him do so, Stella noticed for the first time how deeply callused they were, how scarred, as well as the numerous fresh cuts, gouges, and bruises. They were the hands of a hardworking man.

She couldn't imagine they were the hands of a killer.

She also had to remind herself that most people in a terrible situation might take the life of another human being, either intentionally or accidentally. One could never know for sure what they might do in such a circumstance.

What would she do if someone had attacked her Savannah in the same way?

She shuddered to even think of it. Or how she would react.

Glancing over at Manny, she saw that he was still watching Raul, studying him, evaluating, no doubt, as she was.

Finally, Manny said, "Okay, tell me one thing, Mr. Ortez, and tell me the truth."

Raul nodded. "I will. I swear. What do you want to know?"

"Why?"

For a long time, Raul stood, thinking. Stella wondered if he was trying to come up with a lie, but something told her he wasn't. That he was simply choosing his words carefully, trying to be as forthcoming as possible.

At last he looked into Manny's eyes and said simply, "I think it was because I had to make sure he was dead."

Manny considered his words, nodded, and said, "I understand."

Raul released a sigh of relief. "Thank you, Sheriff. Thank you so much."

Manny pointed to the front door. "Go back to your girl, Raul. Tell her what you saw with your own eyes."

Raul wasted no time doing as he was bid. Within seconds he was out the door and gone.

Manny turned back to Herb and said, "Don't think for one minute you're going to get off that easy, Coroner Jameson."

Herb held up both hands in surrender. "It never occurred to me I would, Sheriff. Bring out the tar and feathers."

Chapter 19

As Herb led Stella and Manny to the rear of the funeral home, he tried to make his case to Manny. "I swear to you, Sheriff, I never would have let Raul touch that body. He didn't try to either. He understood that he was asking a lot just to be in the same room with—"

"He certainly was," Manny interjected. "Do you understand why, as coroner, you should never have allowed a suspect into the room with a homicide victim's body on your table?"

As Herb paused, his hand on the doorknob of his preparation room, he looked confused. "I guess so he couldn't tamper with anything. But he wouldn't have. I was standing right next to him the whole time. Not that it was a long time, but . . ."

"I'm sure he didn't touch anything, and I'm sure you were keeping a sharp eye on him," Manny assured him. "That's not the reason."

"Okay. I'm sorry. What is it?"

Herb looked miserable, and Stella felt bad for him. Herb took being coroner very seriously. Since being given the job, he'd studied his craft night and day and become much better at it. She could tell he was deeply upset to think he had let Manny down.

Manny appeared to sense the man's discomfort, too, because he softened his voice when he said, "Suppose we solve this case, Herb. We figure out who did it and gather enough evidence to take him to trial. Then his defense attorney gets wind of you bringing yet another suspect into your examination room."

Herb nodded and swallowed hard.

Manny continued. "We could argue that Raul never touched the body, couldn't have altered anything to his own advantage, but you broke protocol. A sharp defense attorney could make it look like you and Raul were in cahoots, trying to frame the defendant or whatever. The simple fact that you didn't follow the rules is enough to muddy otherwise clear waters."

"I understand, Sheriff. Really, I do. I just felt so sorry for Raul. I've got daughters myself. If someone hurt them, I'd want to see for myself that . . . You know."

"Yes, I know. We're just going to forget this ever happened and carry on." Manny nodded toward the preparation room's door. "Let's see what we've got in there. What you figured out so far."

Herb brightened in an instant, swung the door open wide, and ushered them inside.

Stella had been in this room before. Several times, in fact. But she thought she would never grow accustomed to the abrupt change—stepping from the public area of the funeral home with its dark, calming colors and elegant furnishings into a sterile, clinical setting of stainless-steel, hard and shiny surfaces.

Instead of overstuffed chairs and dim lighting that was designed to be comfortable and soothing, she saw harsh, bright lights, cabinets filled with bottles, and boxes bearing chemical-sounding names. There was equipment everywhere with dials, buttons, hoses. She didn't even want to think about what they might be used for.

But today, the simple body preparation room had been used for a far less everyday purpose.

While murder was hardly commonplace in the tiny town of McGill, this ordinary funeral parlor had doubled as a coroner's autopsy suite a few times, including today. As Stella, Manny, and Herb entered, all eyes went directly to the guest of honor, who lay on a large stainless-steel table, covered with a white sheet.

"I am looking forward to hearing what you found," Manny said.

Stella couldn't help noticing the kindness in Manny's tone. She could tell he was trying to make up to Herb for any former sternness. Not that Herb hadn't deserved his scolding. But the gentle undertaker was a sensitive man, a good man, who genuinely tried to serve his community and had done so for many years.

Stella knew that Manny hadn't wanted to wound him, but simply correct him for future situations.

She wondered if either man had considered that Manny was breaking the rules, too, by allowing her into the room. She assumed Manny saw the two situations differently because she wasn't considered a suspect. But she was a civilian with no official duties. She figured that, for Manny to make such an exception for her, he must have valued either her opinion, her company, or both.

She found both possibilities flattering and unsettling. But when she thought of the new baby who might soon be in her arms, she knew these little forays into the world of law enforcement would be coming to an end.

She couldn't imagine bringing a sweet infant into such a situation.

Putting thoughts and concerns of the future aside for the moment, she watched with keen interest as Herb hurried over to the body and pulled the sheet down from the head to its waist.

Stella had the impression that, had she not been present, he would've removed it entirely. It might be the mid-1980s in the rest of the world, but in little McGill, modesty was still considered a great virtue that needed to be practiced at all times. Especially in what was still called "mixed company."

Manny walked up to the table and studied the body carefully. "Can we get a bit more light here, Herb?" he asked.

"Sure." Herb flipped on a light that was hanging over the table, then turned it to its highest setting.

The result was jarring. The sight of the body on the table had been upsetting already, eerie in its stillness, a pale and empty shell, abandoned by the spirit that had occupied it. But the moment the searing light came on, more unsettling details were revealed with stark clarity.

"His eyes, they're awful red," Stella said.

"Looks like quite a bit of discharge or whatever from his mouth and nose, too," Manny remarked. "I didn't notice that back at the motel."

"Even with those lights you brought in, it was pretty dark in there," Herb said. "I didn't see this myself till I had him in here."

The undertaker put on a pair of surgical gloves, reached over, and opened the body's mouth. "If you look in there, you'll see it's all red and irritated, like the eyes. Only even worse."

Stella and Manny saw the inflammation in an instant. It reminded Stella of the worst sore throat the children had ever had and much more.

"That ain't from no sickness I ever saw," she said.

"Me either," Manny said. "It almost looks like he drank some kind of poison or acid."

"Funny you should say that," Herb replied. "When I saw this, it reminded me of Carrie Strothers. Do you remember her?"

Manny nodded. "Used to be a waitress at the Igloo. Long time ago."

"That's right. I was in Doc Hynson's office one day, getting some stitches in my thumb. A scalpel cut." He grinned. "You think it's dangerous being a sheriff, try being an undertaker. Anyway, while he was sewing me up, Carrie's daughter brought her in. Her eye was a mess, and she wasn't breathing right. She'd been kneeling on the floor next to the toilet, cleaning it. She set the bottle of cleaner down on the floor a bit too hard, 'cause she was in a hurry to get to work. This stuff inside kinda blurped up and outta the bottle. It got her right in the face. Quite a bit of it. She was really suffering. Her eye was all red like Billy Ray's here, and where she'd got some in her mouth, it looked like this, too, only not as bad."

"A caustic solution of some sort in the face. Hm-m," Manny said, thinking it over.

"But we didn't see no bottles of toilet bowl cleaner there in the bathroom or even in the bedroom," Stella observed. "There wasn't much of nothin' there in that bathroom, except Billy Ray and a towel that was fixin' to fall to pieces."

"I doubt that he drank something poisonous, and then walked into the bathroom to take a shower," Herb said. "From what I can see there in his mouth and that eye, he would've been in quite a bit of pain."

Stella agreed. "I reckon bathroom sanitation would've been pretty low on his list of priorities at a time like that."

"I'll have to go back to the scene again," Manny said, "and check the drains for anything like a cleaner. Anything that could do that much damage to human flesh on contact."

Stella leaned closer, looking at the side of his head. "I'd forgot he had blood in his ear."

Herb nodded. "He's got some in the other one, too. I took a look inside and the inner ear looks as inflamed as his eyes, nose, and throat."

"Did you find any signs of injury on the body," Manny asked, "defensive wounds or whatever?"

"Not injuries," Herb said, pulling the sheet a bit lower and exposing part of the abdomen. "But look at this. I never saw anything like that before."

He pointed to some strange pink and green spots on the skin.

Stella looked at the discolorations. "I can't say as I ever saw anything like that either."

"Weird," Manny said. Pointing to a spot where a small patch had been cut away, he added, "Is that where you incised a sample, Herb?"

"Yes. I took samples from his mouth, throat, lungs, even his heart, along with the usual blood and other bodily fluids like that foam that's around his mouth."

"Good. You get those packaged up, labeled, and ready to go. I'll send them off to the lab in Atlanta, ASAP. We're going to need help with this stuff. It's obviously outside our realm."

"I don't mind saying I'm out of my depth, Sheriff. I'd appreciate all the help you can get us."

Manny looked over the arms and hands. "Is that it when it comes to signs of injury, Herb? Nothing else?"

"No. Just the mess he made of his fingers trying to get out."

"We can see why now," Stella said. "That hurt eye and sore throat must've been pretty painful. He was probably trying to get out so's he could find him some help."

"Then we don't have an actual cause of death," Manny said with a tired sigh. "Somebody must have murdered him, but we don't have a clue as to how or why."

"That's about the size of it," Herb admitted, looking about as defeated as Stella had ever seen him.

"Okay." Manny turned to Stella. "Want to go back with me to the motel and check the plumbing for some sort of drain cleaner?"

"Sure," she said, eager to get out of the funeral home and away from the sight of the body on the table.

Turning to Herb, Manny said, "Get those samples all packed up nice and official. I'll pick them up on my way back."

"Will do." Herb hesitated, then added, "Again, I'm sorry for that business with Raul. I should've known better. It'll never happen again."

"I know it won't, Herb. Forget about it. I have."

"Thank you, sir."

A moment later, Manny and Stella were hurrying down the long, dark hallway toward the front door, and Stella was grateful.

She couldn't recall when she'd been in such desperate need of a bit of fresh Georgia air and sunshine.

Chapter 20

"Sometimes I wonder how you can stand to do this kinda thing all day long," Stella told Manny as she watched him pulling the plumber's snake out of the toilet in the bathroom at Mabel's.

He groaned as he straightened his back and tossed the snake onto the floor. "I don't do that sort of thing very often. Usually, my duties don't include toilet plunging in derelict motels. Mostly, I get to do glamorous stuff like pull cats out of trees and hose out the back of my cruiser after I've given some drunk a ride home."

"Hey, that's why they pay you the big bucks."

He walked over to the sink and began to wash his hands as well as he could without soap.

"There's nothing in that toilet drain but what you'd expect to find there," he said. "The same with the sink and the shower drains. The showerhead's got nothing on it or inside it but a ton of rust. So much for Herb's idea of some sort of cleaning fluid or chemical drain opener causing Sonner's death."

Stella watched the water as it sputtered and spit into the dirty sink. "This place has been deserted for ages," she said. "The electric's turned off. How come the water's on?"

Manny dried his hands on his pants legs. "I'm sure it has something to do with the fact that Billy Ray's old man worked for the water company."

"Oh, that's right. He did . . . before he got sent off to prison. Reckon among all those wise life lessons that Billy's daddy imparted to his son along the way, there were some tips on how to steal water from the city."

"I'm sure he either turned it on or had one of his flunkies do it. In one of the other rooms I saw enough beer cans, marijuana roaches, and girlie magazines to suggest that they had some get-togethers here."

"How do you know it was the Lone Wolves?"

"The swastika flag on the wall was a tip-off, along with the initials LWWP spray-painted on the wall."

"Those boys had a real talent there, decorating with spray paint cans. They missed their callin's as graffiti artists. Speaking of, where's that ugly pickup of theirs?"

"I had it towed over to Flo's garage, and I went over it. Didn't find anything, but I didn't really expect to, after I'd talked to Deacon and Earle."

"You interviewed those hooligans?"

"Sure. I figured they were the ones who took Billy Ray his truck and a change of clothes."

"Did they?"

"Deacon did. Billy Ray broke into the Hodge house—they're away on vacation—and called him. Told him to get the truck to him on the double, so he did."

"Could you arrest Deacon for aiding a fugitive or somethin'?"

"I could, but he swore he was in fear for his life. I'm keeping the possibility in my back pocket, in case I need it later."

Stella looked around and shuddered. "Are we done here? I've had enough of Mabel's for a while."

"Me too. Let's boogie. I've got to get those samples from Herb and off to Atlanta. Hopefully, that'll prove more helpful than snaking an old toilet."

As they locked up the motel room and Manny strung the yellow police tape across the door, Stella thought about Billy Ray and his father. Both were dead now, and it could be argued they contributed to their own untimely demises.

Live by the sword, die by the sword, Stella thought, recalling Pastor O'Reilly's most recent sermon.

"That daddy of Billy Ray's, he never had a lick o' sense, bless his heart," she said as they got back into the cruiser. "He beats that guy in the pool hall nearly to death and winds up in prison. What sort of example was he setting for his young son? What age was Billy when that happened? Ten?"

"About that, I'd say, and Billy's mom wasn't much better. Died in that car wreck."

"She'd been drinking, as I recall."

"She was. Broadsided old Mr. Hayworth. He suffered to his dying day from the injuries she inflicted on him."

"Some folks lead sad lives, that's just all there is to it. I hate the way Billy Ray was, but it ain't too hard to see how he got that way."

Manny started up the car and drove it around the motel and onto the highway. "That's very true. I believe he was about fifteen when his dad got killed in that fight."

"I remember hearin' about that. A fight there in the prison yard, I believe."

Stella was silent, as yet another part of the story came to mind. A disturbing detail.

Manny was the first to speak of it. "The guy who killed him was a Latino, as I recall."

"I remember that, too. I also heard that Mr. Sonner was the one who started the fight."

"Not too hard to see where Billy Ray's nasty attitudes came from. Especially if he didn't take into account the fact that his daddy caused his own problems in life."

"Folks have a tendency to overlook details like that, when it's to their advantage to do so."

Stella thought about the young man stretched out on the stainless-steel table in Herb's preparation room, his hateful tattoos and the strange pink and green spots on his skin.

He'd been strong and healthy . . . except in his mind and spirit. He should have lived a full life, enjoyed raising a family, and contributed something to the world before he left it. What a waste.

"The apple didn't fall far from the Sonner tree," Manny said.

Stella nodded solemnly. "Apples seldom do . . . even on a windy day."

Chapter 21

No sooner had Manny driven himself and Stella back to the funeral home than his radio crackled with a message from Mervin.

"Sheriff, is Mrs. Reid still with you?"

"She is. Why?"

"The school called. Seems Mrs. Reid told the secretary there that, if they needed her, she might be here at the station or out runnin' around in the cruiser with you."

Stella's heart sank. "I did, Manny," she said. "Alma's not been feeling well. I told them to contact me through you if need be."

"Okay, Merv. What else did the school say?"

"Just that one of her granddaughters ain't feelin' up to par, so she oughta come get her."

"Okay. Call them back and tell them she's on her way."

An instant later, Manny was leaving the funeral home and driving toward the town center. "I'll take you to the school," he said, "and if she needs to go to the doctor or the hospital, we'll take her there, too."

"No," Stella objected. "It's bad enough that I interrupt your important business with you having to take me back to the station to get my truck. Then you're gonna have to turn back around and head back to Herb's when you were there already. That's a waste of time on a day when you're so busy. I'm really sorry."

"Don't be silly. Those samples can wait a while. We'll get you and yours taken care of first."

"I won't have it, Manny! Listen to me. That child's had a bellyache off and on for days, and I'm pretty sure we can chalk it up to her being in a dither about that spelling bee and too many rich desserts in a row. You take me to the station."

She gave him a little grin. "You won't even have to stop. Just slow down as you drive by, and I'll bail out. I've rolled outta a few cars in my day."

"You have? How many?"

"Well, none. But how hard could it be? Never too late to learn a new skill, I always say."

"I never heard you say that before."

"Manny, hush up."

"Yes, ma'am."

When they neared the station, Manny made a big show of putting his arm across her so she couldn't jump out. So, of course, she had to pretend to try.

Once the cruiser was stopped next to her truck, he said, "I'll wait to make sure you can get that jalopy going."

"Thank you. Good luck with . . . whatever you're doin' for the rest of the day."

"It won't be as much fun as feeding Alma chicken soup and reading her stories to keep her mind off her tummy, but I'll try. I'll call later to see how she's doing."

"I appreciate it, Manny."

"I know you do. I hope she's okay."

"She will be. Toodle-oo."

"You too."

As he'd promised, he waited until her truck was started and she had pulled away from the curb to make a U-turn and head back the way they had come.

She watched in her rearview mirror as the black-and-white cruiser disappeared down the road.

She felt lonely, as she always did when he left her presence these days.

How on God's green earth can you feel lonely, Stella Reid? she asked herself. *You live in a tiny two-bedroom house with seven young'uns and now there's another one on the way. How lonesome can a body feel under those circumstances?*

Mighty lonely, was her heart's quiet reply. *Mighty lonely, indeed.*

Stella expected that she would need to go inside the school to collect her ailing granddaughter. She couldn't bear the thought of her gentle little Alma suffering—spelling bee stress or coconut cake and brownies aside.

But to her delight, the moment she drove in front of school and parked in one of the spaces reserved for visiting parents, the tiny girl came bounding out the door and down the steps to greet her with a wide smile.

Her glossy black curls, so like Stella's and Savannah's, bounced as she scurried around to the passenger's side of the truck and climbed inside.

"I thought you were in a real pickle, girlie," she said, reaching over and giving her a kiss on the cheek. "I came tearin' over here like a Kansas tornado to get you, and here you sit, fit as a fiddle."

Then Stella noticed the brown stain on the front of the girl's white blouse. "Uh-oh," she said. "That looks like chocolate milk."

Alma grinned and nodded. "It is."

"When it got spilt, was it on its way in or on its way out?"

"On its way out. That's why my teacher wanted me to go home."

"I'll bet she did."

"She had to call the janitor to clean up the, um, spilt milk. She wasn't too happy about it and neither was he."

"So you were just spreadin' sunshine all over the place, huh?"

"Just on my desk and Sally's back and hair."

"You mean Sally Kapensky, whose momma sings alto with me in the church choir?"

"Yeah. She sits in front of me. Well, she used to. She'll probably ask the teacher if she can move to another desk now."

"Ain't that just . . . lovely."

"She probably won't wanna be my best friend no more neither."

"Go figure."

Several hours later, all of the children were home, having returned from school at their regular time. Stella had given them strict instructions to remain in the kitchen until they finished their homework, then to play quietly either in their bedroom or outside.

As always, Savannah remained nearby to help nurse and entertain her ailing sibling. At such a time, Stella always experienced mixed emotions about having the girl so involved in the younger children's upbringing. She felt guilty for relying on a child and asking her to perform what should have been adult duties. Yet, Stella felt enormously grateful, because she couldn't imagine how she could have managed without her help.

Stella placed Alma on the sofa next to her own comfy chair. The child was lying down, her head was resting on Stella's best feather pillow. Well plumped, of course.

Stella covered her with her best quilt, the one her mother had made. Stella gave her strict instructions not to deposit any leftover chocolate milk on it. A waste basket, lined with two layers of plastic grocery bags, sat on the floor next to her for that exact purpose.

"I like this quilt," Alma said, tracing the colorful rings that intersected each other, swirling toward the center.

"It's a very special quilt," said Savannah, who was sitting on the couch, down by Alma's feet. She looked up from the book she was reading. "Our great-grandma Gola was a real Cherokee, and she made that Cherokee wedding quilt for Granny when Gran was just a little girl. But she didn't show it to her when she made it. She wrapped it up in brown paper and tied it with a string and told her not to open it until the day she got married. She said it was her wedding present to her."

Alma turned to Stella. "Did you? Did you wait until you married Grandpa Art to open it?"

"I did."

"That's so nice," Alma said, stroking the fabric with her palm. "A real, honest-to-goodness, Cherokee wedding quilt, made by a real Cherokee momma. No wonder it's so pretty."

Stella gave Savannah a smile that was tinged with sadness. Savannah knew the rest of the story, but she was wise enough not to share it with her younger sister. Gola must have had a premonition that she wouldn't still be alive when her daughter was grown and getting married. Why else would a mother make a quilt, wrap it, and give it to her young child, to be opened many years later?

But Stella had told Savannah the story only recently, and she had warned her then that her siblings were too young to hear how their beautiful, young Cherokee great-grandmother had left this world.

It was best that they thought of her simply as the lady who had made the lovely, colorful quilt, which they all enjoyed now.

Especially when they needed a bit of coddling, as Alma did at that moment.

Savannah returned to her reading, and Stella sat in her chair and crocheted, allowing Alma to rest. Stella hoped she might drift off into a peaceful, healing sleep.

But instead, the child tossed and turned, as though she couldn't get comfortable, special quilt and pillow or not.

"Would you like to hear a story, sugar?" Stella asked her. "I could read you a nice fairy tale from that old book you kids gave me for Christmas last year. It's got some good ones in it."

"No, that's okay." Alma looked up at Stella with eyes that seemed less bright than usual. Less lively than they had been even a few minutes before.

"Are you feelin' any better?" Stella asked. "Did that medicine I gave you help your tummy at all?"

"I think it might've made it worse." Alma touched her belly gingerly.

Stella wondered if she should call Dr. Hynson's office again. She had done so as soon as she returned home with the girl, but the doctor's wife told her that he had gone to the hospital to deliver Debbie Lockland's baby. Mrs. Hynson couldn't say when he might return. Since it was Debbie's first, it might take a while.

Stella reached over, placed her hand on the child's forehead, and frowned, unhappy with what she felt. "Let me take your temperature again, babycakes. You feel hotter than before."

On her way to the bathroom, Stella passed the girls' bedroom and overheard Marietta and Vidalia quarreling about something. This time, even Cordele and Jesup had joined in the affray.

"Y'all keep it down in there like I told you!" she shouted as she passed by. "Your sister ain't feelin' good, and she don't need to hear that malarkey! Neither do I."

To her surprise, they did as they were told instantly. By their tone, she could tell they were still arguing, but at least they were doing so quietly.

She hurried into the bathroom, took the thermometer from the medicine chest, and returned to the living room. She couldn't help being worried. A tummy ache was one thing. A fever, too? That could be bad. More than nerves or an overindulgent diet.

She knelt beside the coach, shook down the thermometer, and stuck it in Alma's mouth, placing the end under her tongue. Then she stroked her hair as they waited for the result.

"That's it, sugar," she told the girl. "You're gonna be just fine. I wouldn't have it any other way, you hear?"

Alma nodded, but Stella didn't like how pale she looked or how quickly she had gone from the chatty, energetic little girl they all loved to this lackadaisical, faded version of herself.

Just as Stella was getting ready to remove the thermometer and check it, there was a soft knocking on the door.

She wasn't expecting company, but in a town as small as McGill, neighbors frequently dropped by unannounced.

Today, of all days, she wished they wouldn't.

Savannah answered it, and Stella was surprised to hear Dolly Browning's voice from the porch saying, "Hello, Savannah. Is your grandmother at home? I dropped by to give her some fresh tomatoes. Just picked them this morning. I've got so many this year, I don't know what to do with them."

Savannah turned and gave Stella a questioning look. Stella nodded, and Savannah said, "How nice of you, Miss Browning. Please, do come in."

To Stella's mortification, it was the exact moment when Dolly stepped into their house that the thermometer came out of Alma's mouth.

It came flying out, along with whatever remained of the chocolate milk she had consumed during her school milk break.

Fortunately, it missed the quilt and most of it landed in the trash can next to the couch.

But Stella was less concerned about the spectacle it must have presented to their visitor and more worried about the fact that her granddaughter wasn't as far along the road to recovery as she had hoped.

Apparently, quite the contrary, in fact.

"I'm so sorry, Miss Browning, but it might notta been the best time for you to come callin'. We ain't at our best, I'm afraid. We've got us a sick girlie here," Stella said as she stroked Alma's forehead, which was now definitely hotter than it had been before. Stella certainly didn't need a thermometer to tell the girl had a fever.

With a look of deep concern, Dolly handed a large bag filled with tomatoes to Savannah, then hurried over to Stella and stood beside her, next to the couch. "What's going on here?" she asked Alma. "We can't have sick girlies around here. We don't allow such a thing."

"She's got herself a fever and her tummy aches," Stella said. "She seems awful tired all of a sudden. She was bright-eyed and bushy-tailed a couple of hours ago."

Dolly laid her hand on Alma's forehead. "How long have you had a tummy ache, sweetie?" she asked her.

"A few days. Off and on."

"Has it been about the same or getting worse?"

"Worse," Alma replied in a voice that sounded so small and weak that it frightened Stella.

With seven grandkids, she was accustomed to nursing sick children. But she didn't like how quickly Alma seemed to be going downhill.

"Stella, have you spoken to the doctor yet?" Dolly asked, moving closer to the couch and Alma.

Stella had to step back a little to make room for her.

"No," Stella told her. "Doc's out of town. His wife says he's at the hospital delivering a baby."

"Aren't they always when you need them," Dolly said. "She definitely has a fever, and I don't like the way she looks."

"Me either, but I—"

"Would you mind if I examined her?"

Dolly's question took Stella aback. Why would this woman, who had just walked into her home to deliver some tomatoes, want to examine her granddaughter?

"I don't mean to overstep, Stella," Dolly said, as though reading her mind. "I just want to help if I can."

Stella studied Alma for several moments. The child looked as though she was about to drift off to sleep. "Would that be okay with you, darlin', if Miss Dolly here checked you over a little bit?"

Alma gave a faint nod, so Stella said, "Go ahead, Miss Dolly. If you think you can . . ."

But Dolly Browning had already raised the hem of the girl's pajama top and lowered the elastic of the bottoms a couple of inches, exposing her belly.

Bending down, Dolly placed her ear on the child's abdomen and listened intently for what seemed like a terribly long time to Stella.

What on earth is she trying to hear? Stella wondered. *Seems like a strange thing—listening to somebody's tummy—to be doin' at a time like this. But she appears to know what she's doing, so . . .*

Finally, Dolly lifted her head and murmured, "Hm-m. Bowel sounds . . . absent." To Alma she said, "Stick out your tongue for me, honey. Let me have a look at it."

Alma did so and Stella noticed it was white, rather than a normal pink.

"Okay, coated tongue," Dolly muttered under her breath. Placing her fingertips on Alma's neck, she said, "Fast pulse."

She placed her index finger of her right hand on Alma's navel and her left in the area of her pelvis on the right side.

It seemed to Stella that Dolly was measuring the distance. Stella watched carefully as Dolly pressed down gently on a spot between the two points that was about two-thirds of the way down.

Alma let out a terrible yelp, and Dolly instantly released the pressure.

Dolly turned and looked at Stella, and the expression on her face made Stella feel suddenly very cold inside.

"We need to call the ambulance," Dolly said, her voice calm and measured. "Hopefully, it will be available. If it's not, we'll drive. Fast."

"Why?" Stella said, afraid of the answer she would receive.

"What's wrong?" she heard Savannah ask, even as the girl hurried to the telephone.

"We have to get Alma to a hospital. I believe she's experiencing the late stages of appendicitis."

Chapter 22

As both Stella and Dolly feared, the town's only ambulance was unavailable when Savannah called for it. But Dolly was kind enough to not only drive Stella and Alma to the hospital, but to remain with Stella as she waited for news of her granddaughter's condition.

They sat in a tiny, claustrophobic waiting room, on a couch that had once been quite fashionable in the seventies with its velvet, floral design and diamond-tucked back. But now, ten years later, the piece of furniture looked as tired and depressed as most of the people who sat on it, waiting for word about their loved ones' conditions.

Stella was no exception.

Just when she thought she had this child-raising duty all figured out, something would come along and show her how little she knew about anything.

If it hadn't been for Dolly Browning, she would still be sitting in the living room with Alma on the sofa, having no idea that the child was seriously ill.

Stella reached over to Dolly, who was sitting next to her, and grasped her hand. "If I live to be a hundred years old, Miss Dolly, I'll never be able to repay you for what you did today."

Though she tried to fight them back, Stella couldn't keep the tears from filling her eyes and running down her cheeks.

One of her grandangels in the hospital.

It was almost more than she could bear.

Dolly chuckled, and the sound of simple laughter gave Stella more comfort than she would've thought possible.

"By the time you're one hundred years old, Stella Reid, I'll be long gone. So you're going to have to repay me with one of those amazing apple pies you make. But I'm old, so don't wait around too long."

"Oh, I won't, believe me. As soon as my little grandgirl and me are outta this place and back home again, you'll be gettin' that pie. Maybe a cake and some brownies, too."

"The pie will be enough, that and seeing your little one running around, full of vim and vigor again."

"From your mouth to God's ears."

They both jumped when the waiting room door opened and the emergency room doctor who had first examined Alma upon their arrival walked in.

He was young. Far younger than Stella would have liked. But then, long ago she had noticed that they were making doctors, lawyers, and policemen far younger than they used to. At least in the eyes of a person who had passed the age of fifty and was old enough to be those professionals' parent.

Both Stella and Dolly jumped up from the old sofa and rushed over to him.

Anticipating their question, he immediately said, "She's fine. As fine as a kid can be whose appendix has to come out. Right away."

"I was afraid of that," Dolly said. "Her white blood cell count is elevated?"

"Very," the doctor replied. "You brought her in just in time."

"Can I see her?" Stella asked. "They grabbed her away from me almost as soon as we brought her in the door. The nurses shooed me right out and told us to wait up here."

The doctor shook his head. "I'm sorry, Mrs. Reid. But she's already been taken to surgery. We couldn't wait. But as soon as she's stable and awake, we'll be sure to let you know. Try not to worry. It's a fairly common surgery, and the surgeon who's working on her has done hundreds of them."

"Hundreds?" Dolly asked.

The doctor smiled. "He did fifty before breakfast this morning." He pointed to the old couch and said, "I'll have somebody come tell you when it's over, but it's going to take a while. So you might as well have a seat over there and try to relax."

"You ever had a baby that you loved going under the knife, Doctor?" Stella asked, trying not to sound bitter or angry. After all, it wasn't this young man's fault that Alma was in surgery.

"No, ma'am, I haven't," he said. "But I can imagine how awful it must be."

No you can't, Stella thought, as she walked back to the couch and collapsed onto it. *Unless you've actually been through it yourself, unless it's your little one, your own flesh and blood, who's in danger, you can't possibly imagine what it's like.*

Three hours later, Stella was in the hospital chapel on her knees, leaning her elbows on a pew seat, and praying, when she heard the door in the back open and close.

Looking up, she saw Manny hurrying toward her.

She jumped to her feet and met him halfway, where he gave her a long, tight hug.

"I came as soon as I heard," he said. "I stopped in the ER, and they told me little Alma's surgery was over. They said everything went well, so I figured you'd be here in the chapel saying, 'Thank you!' "

"Of course I was," she said. "After begging for a good outcome all that time, I figured I'd better come here and give thanks for answered prayers. It's not nice to bend somebody's ear for hours, beggin' and beggin' them for somethin' and then not even say, 'Thank you,' when they deliver the goods. Not even when it's God above."

Stella looked around. There were several other people, who were praying or simply sitting and soaking in the sacred peace and comfort of the place. Some of them looked worried, as though they hadn't received their good news yet.

"Let's go outside," she whispered, taking him by the arm and heading toward the door.

Once they were out in the hallway, he said, "I called your house to see how Alma was feeling. I was surprised when it was Elsie who answered the phone."

"Oh, good. She's over there already. I called Savannah when we got here and told her to get hold of Elsie and ask her if she could come over there tonight to watch them. Savannah's fine watching them for a while in the daytime, but come nightfall, I want an adult there."

"That's what Elsie said. She told me she'd be spending the night. She figured you'd stay here at the hospital with Alma."

"I sure will. They told me I'd have to go home as soon as visitin' hours are up, and I told them they'd better have a whole herd of burly security guards standin' by to throw me out, 'cause that'll be the only way I'll go."

Manny laughed. "At least those guards will be near an emergency room. They can get their wounds tended to right away, once you've finished with them. I don't envy those guys their task, tossing you out on your ear."

"Ain't gonna happen. I won't press my luck by trying to sit there in her room all night. But I promised my sweet girl that anytime she wakes up tonight, she can rest assured that I'll be in the chapel or that waiting room, stretched out on their beat-up old couch, and if she needs me, all she has to do is tell a nurse to come get me."

"Good for you. How did she look, your Alma, when you saw her after the surgery?"

"She was still pretty groggy, but I managed to get a giggle outta her when I told her she could bring that ol' appendix home, put a leash around its neck, and keep it for a pet. She says she's gonna name it, "A. P. N. Dicks."

He reached out and ran his fingers through her curls. "You're a wonderful grandma, Stella. I'm so sorry I dropped you off like I did there at the station. I should have taken you to the school, grabbed her, and got you both to the hospital."

"There was no reason to think she was so awful sick at that point. I had no idea it was serious. Not until Dolly Browning dropped by our house to give us some tomatoes. She looked her over good and figured out it was appendicitis in two shakes of a lamb's tail. I'm tellin' you, you shoulda seen the way she checked that child out. Like she knew exactly what she was doin'. I was mighty impressed, I tell you."

"She's a strange one, that Miss Dolly. Sometimes she's crazy as a bedbug, thinking somebody snuck into her house at night and hid her glasses just to torment her."

Stella chuckled. "Then they creeped back in the next night and left them in her freezer."

"I guess it's easier to blame missing objects on some imaginary enemy than admit you're slipping some mentally and leaving your stuff in weird places."

"Then she goes and does somethin' like she did today, savin' my baby's life with knowledge that I didn't have, and most people wouldn't. She's an odd one, that Dolly. You never know what to expect outta her."

He glanced up and down the empty hall. "Where is she now?"

"I sent her home. She didn't wanna go. Put up quite a fuss about it. She even offered to stay the night with me. But I told her to go take care of her animals, they'd all need feedin' and the dog would need walkin'. I told her I was fine, since I knew my Alma was gonna be okay."

"You must have been so worried. Surgery. On a child so young."

"Oh, I was beside myself, Manny. Turns out it was just as serious as Dolly feared, too. They said that appendix was so swollen up and infected and fragile that when the surgeon took it out, it fell apart right there in his hand. I tell you, if it hadn't been for Miss Dolly Browning, I don't think I'd have my baby girl no more."

"That's wonderful, honey. Thank goodness for Dolly. I'll be sure to thank her next time I see her. In fact, I believe I'll ask the mayor to give her some sort of medal or prize. Name her McGill's Citizen of the Year or whatever."

Stella couldn't tell if Manny was joking or serious, but something told her that Dolly wasn't the sort to want a medal or anything else as a reward—other than a home-baked apple pie.

She glanced down and realized that Manny was holding a brown paper grocery sack in his hand. It appeared to be full of something and its top was folded closed.

"You didn't need to bring me food," she said. "They've got a good cafeteria here, and I'm on friendly terms with the gal who runs it. I ain't likely to starve."

"It's not food," he said, handing it to her. "Savannah asked me to swing by your place on my way here, pick this up, and bring it to you. She said it had 'girl necessities' in it. I figured I'd better not ask for particulars, but just do as I was told."

Stella unfolded the top and peeked inside. On top of what appeared to be a stack of clothes and toiletries, she saw her purse, some panties, and a stick of deodorant.

"God bless that child," she said. "I was wondering how I was going to brush my teeth tonight or comb my hair tomorrow morning. I ran out of the house with nothin' but my ailin' granddaughter in my arms. Thank you, Manny. I sure appreciate this."

"No problem. Did they say when they might release her? I know you'll be anxious to get her home."

"Oh, I sure am, and they said, if all goes well, she can leave day after tomorrow."

"That's great. You just let me know when you think you and she will be ready to travel, and I'll be here. I can get you home in record time."

"Lights and sirens?"

"For our little Alma, you betcha. She gets the works."

Suddenly, their cozy conversation was interrupted by an angry voice shouting, "Sheriff Gilford! What the hell are you doing here? You've got a lotta gall showing your face here, now of all times!"

They turned toward a door at the end of the hall where several people had just entered. The one who had yelled was Donald Barton, Daisy Tucker's fiancé. He was accompanied by Gertrude Tucker and Daisy.

All three seemed highly upset about something and the target of their wrath appeared to be Manny.

"I beg your pardon?" he asked in a tone that was as calm and smooth as Donald's was loud and abrasive.

"You just can't leave him alone, can you?" Daisy shouted as the irate trio rushed down the hall toward Manny and Stella.

"I hope you're satisfied now, Sheriff." Gertrude stopped only a few feet from him and said with tears in her eyes, "You just kept at him and kept on until you finally—"

"Mrs. Tucker, Daisy, Donald, what's wrong?" Stella asked them. "What's happened and why are you tearin' into Sheriff Gilford like this? I saw the talk he had with y'all there in the station. He was most respectful to each and ever' one of you. Why're you givin' him such a rough time?"

"He wasn't all that respectful when he went by the bank today and accused my husband of murdering that terrible Billy Ray Sonner boy," Mrs. Tucker said.

"Actually, I think I was respectful," Manny said. "I didn't accuse your husband of anything. I only asked him a couple of questions, quietly, privately, there in his office."

"Well, I don't know what you said, but it really upset him," Daisy said, also starting to cry, "and now he's here in the hospital."

"He's had a heart attack," Donald added. "A bad one. They don't know if he'll make it or not."

Stella gasped. "Oh, no!"

Manny said, "I'm sorry to hear that. Very sorry. I think a lot of Mr. Tucker. I assure you I never meant to do him any harm at all. I thought we parted on good terms. We shook hands and—"

"His secretary said that less than fifteen minutes after you left his office, he collapsed. He would've died if the bank manager hadn't given him CPR."

Oh, Stella thought. *I'll bet that's why the ambulance wasn't available for Alma.*

"I've just got one thing to say to you, Sheriff Manny Gilford,"

Mrs. Tucker said, poking her finger at Manny's chest. "Don't you come anywhere near my husband again. I mean it! If I hear you've approached him for any reason whatsoever, I will sue you for endangering his life or something like that. Or better still, I'll just beat the tar out of you all by myself."

She glared up at him, her dark eyes glittering with undiluted hate and fury. "You'd better believe me, I can do it!"

Apparently satisfied with having said her piece, Gertrude Tucker spun around and headed back down the hall with her daughter and future son-in-law behind her. They left through the door they had entered by.

Stella and Manny stood in stunned silence in their wake.

Finally, Stella said, "What in tarnation was that all about?"

Manny stared at the closed door at the end of the hall, looking confused and troubled. "I'm not sure," he said. "I dropped by the bank earlier as they said. After I got those samples off to Atlanta, I got to thinking about that blue fuzz on the tape and the sweater Franklin was wearing when we saw him. So I did a bit more research on him."

"Anything interesting?"

"Yes. He wasn't always a mild-mannered banker."

"Really? Do tell."

"He served in the Vietnam War. More than that, he was a Green Beret. Decorated several times for acts of bravery that saved his fellow soldiers." Manny paused, then added, "Most of those acts of bravery included killing the enemy in one-on-one, hand-to-hand combat."

Stella digested that information, trying to square it in her mind with the gentleman she knew who ran their local bank. Calm, kind, easygoing Mr. Tucker. A trained killer?

"Reckon you don't have to ask yourself now if he was capable of killing somebody? Apparently, he could've if he'd wanted to bad enough."

"But a former Green Beret could have taken Billy Ray out with a single jab to the heart, bullet to the head, or even a twist of his neck. Why the whole bathroom–taped door routine?"

"I don't know," Stella said, her own mental wheels racing. "But if Mr. Franklin Tucker, former tough guy, special ops soldier, was so upset by your questions that he had a heart attack after you asked them, you gotta ask yourself why."

Chapter 23

That night, after Manny had left and Stella had said good night to Alma and tucked her in with a kiss, a bedtime prayer, and a wish for sweet dreams, Stella made her way to the reception area at the entrance to the hospital. She used the ladies' room there to brush her teeth and wash her face.

Since Savannah had been kind enough to include her jar of cold cream, she applied a bit of that, too.

Looking in the mirror, Stella realized that no amount of moisturizer was going to perk up a face as tired as hers, but she found a degree of comfort in following her nightly routine. Even if it was in a hospital restroom.

The sink and some paper towels, applied in the toilet stall, were a far cry from her relaxing soak in her bathtub at home, but Savannah had thought to send her lilac soap along, tucked into a plastic sandwich bag, so she smelled nice once she was finished.

Having completed her toilette, Stella changed into her fresh clothes and felt like a new woman . . . as long as that new woman had been dragged backwards through a patch of scrub brush and left on the side of a dirt road.

She knew what was weighing her down so badly. It wasn't the fact that she was in a hospital with a sick child. After the doctor's good report and seeing Alma very nearly her feisty self again, that wasn't what was making Stella sick at heart.

It was a task she had put off since the moment she had first arrived at the hospital and placed her beloved grandchild into the hospital staff's care.

She had put it off as long as she could.

It was time.

She pulled her purse out of the bag and collected every coin she could find inside. There wasn't much. Expendable income wasn't a concept she was familiar with. At any moment, Stella knew almost to the penny how much money she had and where it was supposed to go.

But it wasn't the expenditure that was bothering her.

No, her task was far more bitter, more hurtful than any issue having to do with money.

Long ago, she had heard a wise saying: "If you have a problem that money can solve, you don't have a problem."

This was a problem she'd had for years, and she knew of nothing, other than divine intervention, that could fix it.

With her fist full of coins and her bag of clothing and toiletries under her arm, she made her way out of the bathroom and walked back to the waiting room area and the phone booth she had used before to call home.

Fortunately, it was empty. Now that she'd made up her mind to do it, she wanted to get it over with.

As before, she was happy that the booth had a folding door for privacy and a seat for comfort. She sat down and dumped the change on the tiny shelf beneath the phone, making sure the coins didn't roll off. Then she reached into the paper bag again.

Often, her granddaughter amazed her. Savannah was more thoughtful and showed more common sense than most adults

Stella knew. The girl had put her little address book in with the rest of her necessities, anticipating she would need it.

She took it out, flipped to the "M" page, and looked at the lengthy list of telephone numbers she had written beneath the name "Macon."

For the fourteen years that her son had been a long-distance truck driver, she had never known for certain, from moment to moment, where he was or how she could reach him.

During the first ten of those years, Stella had assumed it was just a part of the job, being unavailable to family and friends for most days of the year. But over time, Stella had spoken to other truckers, some of whom had the same routes as Macon's, and somehow, they managed to be with their loved ones for most major holidays and make regular phone calls home.

Finally, Stella had stopped making excuses for her son. Macon preferred to be out of reach, unaccountable, with little or nothing expected of him.

She thought of how responsible her Art had been and what a great example he had set for his boys. She thought of their other son, who had laid down his life for his country.

For so many sleepless nights she had pondered the question, but she simply couldn't figure out how she had gone wrong when raising Macon. Surely, when she was teaching him table manners, how to do his math lessons, and to be sure to wash behind his ears, she must have mentioned the importance of taking care of one's family. Especially the innocent, dependent children you brought into the world.

Now he had another on the way and one in the hospital, and she had no idea if any of the numbers in her book would reach him.

She shoved coins into the phone, tried one entry after another, until on the seventh, a woman answered with a simple "Yeah?"

"Hello," Stella said. "Is Macon Reid there?"

"Who's this?"

Stella took a deep breath, tamping down her temper. It wouldn't do to fly off the handle and say something like, "None of yer business, ya brazen hussy! Put 'im on the dadgum phone! Now!"

Instead, she managed to disguise her annoyance behind a syrupy sweet, "This is his mother, darlin'. Please ask him to come to the phone. There's a family emergency."

"Macon," she heard the voice with soothing, dulcet tones bellow like a foghorn, "get off the john and come answer your damned phone. It's your mother!"

Eventually, after Stella had deposited still more change into the phone, she heard her son pick up the receiver and say, "Hi, Mom. What's up?"

"I'm calling you from the hospital. Alma just had surgery. I thought you should know."

You coulda broke that to him a lot easier there, Stella, ol' girl, she told herself. *If I didn't know better, I'd say you're deliberately tryin' to scare him plum to pieces.*

"Oh," he said, like a boxer who had just received a slug to the solar plexus.

"Yes. Oh."

There was a long pause, then he said, "What happened?"

"Appendicitis."

"Okay. Is that serious?"

"Can be. It was. But they took it out, and they expect she'll be all right."

"Oh, good."

"Are you anywhere around here at the moment? I know it'd do her a world of good to see you. It'd be nice for all the kids. Waycross misses you somethin' fierce."

"I'm headin' out to the West Coast tomorrow. Got a load of beef for a big restaurant chain out there."

"Then maybe a phone call? Like I said, it would mean so much to her."

"I'll see what I can do, Mom. I'll be driving straight through. I have to. Don't want all that beef to go off."

He wouldn't call. Stella knew it was pointless to nudge him. In fact, if anything, he would be less likely to cooperate if he thought it was expected of him.

"I heard about the baby." She was surprised to hear the words come out of her mouth. She'd decided she wouldn't say anything about the pregnancy to him, for fear she might lose control and give him a much bigger piece of her mind than he could handle.

Maybe the stress of the day had clogged some of her mental filters that kept those sorts of words from pouring forth.

Maybe she'd finally reached a point of no return with her son and no longer cared if she offended him or not.

To her shock and relief, she heard herself saying, "Did you give it one single thought before you started bangin' that hair-brained wife of yours like a screen door in a windstorm there in the jail and makin' another baby that neither one of you wants or can take care of? She's locked up now for mistreating these I'm raisin'. But you and her get two minutes together alone in a cell and what do you do? You jump on each other without any protection and come up with another one. Did you think I don't have enough on my hands, raisin' these ones I got already, without you two adding a tiny, helpless infant to the picture?"

There was dead silence on the other end. She thought he might have hung up on her, and she wouldn't have blamed him if he had. But the words, so long held back, were gushing from deep inside her, from a place of great pain, frustration, and exhaustion. She couldn't stop them.

"Let me tell you somethin', Macon Reid. Your sweet little Alma is layin' in a bed upstairs with her belly cut up, hurtin' bad. She's in room number fifteen, and there's a phone right next to her bed. If you don't call her sometime in the next twenty-four hours and tell her you love her and wish her a decent 'get well' then don't bother to contact me again. Not for nothin'. Do you hear? I mean it, Macon. I've had enough of this crap. Your children deserve better, and you start givin' them some. Now!"

When she slammed down the phone, her hand was shaking so badly that she missed and had to try twice more before she had the receiver cradled.

Her pulse was racing, her breath coming in ragged gasps.

She waited for it to hit her—the wave of guilt that would overwhelm and suffocate her.

She waited for the lightning bolt from heaven that would zap her, punish her for not being "nice" enough to her own son.

She, who had always prided herself on not being judgmental, for showing kindness when provoked, love when being mistreated, and patience when being tried.

Ah, to hell with it, she thought, as she gathered up her leftover coins and tossed them into the bag with her dirty clothes. *He deserved ever' bit of that and more. "Nice" is overrated.*

Chapter 24

Of course, Stella had seen her little granddaughter happy many times. Alma was a child who just naturally chose joy over sadness in all circumstances, even trying ones. She had been cheerful since the day she was born.

But Stella couldn't ever recall seeing her sweet face shining quite so brightly as it was two days later, when Stella stepped into the girl's hospital room to tell her that she had been cleared to go home.

The drab room looked as though a wonderful party had been thrown inside its jail-cell gray walls.

On the nightstand next to her bed was a spring bouquet of daisies, carnations, tulips, and a couple of Stargazer lilies, whose spicy fragrance chased away all the medicinal odors in the room.

To her delight and astonishment, Stella had seen the flowers delivered the very next morning after her talk with Macon. The deliveryman had handed them to Alma with much pomp and circumstance, along with a card that told her they were from her daddy and that he loved her very much.

Alma had been thrilled beyond words.

That afternoon, Stella had overheard Alma's end of the telephone call that Macon had placed to his daughter. The call was fairly short, but Stella could tell by the smile on her granddaughter's face that Macon was saying the things the child so desperately needed to hear: He loved her dearly, and he wanted her to get well right away, if not sooner.

Alma had been positively overwhelmed by the attention and told Stella, "Daddy said I was his princess, Granny. That's why he sent me the flowers, because princesses should have flowers in their room, he said, especially ones who just had an operation."

Witnessing this overnight change in her son's behavior, Stella told herself, *Just think of all the times you forced yourself to be kind to him, when you felt like clobbering him upside the head with a rolling pin. All the nights you laid awake prayin' for wisdom about how to deal with him. Who'd have thought all you had to do was get real tired, real mad, real sick of the whole thing, and just tell him off? Remember this, girl. It's a Life Lesson!*

Before the day had passed, even more presents arrived. Dolly Browning popped into the room, carrying an orange Care Bear with a couple of smiling flowers on its tummy. She gave it to her "special patient," as she called Alma, when she placed the toy in her hands and a kiss on each of her now rosy cheeks.

Then a dozen balloons arrived. One of each color of the rainbow and more besides. They floated at the top of the ceiling with curly ribbons streaming down. One was a silver and pink heart with a message that encouraged her to "Get Well!"

They were from Manny.

Stella wasn't surprised. Manny loved her grandchildren. She had no doubt of that. Which made it particularly difficult for her not to love him.

"Can I really go home now?" Alma asked as Stella scurried around the room, gathering up their personal items. "Can I take my flowers and my balloons and my Care Bear with me?"

"Of course you can, sugar," she replied. But even as she spoke the words, she wondered how Manny was going to get two extra people, a stuffed bear, a large bouquet of flowers, and especially the dozen balloons he had sent, all inside the cruiser.

Oh well, she thought. *He sent 'em to her, and he knew he'd be bringin' her home. He must've had a plan.*

If there was anything Sheriff Manny Gilford was good at, it was thinking ahead.

"What the heck was I thinking, sending her a zillion balloons like that?" Manny whispered to Stella as they rode down the highway, surrounded by the colorful orbs floating eerily around their heads. "If I saw anybody driving down the road with their vision obstructed like this, I'd pull them over in a heartbeat and write them a ticket for being stupid."

"Good thing you're the sheriff then." Stella laughed at him as he swatted away a red one that was drifting in front of his face. "You're generous to a fault, Manny Gilford. That's your problem. Always has been."

He sniffed. "I know a few miscreants in our town who would beg to differ with you there."

"They don't know you as well as I do."

"I'll give you that."

Stella grabbed the offending balloon that was tormenting him more than the others and tried to tuck it under her knees, along with four of its siblings. It wouldn't stay, she knew, but she was trying.

She glanced over her shoulder to the rear seat of the cruiser, where Alma was sleeping, Manny's jacket thrown over her. Her bear was hugged tightly to her chest, her flowers on the seat beside her, and she was surrounded by as many balloons as the area would hold.

She looked every bit the princess that she was.

Turning to Manny, Stella said, "I've been dying to hear where you're at now, with the investigation that is, since I've been out of commission. She's asleep back there, so tell me everything. Don't hold back."

Manny laughed. "Like I could withhold anything at all from you. You'd wring it outta me if I even tried."

"That's true, so let 'er rip."

"I'm flattered that you'd think I've wrapped this case up by myself in forty-eight hours. I'm sorry to disappoint you, but I've got as many, or more, questions than I had the last time we discussed it."

"I'm sorry to hear that. I figured you'd have it all solved and somebody behind bars by now."

"I wish. No such luck. But I did hear from the lab in Atlanta."

Stella perked up. "Great! What did they say?"

"I actually got some interesting information. Made me glad I sent it off to them."

"That threatening letter that Dolly got?"

"No fingerprints on it but hers, a partial of mine, and the mailman's. The sender must have used gloves."

"Okay, then that rules out Deacon or Earle. They ain't got the good sense God gave a sock full of rocks.

He cut her a funny sideways look. "A sock full of rocks? Where do you come up with these, girl?"

"Make 'em up as I go along. Just part of the wonder that is me."

"That's what I figured. Anyway, the lab says the fibers are just what Savannah said. They're from an angora rabbit."

"A blue rabbit. That shouldn't be too hard to find. Can't be a lot of blue bunnies hoppin' around town."

"It was *dyed* blue, Stella. Most likely from a ball of fancy knitting yarn, they said."

"I figured. Duh, Manny. Don't you know when your leg's gettin' tugged?"

He rolled his eyes and batted a balloon away from his face. "Then there's the bodily fluids and tissue samples that Herb collected. Those are the most interesting of all."

"How so?"

"At least we know the cause of death now. A toxic chemical called hydrogen cyanide. They found it in that discharge around his mouth and also from the tissue samples Herb took from his mouth, nose, and throat."

"Nose? Then it's not somethin' he drank. It must've been somethin' he breathed in."

"That's right. Now we know the reason for the duct tape. They didn't put it there to keep him in. It was to seal off the room."

"But we didn't find any sort of chemicals inside there. Not even down the drains when you snaked them."

"I know. I went back, checked everything again—the toilet, the sink, the showerhead. I didn't find a single thing out of the ordinary."

"The killer couldn't have removed the toxin after Billy Ray expired, or the tape would've been torn off."

"It's a stumper. That's for sure."

"I never heard of that hydrogen cyanide before. What is it? Where would you get such a thing."

"I checked around and found out that it's a pesticide. It's been used to delouse places and to kill other insects. Farmers used it quite a lot, but not so much now because it's so toxic and dangerous to handle."

"Farmers, huh?" Stella didn't want to hear that. Instantly, she thought of Raul and his calloused hands.

"Yeah. I know," Manny replied. "It got me to wondering if maybe Raul went to the funeral home for a different reason."

"To try to find out how much Herb had or hadn't figured out?"

"Something like that."

"It weren't him. I just don't believe it of him. He'd already beat Billy Ray up. I think he'd got it outta his system already."

"I expect so, too."

"But even if Raul wasn't satisfied and wanted more, he would've just given Billy Ray another poundin', not rigged up a fancy poisonin' like that."

"We can't discount anybody, Stella. No matter how much we might like them. People are people, and there's just no telling what they'll do at any given time."

"That's true. Folks surprise you. Good ones go bad and once in a blue moon, bad ones do somethin' good."

Manny chuckled. "Don't see the latter as often as the former though."

"That's for sure."

Suddenly, she recalled something she had intended to tell him. "By the way, when I was filling out the papers to get Alma discharged, I saw Franklin Tucker leaving. He had his gang with him, and they were handling him like he was the King of Siam when they put him in and outta that wheelchair."

"I'm relieved to hear he's all right. I didn't cause that heart attack, Stella," Manny said. "I'm sorry he had it, but it wasn't my fault. I swear I was gentle as I could be with him."

"Then why do you figure they thought you roughed him up?"

"Probably because he got so agitated when I brought up his war record."

"A lot of men who served in Vietnam—and other wars, too, for that matter—don't like talkin' about it."

"I know. Yesterday I was looking deeper into his record. I

found out that when he was a Green Beret, he had some special training. Chemical warfare."

"Chemical warfare? Like mustard gas and such?"

"No. Not things that kill human beings. Stuff like Agent Orange that was used as a defoliant, to cause the leaves to fall off the trees the enemy soldiers were hiding under."

"But he might have learned some other things, too," Stella suggested.

"He certainly might have. The fact that he got so upset about the topic makes me wonder."

Stella sat quietly as they passed through the countryside, which was mostly farmland. Many of the spring crops had sprouted and taken hold, bright green against the red Georgia clay earth.

Already, she could feel a hint of the summer heat and humidity that was to come.

She thought of the baby, who would be arriving at the height of that hot weather. She had no air-conditioning in her house or her old truck, and sometimes it was hard to keep little ones comfortable at a time like that.

But she'd done it before. She could do it again.

Somehow.

Manny glanced up at his rearview mirror, at the sleeping child in the back seat. He whispered, "You're thinking about the baby, aren't you?"

"I am. Never far away in my thoughts, as you can imagine."

"Have you told the kids yet?"

"No. I was waiting to find out for sure what's gonna happen to the little one. For all we know it might have to go to a—"

"Your house, Stella. Not a foster home. As soon as it's born, they're going to give it directly to you."

Stella gasped. "How do you know this, Manny Gilford?"

"I know it because I had a long sit-down with Judge Patterson yesterday, and it didn't take much arm-twisting at all to get him to agree that would be best for everyone concerned. I mean, it'll be hard for you, providing the caretaking for a newborn, but—"

"But that's what I want, hard or not!"

"Then that's what you'll get. He told me to tell you it's a done deal. Get out those old baby clothes and dust off the cradle."

Stella could hardly contain her excitement. Now that it was settled, she found the mixed feelings had disappeared. Only joy remained.

"Oh, thank you, Manny! Thank you, thank you!" She heard Alma stir behind her and lowered her voice. "Since it's decided, I'm going to tell the kids today. I'd planned to invite Elsie and Dolly over and have a little welcome home party for Alma. It's the perfect time to announce it."

She tried to stick yet another balloon under her legs, but only succeeded in releasing two more. "We got the decorations already, thanks to you. Might as well put 'em to good use."

In the distance she could see her tiny, humble house, and a wave of contentment swept over her. Home. It had only been three days since she'd left it, but oh, how she'd missed it.

"I'll be baking brownies again," she said. "Alma never tires of 'em. We'd be happy to have you celebrate with us, if you've a mind to."

"I believe I will," he said. "The day I turn down something that you baked, Stella, is the day you'd better check my pulse."

Chapter 25

Stella looked around her living room and thought she couldn't recall when it had appeared so festive. Not even at Christmas, when she and the children went all out and decorated everything from the tree, to the doorknobs, table lamps, and tissue dispensers. All sparkled with gobs of glitter, ornaments made of Popsicle sticks, and gold and silver tinsel, which she bought on sale at the end of each holiday season.

The Reids knew how to celebrate.

No doubt about it.

Long ago, Stella had decided that no holiday or special occasion would pass without her making it memorable for her grandkids. You only had one chance to create childhood memories, a limited window of time when the human heart was still young enough, trusting enough, to believe in magic.

But tonight, she'd had help with the decorations, thanks to Manny, her son, and Dolly Browning.

Earlier, she had called Dolly Browning and invited her to their little "shindig." But Dolly had graciously declined, saying she had an errand to run. Stella thanked Dolly for all she had done and promised to invite her again soon so she could see how well her special patient was doing.

But Elsie had jumped at her invitation and had shown up with one of her famous gumdrop coconut cakes in hand. As if they needed any more sweets, considering the plethora of brownies adorning Stella's company platter on the kitchen table.

Now, as Stella looked around her crowded living room, she realized it contained the people she loved most in the world. Elsie was sitting on the end of the sofa with Alma's head in her lap. She was winding Alma's curls around her fingers, and in her soft, sweet voice, she was telling Alma what a brave girl she had been.

Manny was sitting in the rocking chair, having a deep, man-to-man conversation with Waycross about school bullies and how to handle them. From his seat on the floor next to Manny's chair, Stella could see Waycross was drinking in every word.

She smiled, blessing Manny for helping a little boy who, due to his bright red curls, copious freckles, and feisty disposition, knew far more than his share about bullies and being teased.

"Come by the station after school sometime," she heard Manny tell him. "I'll show you some special moves I've got for handling situations like that. But you've gotta keep what you learn to yourself."

Waycross nodded vigorously. "Sure! I won't tell nobody. We don't want it gettin' back to the bullies. They'd use them moves on me!"

"Exactly, and we sure don't want that!"

The other children were scattered around the room. Jesup and Cordele were in the middle of the floor, playing a fierce game of jacks.

At Marietta's insistence, Vidalia was ratting, spraying, and spiking her sister's hair in an attempt to make Marietta look like her latest celebrity idol, Cyndi Lauper. As long as Marietta didn't attempt to color it bright pink, Stella decided she'd just let it happen.

With seven children in the household, Stella knew she was severely outnumbered. For the moment, she had her bluff in on all of them. But the tide could turn at any time. So, one had to pick their battles.

Only Savannah was alone, sitting in the corner, propped up on one of Stella's big floor cushions that was pressed into service when all the chairs were taken. She had been absorbed in a certain book for days now.

When Stella and Manny brought Alma into the house, Savannah set her reading aside and helped them get her little sister situated. But once Alma was settled in, Savannah had instantly returned to her book.

It must be a good 'un, Stella told herself. *She's sure got her nose buried deep in it.*

But the girl's reading had to be interrupted for a bit, and Stella suspected that, once she had delivered her news, neither Savannah nor any other child in this room would be able to concentrate on anything else.

Stella clapped her hands to get their attention, which they reluctantly gave. "I have an announcement," she said. "A very, very important one. So y'all listen up."

One by one, with great reluctance, they set aside their various forms of entertainment and turned to Stella, their expressions only mildly interested at best.

Elsie gave her a brief smile, but her attention was still on Alma as she continued to stroke her hair.

Only Manny showed any genuine concern, and Stella knew that was because he was aware what was coming.

The children's lives would be changing in the next moment, and they had no idea and no control over it.

"What's up, Granny?" Waycross asked in his typical, little smarty-pants way that she found most endearing.

"Something big. Something important." She paused, steeled herself, and added, "Something miraculous and wonderful."

"You won the lottery!" Marietta shouted. "Buy me a Glitter and Gold Jem doll!" With her hair standing on end and bigger that the width of her shoulders, she looked more like a giant dandelion in full bloom than Cyndi Lauper.

"I want a Teddy Ruxpin!" Jesup announced.

In seconds, other dream toy orders were pouring in.

"I need a Rainbow Brite doll!"

"I want Cabbage Patch twins, a boy and a girl!"

"I already got my present," Alma said, hugging her Care Bear to her chest. "Miss Dolly took good care of me already."

Waycross added his request to his sisters'. "If you've got any money left after buyin' all that sissy, girl junk," he said, "I'd like to have a G. I. Joe Attack Tank."

Stella sighed. "I didn't win the lottery. What I have to tell you is much better than that."

"Nothin's better than winning a ton of money!" Marietta said with great authority.

"Hush up, everybody," Savannah said in a quiet voice from her seat in the corner. "Can't you see that Granny's got something important to tell us? Be quiet and let her say what it is."

"Thank you, Savannah girl," Stella said. Her eyes met her granddaughter's and Stella could see that Savannah sensed this "good news" might not be 100 percent sunlight and roses.

Stella glanced over at Manny and saw him give her a loving, understanding look and a subtle thumbs-up.

Elsie had stopped fiddling with Alma's curls and was watching Stella with concern and curiosity registering on her pretty face.

"We're going to be blessed with a miracle," Stella began, "a miracle that the Lord above must've wanted us to have, 'cause He's the one who brings such things to pass."

She paused and looked around at the blank faces. So far, the kids didn't seem particularly impressed. Elsie looked downright worried.

"Someone gave me some news, and I wanna share it with y'all. It's about your momma."

The faces went from blank to frowning in a heartbeat, and Stella couldn't blame them. Since when was Shirley the source of any news to celebrate?

"I don't wanna hear about Momma," Jesup said. "Stuff about her makes me feel sad, and I wanna be happy that Alma's home."

"I'd rather have my Cabbage Patch twins than hear about Momma," Cordele added.

"No more about toys, Cordele," Elsie said softly. "Be quiet and listen to your grandma. This is important."

"We're all gonna be gettin' a doll, all right," Stella said, forcing a smile. This wasn't going at all the way she had envisioned it. "In just a few months, we're fixin' to get us a real live dolly!"

"A live dolly?" Vidalia said, looking highly suspicious and sounding somewhat alarmed. "You don't mean, like a real *baby*, do you?"

A calm, quiet voice from the corner said, "Gran, is Momma pregnant again?"

"Yes, Savannah," Stella told her. "Come mid-August, you're going to have another sister or brother. Isn't that wonderful?"

Instead of cheering, there was silence. The ominous quiet stretched on and on, growing more uncomfortable by the second.

Stella saw tears in Elsie's eyes. She couldn't tell if they were from joy or sadness.

Then Marietta said with a completely sarcastic and deadpan delivery, "Well, that *would* be a miracle, since she's locked up in a prison with just women. Too bad it won't be born in December. We could name it Jesus. Even if it's a girl."

"Marietta Reid, that's durned near blasphemous," Stella told her. "I'll ask you to watch what you say."

"I don't wanna change dirty diapers," Vidalia piped up. "I had to do enough of that with Jesup. I hate diaper duty."

"We'll all have duties, and we'll divvy them up when the time comes. But mostly, it'll be me taking care of the baby, and I'm happy about it, so y'all try to be, too."

"You know I'll be helping you," Elsie said. "I'm happy about it. I'm quite partial to infants."

"I know you are, Elsie. Thank you, darlin'."

"Me too," Manny added. "Count me in."

Stella gave both him and Elsie loving, grateful smiles.

"Will it be a boy or a girl?" Alma wanted to know.

"We don't know yet. That'll be part of the surprise on the day it's born."

"I hope it's a boy," Waycross added. "We got girls to spare around here, and I need somebody to play with."

"Whatever it is, girl or boy, it's exactly the one we want, 'cause it's ours."

Marietta sniffed. "Well, it's half ours anyway. It's Momma's, to be sure. Are there any boy guards at that prison?"

Again, Stella shuddered to think an eleven-year-old knew this much about adult matters.

She was debating what to say when Savannah spoke up. "Did Daddy visit Momma in jail? Alone?"

"Seems so," Stella said. "A short visit, I hear."

"A minute and a half is long enough for them," she heard Savannah mumble under her breath.

Stella hated to admit that she agreed with the child's assessment. Even knuckleheads like Shirley and Macon had something they were good at.

Looking around the room at the faces that varied from Savannah's somber expression, to Marietta's indignant puss, to Elsie's and Manny's sympathetic but concerned half-smiles, Stella felt she should end the announcement on a happy note if possible.

"Listen, kiddos," she said. "Every little baby that comes into this world deserves to be wanted. I want this one. Just like I wanted each and every one of you when I found out you were on your way into my life. This child will need each and every one of you, your love, and acceptance. I'm asking you to be happy with me, to celebrate our Alma's homecomin' and the little one who's on the way."

A couple of the faces softened, a few semi-grins appeared, and Marietta seemed a tad less disgruntled.

"Okay," Stella said, deciding to settle with what she had. "Should we tie into Elsie's gumdrop cake and the brownies?"

That did it. Yells of delight and screams of anticipated pleasure filled the room.

The Reid young'uns might not be excited about the new life soon to join their midst, but they went crazy at the mention of dessert.

Stella sighed and shook her head. At least they had their priorities in order.

Chapter 26

Once the party had ended, the dishes were done, and all of the younger children put to bed, Stella, Manny, Elsie, and Savannah sat around the kitchen table. The adults were enjoying a last cup of Stella's strong, after-supper brew, while Savannah sipped her cocoa with marshmallows and continued to read her book.

"I think you did a fine job, informing the children," Manny told Stella. "I figured you'd have some mixed reviews, but you handled the opposition well."

"I don't know about that. One of these days when this new baby's a child and old enough to understand such things, I won't be telling it that their siblings would have preferred toys to their company."

"Probably best not to write that in the baby book," Elsie said, reaching for another sliver of leftover cake. After enjoying a mouthful of her own artistry, she said, "They're little. They don't know any better. They'd fight tooth and nail to keep every one of their siblings if push came to shove. They might quarrel amongst themselves, but thanks to you and your good teachin's, there's a heap of love between 'em, too."

"I tell myself that a lot." Stella sighed. "I can believe it most times, unless blood's been spilt."

"We love each other even then," Savannah said, her eyes still on her book. "If I make somebody bleed, I always fetch them a Band-Aid and some antiseptic ointment. It's just common courtesy."

"See?" Elsie said. "Proof of a child raised with love."

Everyone snickered, then Elsie reached over and patted Stella's hand. "I hope you know that I'm so happy for you, Stella, and, like I said before, I'll be right here, front and center, to help you with the new one, too."

"I know you will, Elsie," Stella said. "You're the best friend in the world. I'll never be able to repay you for what you've done for me and these kids."

"Oh, I love it! Every minute of it!" Elsie said. "I'm lookin' forward to this new baby as much—well, almost as much—as you are. I was just thinkin' the other day that I miss them bein' babies. Now we get to go through it again. Baby shampoo and lotion, cute little outfits, the sweet little googly sounds they make, the wonderful way they smell . . ."

"Only when their diaper's clean," Savannah added, turning a page.

"It's going to be so much fun," Elsie said with a degree of enthusiasm that Stella wished she could feel. But she was too tired. The past couple of days had taken too much out of her.

"You look exhausted, Stella," Manny said. "I'll leave and let you get some rest."

"You don't have to go on account of me," she said. "I'm too wound up and excited to sleep anyway."

He walked over to the stove, got the coffeepot, and refilled her cup.

"Don't wait on me, Manny Gilford," she said, playfully swatting his hand. "This is my house and that's my job."

"This is your first night home from the hospital," he told her, moving the sugar bowl closer to her. "You could use a bit of pampering. Lord knows, you've helped me plenty in the past week. I owe you more than a coffee refill."

He topped off Elsie's cup and replaced the pot on the stove. Turning to Savannah, he said, "You've barely looked up from that book all night, kiddo. What is it? A whodunit? One of those mushy romances?"

"It's about the Holocaust."

Her answer surprised everyone at the table, including Stella. The book's cover was simple, just plain, red cloth with no dust jacket to reveal what was inside. Stella had surmised it was one of Savannah's detective novels.

"The Holocaust?" Manny said. "That's some heavy reading."

"Very," was Savannah's reply.

"Why are you readin' somethin' like that?" Stella asked, wondering if the book contained the most chilling and graphic details about that horrible event. She hoped not, for her granddaughter's sake.

"Because I wanted to know what the big deal was about the Nazis." Savannah looked up from her reading for a moment, and Stella saw, reflected in her granddaughter's eyes, the same sickening awareness that she had felt when she had first studied the subject, so many years ago.

Stella remembered, all too well, when she was a teenager, how learning about the Holocaust had changed her. Changed her to the marrow of her soul.

Finding out the depths of evil that human beings were capable of doing to each other had caused the young Stella to lose her respect for mankind. Having read the heartbreaking accounts, having seen the devastating pictures, Stella had never felt completely safe in the world again.

She had hoped her grandchildren would be spared that experience, at least until they were a bit older.

But Savannah had always been a precocious child, so eager to learn and absorb all the world had to offer.

In this case . . . unfortunately.

"So, what have you learned about the Nazis?" Manny asked.

"Enough to know that Billy Ray and his friends are stupid and meaner than mean to think they were good guys. They were horrible." She slammed the book closed. "How could anything like that even happen? How could anyone ever read these things, see these pictures, and then say it never happened, or if it did, it was a good thing?"

"You never will understand it, child," Stella said. "You could think about it ever' minute of ever' day for the rest of your life, and you wouldn't understand. You can't, because it's just not in you to think that way. You're not made like that."

"No, I'm not! I would die, literally die, to keep something like that from happening!"

"A lot of soldiers did," Manny told her. "In fact, some of them are buried right here in our cemetery in McGill."

"I wonder if people who are alive now would be brave enough to do that," Savannah said, "to die to stop something like that from happening."

"I wonder that myself," Elsie admitted. "Seems like folks won't even speak up against that kind of thing anymore, for fear they might offend somebody, or 'cause someone else might not like them. That's a long, long way from being brave enough to die to stop the powers of evil."

"There better be people like that left in the world," Stella said. " 'Cause it'll show up again. Evil don't stay buried. It always rises up again, sometime, somewhere, and if there's not good, strong, brave people there to force it back down into its grave . . . heaven help us all."

A half hour later, Manny stood up from the table, stretched his long arms and legs, and said, "I'd best be going. That motel bathroom isn't going to check itself."

At first, Stella felt an overwhelming urge to ask if Manny would like some help with the motel, but one thought of her precious Alma lying in her bed in the other room just home from the hospital and Stella wondered what was wrong with her.

This was why she had to watch how involved she got with Sheriff Manny Gilford. She found both him and the life he led far too exciting. At least, too exciting and tempting for a woman with seven . . . soon to be eight . . . children to raise.

There was a momentary silence, as though Manny was waiting for her to invite herself.

Elsie, always the mind reader, filled in the blank. "Why don't you go with him, Stella? He could probably use a hand. The children are all in bed but Savannah, and I'd be happy to visit with her till you get back."

Stella looked up at Manny. She could see in his eyes that he wanted her to go with him. After all, Elsie had said it was okay.

"But Alma . . ."

"Alma's asleep and will probably stay that way for the rest of the night. She won't even know you're gone."

For a moment, Stella almost agreed. But at the last second, she thought of how she'd felt and the promises she'd made there in that chapel. Vows that she would never let anyone or anything distract her from her true calling in life, raising her grandchildren.

"I'd better stick around," she told Manny. "If you think you'll be okay over there on your own."

Manny grinned. Of course he would be okay, she reminded

herself. He appeared to enjoy her company, but he'd been the sheriff his entire adulthood without the assistance of Stella Reid. She realized she was being a bit conceited to think he actually needed her.

"I'll be fine, Stella," he said. "I doubt I'll find anything. From what I hear hydrogen cyanide is either pale blue or colorless. I don't know how I expect to actually see it. But I have to try."

"Hydrogen cyanide?" Savannah asked, suddenly very interested in the conversation. "Why will you be looking for hydrogen cyanide?"

"Seems that's what killed Billy Ray. He breathed it in and that was the end of him."

"Oh, my goodness," she said, grabbing her book and flipping the pages as fast as she could, searching for something. "That's what they used in the gas chambers in the death camps. The Nazis used hydrogen cyanide to kill all those people!"

"I think you're mistaken, darlin'," Stella said. "I believe it was something called Zyklon B. Terrible stuff, it was, too."

Savannah had found what she was looking for and showed it to Manny, pointing to the passage on the page. "See, Sheriff. Granny's right, but I am, too. Hydrogen cyanide and Zyklon B—they're the same thing. It's the stuff that came from the ceilings of those fake showers and killed all those poor people."

"Wow!" Elsie said. "Sounds like the murderer wanted Billy Ray to get a dose of the evil he was crowin' about all the time."

Savannah nodded, tapping her finger on the page. "It's right there. It tells how awful it was. Elsie's right! The killer wanted Billy Ray to suffer like they did. *Exactly* like they did!"

Stella felt an excitement welling up in her, but it was quickly doused when she heard herself saying, "But that don't get us any closer to who done it. Ever'body knew what kind of hateful nonsense he was spoutin'." She turned to Manny. "Like we said in the car, Earle and Deacon couldn't pour water outta a boot if the directions were written on the heel, which rules them out, 'cause it'd take a bit of smarts to handle nasty junk like that and not kill yourself."

Manny nodded. "So, that brings us back to either Raul, who, as a farmer, could get his hands on that stuff. Or Franklin, who probably knows more about chemicals and how they can kill than you or I ever will."

"Or it's somebody else in town," Elsie said, "who Billy Ray hurt or offended. Somebody you ain't even thought of yet."

Manny shook his finger at Elsie and gave her a grin that caused her to giggle. "That will be quite enough out of you, young lady," he told her. "I can think up plenty of depressing thoughts all on my own. I don't need help from the likes of *you!*"

With both Savannah and Elsie wishing him good luck, Manny headed for the front door, and Stella walked him out onto the porch.

"Thank you again for bringing Alma and me home today. Nobody else would've put up with those balloons."

"That's for sure." He laughed. "I'll call you tomorrow morning and tell you if I found anything over there."

"You will not," she said.

"Oh, okay. Of course you'd like to sleep in, after the last few days you've had."

"I'll not be sleeping in. But I don't want you to call me tomorrow morning. I want you to drop by here on your way home tonight and tell me what you found."

"You'll be up?"

"I won't sleep a wink until I know."

Chapter 27

Stella, Elsie, and Savannah sat in the living room, chatting about the new baby, what clothes and supplies they had or would need to get. The conversation was light, joyful, and companionable as the three females shared what it would mean to them to have a baby in the house.

"I just want to touch its little cheek," Elsie said. "There's nothing softer on earth than the feel of a newborn's skin . . . except maybe that of a very old person. Seems our skin's the softest when we first enter the world and then again when we're about to leave it."

"I just want to sit and hold it for hours at a time." Stella smiled, feeling her entire body relax at the thought. "There ain't nothin' more peaceful in the whole world than sittin' and holdin' a baby and listenin' to it breathe."

"I want to stick out my finger and feel the baby wrap its little hand around it," Savannah told them. "That's about the sweetest thing they do, I believe. It's like they trust you, even when they're just itty-bitty. Like they love you and want to hang on to you."

"I'll be happy with whatever it is, but I hope it's a boy," Stella admitted. "Poor Waycross is so outnumbered in this family. He'd be tickled to death to have a little brother."

Savannah grimaced. "Just what we need, *another* boy to help him put frogs in us girls' underwear drawer."

The women laughed and continued their baby daydreaming, but all three kept sneaking furtive looks out the front window. They might be talking about infants, but they were all wondering about murder.

Stella kept an eye on the clock. Manny had only about two miles to travel to the motel. So, the driving part of the trip would have been less than five minutes round-trip.

He had been gone forty-eight minutes, so she figured he must have found something.

It wouldn't take forty-three minutes to find nothin', she told herself, as her excitement built by the minute.

She tried not to be too hopeful. After all, both she and Manny had scoured that room twice, looking for anything out of the ordinary, and had discovered nothing unusual inside the bathroom but Billy Ray's dead body. It wasn't logical to think that Manny would happen to discover a poisonous gas lurking about. Anything vaporous was bound to be long gone, probably even before they had first opened the bathroom door.

Suddenly, Stella recalled that her eyes had burned a bit and her throat had felt sore when they had been gathering evidence from the motel room. She wondered if it might have been caused by the same substance that had killed Billy Ray.

Quite a sobering thought.

"Do you think this baby will have black hair, like the others," Elsie was saying, "or red curls, like your Art and little Waycross?"

Stella opened her mouth to answer but caught a glimpse of Manny's cruiser turning off the highway and heading up her dirt road.

"He's back!" she announced, jumping up from the couch and heading to the door.

Elsie and Savannah followed her out onto the porch, then down the stairs, just as the vehicle pulled up and stopped nearby.

The three women ran around the car to the driver's door, and Savannah yanked it open. "Well, Sheriff?" she said. "Did you find something? We've been dying in there, talking about babies, but wondering about you."

Manny chuckled as he stepped out of the cruiser, then shut the door behind him. "I always thought I was the nosiest person in McGill, but you three have got me beat by a mile."

"Not nosey. Curious," Savannah said. "Rabidly curious, that's all."

Manny reached over and tweaked her chin. "That's why you'll make an amazing police officer someday, Savannah. A detective, I'm sure."

Stella grinned, watching her granddaughter beam with joy at his compliments.

Manny was so good with Savannah. With all the kids.

Okay, he's good with all of us, she admitted to herself.

She looked him up and down and, even by the dim porchlight, she could see that his usually spotless and perfectly pressed uniform was wrinkled and covered with dirt and cobwebs.

"Where have you been, boy?" she asked. "Crawlin' around in a swamp somewhere?"

"Nope, but just about as bad."

"I'll say. You'll never get all the grit outta that uniform," Elsie told him. "You couldn't get that clean on a washboard."

"Hey, I don't mind going home at the end of the day with some dirt on me. As long as it's not blood. Mine, anyway."

Savannah started to jump up and down like an excited child

wanting to open gifts on Christmas morning. "I'm dying here, Sheriff. Tell us what you found!"

"I'll do better than that. I'll show you."

As he walked them to the back of the car and stuck his key into the trunk lock, he said, "I checked the bathroom again, like we did the other two times, Stella. But just like before, I couldn't find a thing. Then, Miss Savannah, I remembered what you said about how the Nazis released the gas from the ceilings of those fake showers. So, I looked up."

"I already looked up in that bathroom," Stella said. "It's just one of those old foam tile ceilings."

"Tiles that can easily be removed or slid aside from above."

"Bingo!" Elsie said. "Now we know how you got so dirty. You were crawling around up there in the attic!"

"I was," Manny said, opening the trunk, "and that's where I found them."

"Them?" Savannah tried to look over his shoulder as he bent down into the trunk and pulled out a cardboard box.

"Yes, and I'm going to show them to you. But I don't want you to get too close to them, because I don't know exactly what they are or if they're still dangerous."

He carefully opened the lid of the box, took his flashlight from his service belt, turned it on, and shone its beam inside.

"I picked my way—carefully, I assure you—across the beams in the ceiling of that attic. Right below were those foam tiles and the flimsy frames that hold them up. Finally, I got over the number five motel room, then its bathroom."

"And?" Savannah poked his ribs with her forefinger.

"And these four things were lying on top of one of the tiles that makes up the corner of the bathroom ceiling," he said.

First, he directed the beam of the flashlight on an opaque,

white glass bottle with a label on it that read "Sulfuric Acid." Then he moved the light so they could see a dark amber bottle, which was marked as "Potassium Cyanide Crystals."

"I'm not sure what those are," Stella said, "but with wicked-sounding names like that, I sure wouldn't put 'em in a cake I was bakin'."

"That's good to hear, since I frequently eat at your house," Manny told her.

Next, he illuminated something that reminded Stella of a homemade cheese strainer bag, a bundle made of cheesecloth and tied with a string around the top.

A smell emanated from it that was familiar, but not pleasant. It was what Stella had briefly smelled when they had first opened the bathroom door.

"I remember that," she said. "It's the smell of almonds. Like the almond extract I bake with sometimes, only not nice. Bitter."

"They say that's what the stuff they used in the gas chambers smelled like," Savannah said, looking like she might be sick, as she put her hand over her lower face. "I don't even want it in my nose. I can't stand to think this is what they were smelling as they . . ."

The four of them stood there in the dark, thinking of the victims, even though it pained their souls to do so.

"We have to think about them, Savannah honey," Stella said, putting her arms around her granddaughter's waist and drawing her near. "They had to suffer having it done to them. We can at least honor them by remembering, never forgetting, making sure it doesn't happen again."

Savannah said nothing. She just sniffed, nodded, and wiped some tears away with the back of her hand.

Manny moved the flashlight once more. This time it was a mask they saw. Not a simple dust mask, like the one Stella used when she cleaned out the henhouse. This was a heavy-duty, industrial-looking thing. Stella figured it had probably been designed to protect its wearer in especially dangerous, toxic environments.

"That's how the killer kept himself safe," Elsie said.

"Yes," Manny agreed. "I suspect those two chemicals, when mixed together, produce hydrogen cyanide."

Stella mulled it over, thinking aloud, "Billy Ray was naked and had an old towel with him there in the bathroom. He'd left his clothes outside on the bed. So, he must've been fixin' to take a shower. Once he was in there, the killer coulda barred the door with the chair, and after that, Billy couldn't have got out. So the murderer could've taken his good ol' easy time puttin' the tape around the door and then makin' his way up to the attic."

"Yes. I believe that's how it happened," Manny agreed. "They walked across on the beams, just like I did. Then they put the crystals in that cheesecloth bag, dipped the bag into that liquid acid, slid the tile aside, and then hung the bag down there in the room, where it released its poisonous fumes. It wouldn't be that hard to do. Dangerous and dirty, but not difficult."

"Don't you think Billy Ray would have seen the bag hanging there?" Stella asked.

"He might have, but he couldn't have done anything about it with the door taped and barred. The bathroom had no window to crawl out of."

"Couldn't he have yanked the bag down and dumped it in the toilet, or pulled himself up to the ceiling and crawled into the attic?" Savannah asked.

"No," Manny said. "After I found this stuff I went back down to the bathroom and tried myself. I'm a lot taller than Billy Ray was, and I have much longer arms, but even standing on the toilet, I couldn't have reached the bag, let alone the ceiling."

"He had to just stand there and look at that bag and breathe that awful stuff and suffer," Elsie said.

Savannah shook her head. "I believe this is the only time I ever felt sorry for the likes of Billy Ray Sonner."

"You and me both, kiddo," Manny told her.

"But you still don't know who did it, Sheriff," Elsie said. "You know how, but not who."

Manny gave her a fake stern look. "Now what did I tell you, Miss Elsie, about speaking words of gloom and doom in my presence?"

"Um . . . not to?"

"That's right. I—"

Manny stopped and turned toward the cruiser's door. They had all heard it, the cruiser's radio, asking the sheriff to "Come in."

"Oh, joy. It's Merv again," Manny said as he crawled inside to answer the summons.

Stella listened as the deputy told Manny the purpose for his call.

"She did it again," she could hear Merv saying, "that crazy gal with all them cats who lives in that haunted monstrosity by the graveyard."

"Miss Dolly Browning has a name," Manny told him, "and I'd prefer you use it when you refer to her, Deputy. What exactly did she do again?"

"That crazy gal named Miss Dolly Browning did that stupid thing she does this time ever' year, gettin' drunk as Cooter Brown's skunk and takin' a cab to Atlanta and back," Merv replied. "I got me a mad-as-hell taxi driver here in the station. He wants me to arrest her for theft of service."

"You know the drill, Deputy," Manny told him. "Take whatever she owes him out of petty cash, tack on a nice tip, and send him on his way."

"But that's the town's money."

Stella watched Manny's face tighten. He shook his head and said, "Damn it, Mervin. What's in that shoebox is mostly outta my own pocket, and don't pretend you don't pilfer quarters out of it all the time to support your *Pac-Man* addiction. Do as I say! Now!"

"Yes, sir."

Manny slammed the microphone into its cradle and got back out of the cruiser. He rubbed his hands over his face in a gesture that Stella knew meant their stalwart, never-say-die sheriff had just about reached his limit.

"You oughta go home, Manny, and get some sleep. Tomorrow's another day."

"Yes, unfortunately, it will be," he said with a sigh. "Why didn't I follow my childhood dream? It would've been far less stressful than trying to protect and serve these knuckleheads."

"What was that?" Savannah asked innocently, not detecting the note of sarcasm in his voice. "What did you really want to be when you grew up?"

Stella knew what was coming. She'd heard Manny use this joke before.

"A sword-juggling, tightrope-walking matador who disarms bombs in his spare time."

Savannah laughed. "I think you made the right choice, Sheriff." She turned to Stella. "What's this business about Miss Dolly going to Atlanta every year? I heard she does it, and there's something weird about it, but I don't know why."

"Nobody knows why," Stella told her. "The rest of the year, she's right as rain. I've never even seen the woman tipsy. But for some reason, every April thirtieth, she downs most of a bottle of whisky, dresses up in a fancy dress, hat and gloves, and a mink stole, and she calls a cab to take her to Atlanta."

"Why Atlanta? Does she go shopping?"

"Afraid not," Manny said, as he returned to the trunk and secured the items in the box. "I've gotten more than one complaint from some folks who own a big Tudor mansion, there in the suburbs. She goes to 'visit' them. Uninvited, I might add."

"Why?"

"Again, nobody knows for sure. The first time she did it was about fifteen years ago. She got all spiffied up, like your granny just said, and with that old alligator suitcase in hand, she marched up to their door. And since it was open, she walked right inside and made herself at home. She shook their hands and said, 'Thank you for taking care of my estate while I was gone, but I'm home now, so you can leave.' "

"That must have been a shock for the real homeowners."

"It was. But they're kindhearted people, who realized she'd had too much to drink and was more confused than dangerous."

Manny closed the box and placed some evidence tape across the top to seal it. "After she showed up the second time, they started making sure the door was locked. But every year, like clockwork, a cab pulls up to the mansion, she gets out, struts up there to the door, as bold as you please, and when they don't answer, she yells and pounds on it until they do."

Savannah turned to her grandmother. "That's sad, Granny. Has anybody asked her why she does it?"

"I did, about ten years ago," Elsie said. "But she didn't want to talk about it. Once she sobers up, she's all embarrassed, and she clams up tighter than a flea's butt over a rain barrel. Refused to even discuss it."

"I usually pay her an early morning visit every April thirtieth," Manny said. "I warn her to stay off the whisky and suggest she spend the day at home, all quiet and peaceful like. For all the good it does. The minute my back's turned, she hits the bottle, then carries on with her day, just like she'd planned. With all that's been going on, I forgot this year. It completely slipped my mind."

"You've got bigger fish to fry, Manny," Stella assured him. Turning to Savannah, she said, "No real harm's done. Nobody gets hurt, except the cab drivers who get their noses outta joint when they realize this woman, who was all dressed up like a rich lady and looked like she could afford a taxi trip to and from Atlanta, doesn't have a single dollar bill on her."

"That's when they come to the station and complain to me. Some, like the guy this year, want her locked up."

"*You* pay her taxi bill ever' single year, Sheriff?" Elsie asked.

Manny shrugged. "It's not that much. She's a nice lady, doesn't cause me any trouble the other 364 days a year. I don't mind helping her out a little once in a while."

Savannah studied him with admiring eyes for a moment, then said, "You make a nicer sheriff than you would have a bullfighter."

"I'm sure that's true." Manny winked at her as he slammed the trunk closed. "I wouldn't have gotten far as a matador, shooting foam darts at the bull."

Savannah turned to Stella and said, "I feel funny even mentioning this, Gran. I don't even know why I thought of it, except that I've been reading that book about the Holocaust for days."

"Okay, darlin'. What's on your mind?"

"I was just wondering if any of you know what April thirtieth is. What significance it has in world history, that is."

Stella thought for a moment, but nothing came to mind. She turned to Manny. "I'm drawin' a blank here. You, Manny?"

"I've no idea."

Manny and Stella looked at Elsie, but she shook her head and said, "I can't think of anything either. Is it the birthday of somebody famous?"

"Not their birthday," Savannah said. "The opposite of a birthday, in fact. April thirtieth is the day Adolph Hitler died."

Chapter 28

Stella, Manny, Elsie, and Savannah stood at the rear of the cruiser, silent, as the adults took in what Savannah had just said.

It's probably nothin', Stella told herself. *Who knows why a date is important to anybody? Could be a birthday, an anniversary, any sort of remembrance.*

But something deep inside told her this was a crucial piece of information that they needed to, at least, consider.

"Are you absolutely sure about that, Savannah?" Manny asked her.

Stella could tell by his tone that he was taking it seriously. Apparently, his instincts were telling him it was important, too.

Savannah nodded. "I can take you back inside and show you in the book."

"Would you mind doing that, darlin'? It's not that I don't trust you, but I do need to verify it." He shot Stella a look and added, "It might be important."

Stella's head was spinning as the four of them walked back into the house.

When Savannah ran off to the kitchen to get her book, Stella whispered to Manny, "But Dolly got a threatening letter, and we know it was from the killer, 'cause they knew about Billy Ray's body being at Mabel's Motel."

Manny looked less than convinced when he reminded her, "A letter with only her fingerprints and mine and the postman's on it."

"Yes, but—"

Savannah had returned with the book. She quickly thumbed through the pages, found what she was looking for, and shoved it into Manny's hands.

Pointing to a particular passage, she said, "See there. He gave his girlfriend, Eva, some poison—well, she was his wife by then, because he'd just married her—and then he shot himself. Some of the experts say he poisoned himself first, too. But either way, it all happened on April thirtieth, 1945."

Manny read the section and nodded. "She's absolutely right. I don't know if there's any significance at all, but . . ." Closing the book, he said, "Stella, Elsie, have either one of you ever heard anything, even a rumor, about where Dolly Browning's from? Where she lived before she showed up here that day, back in the forties, with her alligator suitcase?"

"No," Stella said. "I heard she had a little bit of an accent back then, like maybe she was from a different country. But I never heard where. Now she speaks like the rest of us, only maybe better."

"I never heard where she was from neither," Elsie said, "but I could swear, one time I heard her speaking another language."

"Really?" Manny leaned closer to Elsie. "What language?"

"I don't know. It was right after she got that dog of hers, Valentine. She was so proud of her new puppy. Was tellin' ever'body she met about him. I had a ham bone left over from the judge's big Easter feast, so I took it over to her."

"That was nice of you," Savannah said.

"Oh, shucks. I didn't have a dog myself, and I thought he'd enjoy it. Anyway, I knocked on her door, but she didn't answer. Then I thought I heard her in the backyard. I walked around the house and saw her layin' on her back on the grass. The puppy was a big one. He was standing on her chest, licking her face. It was a sweet sight, I tell you. She was talking to him, and I didn't recognize any of the words."

"But you've no idea what language it might've been?" Manny asked, frustrated.

"No. But I remember what she called him. I thought it might be the name she'd given him, so I remembered it."

"What was it?" Stella asked.

"It didn't make sense, but it sounded like, 'Mine Lee Bling.'"

"Mine Lee Bling?" Savannah mused. "That'd be a pretty weird name for a dog."

"No kidding," Stella agreed. "Fido rolls off the tongue a lot easier."

She glanced over at Manny, who was staring at Elsie, as though her words had stunned him.

"Mine Lee Bling?" he asked.

Elsie nodded. "That's what she said."

"*Mein liebling,*" he whispered. "My little darling."

"What?" Stella asked. "What do you mean?"

"*Mein liebling.* It means, 'my little darling' or 'my little sweetheart,' in German."

"German?" Elsie was flabbergasted. "Really?"

"Wow," Savannah said, her mouth open. "That's weird. I mean, with all that's been going on and—"

The phone rang, and they all jumped.

"Who in tarnation is that?" Stella said as she rushed to answer it before the noise woke the children. "It's after nine o'clock. Ever'body I know who'd call me at this hour is here already."

She picked up the phone and said, "Hello."

The person on the other end didn't answer for so long that Stella thought it might be a prank.

"Who's calling, please?" she asked.

"Stella?"

The voice was slurred and weak, as though the speaker was far away, but Stella thought she recognized it. "Dolly? Is that you?"

"Yes. It's me. I'm sorry."

"For what, darlin'?"

"For calling so late. For disturbing you. I know you just got your little girl home from the hospital today."

"It's okay, Dolly." Stella looked around the room and saw that Manny, Elsie, and Savannah were watching with great interest and listening intently. "I'm glad you called. Are you okay? You don't sound yourself."

Stella heard soft laughter on the other end, then, "I've had a bit to drink, this morning and then again a few minutes ago. I don't usually, so it goes right to my head."

"I imagine it would."

Stella's mind raced, wondering the purpose for the call. She couldn't remember Dolly ever phoning her at night, and certainly not when she was inebriated.

"I want to ask you for a favor, Stella," Dolly said, speaking each word slowly and deliberately, as though it was quite an effort. "It's a very, very important favor."

"Okay, I'd be happy to do a favor for you," Stella repeated for the sake of those listening. "Just tell me what it is."

"I have something to give you, and I need to give it to you tonight. Right now, in fact. Could you please come over here to my house?"

When Stella hesitated for a second, thinking of Alma, Dolly quickly added, "I'd drive over to your home, but I'm in no shape to get behind the wheel."

"No, of course you mustn't drive. I'll come right over."

"There's one more thing. It's very important," Dolly said, sounding far more serious than before. "Could you come alone? It's . . . a privacy thing."

"Okay. I'll come alone."

"And you'll come right now? I hate to insist, but—"

"No problem. I'm leaving this instant. I'll be there in less than ten minutes."

"Thank you, Stella. You're a good friend."

Stella heard the phone click. She turned to Elsie and said, "I guess you heard that."

"I did. Don't even ask. I'm here for as long as you need me."

"Thank you."

"I'll stay up and help her," Savannah added with a sly smile.

"The kids are in bed and asleep, Miss Savannah. Elsie don't need no help, and you've got school tomorrow."

"Granny, ple-e-ease!" Savannah looked like she was about to burst into tears. "This is *way* more important than any stupid thing I'm going to learn in school tomorrow. This is real life! Besides, I won't be able to sleep a wink until you get home and tell me what happened. I might as well be sitting out here, talking to Elsie, than tossing and turning in that bunk bed in there, listening to Vidalia snore and Marietta fart."

Stella sighed. "That's true, girlie. Stay out here and keep Elsie company. I'll be back as soon as I can."

As she was putting on her sweater and reaching for her purse on the piecrust table behind the door, she noticed that Manny was sliding into his jacket.

"What do you think you're doin', Sheriff Gilford?" she asked him.

"I'm taking you to see Dolly Browning."

"You must have heard what I told her. You were standing right next to me."

"I did, and I'm driving you over there and going inside with you."

"You can't! She said it was a private matter, and I had to come all by myself."

He walked over to the door and opened it. "Go sit yourself down in my cruiser, Stella May," he said. "You told her you'd be there in less than ten minutes. We can argue about it on the way there."

"Do I look stupid to you, Manny Gilford? If we're on our way, then you've already won the argument!"

He stepped up to her, grabbed her by the elbow, and said, "Mrs. Reid, are you resisting an officer of the law?"

"I most certainly am. He's being overly bossy, and I don't abide such things."

"Ugh, woman! You drive me batty—you know that?"

Manny groaned and ran his fingers through his hair several times in exasperation. When he was finished, he reminded Stella of Marietta's impression of Cyndi Lauper.

With what appeared to be a great effort on his part, he calmed himself and said with exaggerated patience, "Just think about this for a second, and I'm sure you'll agree I have a good point. In the past thirty minutes, Miss Dolly Browning has moved to the top, or at least near the top, of my suspect list. Then she makes a mysterious late-night phone call to you, asking you to come over to her house to do her some unnamed favor, and she insists that you come alone. Alone, Stella. Why would she need to see you alone? Do you really think I'm going to let you go over there by yourself? Seriously? I wouldn't let some two-hundred-pound jerk from the pool hall that I don't even like go over there without my protection tonight. Let alone you. "

Stella mulled it over for several seconds, looked up at him coyly, and said, "I'll make a deal with ya."

"I'm sheriff of this county, Stella May. I don't have to make deals with anybody."

Ignoring his last statement, because it didn't serve her purpose, she said, "Here's my compromise. You drive me over, park a block from the house, so she can't see your cruiser. Then you wait in the car while I go in. If I need you, I'll holler."

"I might not hear you."

"Obviously, you have forgotten who you're talkin' to. I will remind you that when I was sixteen, I won the county fair's hog-callin' contest."

She could tell by the defeated look on his face he had come to his senses. As she had intended, he realized that her sound logic had trumped his overly protective, emotion-based argument.

She reached up and patted his cheek as she walked by him and out the door. "Don't look so glum, darlin'," she told him. "There ain't a thing to fret about. I promise you, if I have cause to scream bloody murder, you and ever'body in town's gonna hear me."

Chapter 29

When Manny and Stella turned down the street where Dolly Browning lived, Stella could feel her pulse rate quicken, and it had been racing since they'd left her house.

Ahead, she could see the cemetery, and overlooking it on the hill, Dolly's old mansion.

"I keep thinkin' about how folks say she paid cash for that house," Stella said as they drew closer. "Like how they say her suitcase was full of cash."

"If she's lived on what was in that suitcase all these years, it would've had to be something more valuable than paper money."

"Jewels maybe?"

"Who knows. It was after the war. Most people lose a lot during a war, their homes, even their lives. But a few actually profit."

"I can't think about that now," Stella said. "For all I know, she's invited me over here to give me more of those garden tomatoes of hers. She saved my grandbaby's life only a few days ago."

"She diagnosed Alma like a professional would," Manny observed. "A doctor or trained nurse couldn't have done better. If she had medical training like that, why hasn't she ever told anyone? Why didn't she continue to practice medicine in some capacity?"

"I know! I know, Manny! It's driving me crazy wondering. I don't wanna accuse an innocent woman, a woman I owe a debt to that I can never repay, of a terrible crime. We don't have any real evidence that—"

"We aren't accusing her of anything," Manny said. "We're just weighing the evidence that we have, sorting through it, and seeing what it shows us. No accusations involved."

"Not yet. But that's what you're thinkin', ain't it?"

"What I'm thinking isn't important right now. At the moment, all that concerns me is your safety, and it should concern you, too. Never mind what you mean to me and your friends. Those grandangels, as you call them, depend on you. They depend on you *hard*, Stella. I can't stand to even think about what would happen to them if anything happened to you."

"Do you think that hasn't crossed my mind, too, Manny? Crossed it, churned it up, and spit it out. I can't stand the thought either. But I could hear it in her voice. Dolly's in trouble. I have to go in there and see if I can help, 'cause if I don't, I won't be able to live with myself."

Manny pulled over to the curb and parked the vehicle in an area that was poorly lit. "Okay," he said, turning off the key. "This is as close as I can get without risking her seeing me."

"It's fine. You just stay here and wait for me. Hopefully, I won't be long."

When he didn't reply, she said, "You're gonna do that, right? You're gonna wait here in the car till I come out, like I waited for you at the motel. Promise me, Manny."

"She won't see me. I promise you that."

She held up her little finger, as they had when they'd been children. "Pinky swear."

He grinned, crooked his finger around hers, and gave it a squeeze. "Pinky swear."

Their ritual finished, she took a deep breath and said, "I'd best get goin'."

"Go. Be careful!"

"I will. Jeepers creepers, you sound like a broken record."

As she climbed out of the car, he blew her a kiss, which she "caught" with her hand and blew back to him.

Then she was on her way. Where to, she wasn't sure. But Manny was right. She had to be very careful; those grandbabies were depending on her to return home to them safe and sound.

She thought of Savannah and Elsie sitting on her couch at home, no doubt, making small talk to cover their nervousness as they waited.

Yes, she was important to a number of precious people—one being the man sitting in the cruiser, watching her every step.

She was grateful for their love, but more nervous than she had let on to any of them.

As she climbed the loose, splintery steps leading to the ancient house, she had a bad feeling. Deep inside, the calm voice that abided in her spirit, the source of what she and others called her "intuition" or her "higher self," told her that what was about to happen next was going to haunt her for the rest of her days.

However many of them remained.

Chapter 30

No one answered when Stella knocked on the door of the old mansion. She heard Valentine's toenails on the tile as he approached and his sniffing around the doorframe. She hoped he would remember her scent and the fact that she had patted him on the head and scratched behind his ears on her recent visit.

Knocking the third time, she said, "Valentine. Go tell your mistress she's got company, okay?"

All she heard in response was more sniffing, but no human footsteps or voice bidding her to open the door and come in.

She twisted the knob and pushed a little to see if it was unlocked.

It was. It creaked open an inch. Enough for her to see the quivering black nostrils of the gigantic dog on the other side.

"Hey, Valentine," she whispered. "Don't eat me now, 'kay? I'm a friend, and your mistress wouldn't take kindly to you rippin' the arm off somebody she'd invited over."

She opened the door a bit more and could see the dog's tail waving vigorously. She reminded herself that, although that was usually a good sign, some dogs wagged their tails while chomping on a burglar's leg, simply because they liked the taste.

"You gonna let me in?" she asked him. "Can I come into your house, big boy?"

She held her hand out so he could smell the back of it. She wished she'd rubbed some bacon grease on it before she'd left the house.

"Dolly?" she called out, "it's Stella Reid. I'm here in the doorway . . . with Valentine," she added, hoping the mistress of the house would take the hint and come rescue her.

When there was still no response from inside the house, Stella slowly opened the door the rest of the way and gingerly stepped inside.

The moment her foot crossed the threshold, Valentine growled. A chill went through her as the sound rattled deep in his chest. It touched some primitive part of her being that recognized it as a critical warning. A life-threatening warning, coming from a dog that was twice the size of a German shepherd or rottweiler.

She stood very still, wondering what to do, then she recalled what Elsie had said. One quick look into the house told her that Dolly wasn't within earshot, so she whispered to the dog, "Aw, it's okay . . . *mein liebling.*"

Instantly, the dog stopped growling and started to whimper like a joyful puppy who had been waiting all day for his owner to come home and play with him.

He began to gamble about, clumsy, all legs, tripping over himself. He gave a joyful bark and licked her hand, covering it in an instant with saliva from her wrist to her fingertips.

"Atta boy," she told him as she walked on inside and shut the door behind her. "Where's your mistress, huh?"

She saw several cats—a tuxedo kitty, an orange tabby, and a solid black mini-panther—scurry away and hide behind some boxes, where they sat, peering out at her with golden eyes.

"Dolly!" she called out, louder than before. "It's Stella, honey. I'm here. Where are you?"

"In here," was the reply, but the voice was so soft, Stella barely heard it.

She walked into the parlor, where Dolly had entertained her and Manny before, and there she was, reclining gracefully on the sofa.

To Stella's surprise, Dolly was wearing a beautiful, peach-colored cocktail dress that appeared to be from the forties. The shoulders were generously padded, the velvet bodice heavily embroidered with lace and iridescent crystals. It fit Dolly's slender figure perfectly, the color lending a comely glow to her otherwise sallow complexion.

She looked like a vintage movie star, relaxing after having attended some regal ball where she had danced the night away with royalty.

Stella hurried over to the sofa and knelt beside her. It was only then that she noticed the mink stole lying beside her. It was one of the old-fashioned sorts that included the heads, legs, and feet of the animals who had, no doubt unwillingly, contributed their pelts to the making of the piece.

Stella shuddered and looked away, as she realized this was probably the very outfit Dolly had worn on her trip to Atlanta today to "reclaim" her home.

How very eccentric, indeed.

As Stella leaned over to take Dolly's hand in hers, she smelled the strong odor of whisky that seemed to be not only on the woman's breath but emanating from her very pores. Mixed with the exotic scent of Dolly's heavy, floral perfume, it was a strange odor and not a particularly pleasant one.

"Thank you for coming, Stella," Dolly said, grasping her hand and holding it tightly. "I was afraid you wouldn't. You've always been so kind to me. Kinder than I deserve," she added, tears filling her watery blue eyes.

"Now, now. No crying. What's this favor you want me to do for you?"

"We'll get to that in a minute. But first I want to give you your present. I've only just started it, so it's far from finished. I ran out of time. For everything."

"What do you mean?" Stella said, feeling a bit chilly, in spite of the warmth of the space heater glowing in the corner.

"Over there. In my knitting basket. I can't get up now. Will you fetch it for me?"

"Sure. You just rest." Stella rose from her knees and walked across the room to the large wicker basket Dolly had pointed to.

"In here?" she asked, looking down at the assortment of yarns, half-finished projects, and miscellaneous stuff that had been tossed into the oversized hamper.

"Yes, it should be close to the top. I was working on it yesterday. Just throw the junk out and you'll find it."

Stella wasn't listening. Her mind was frozen as she stared at the first bit of so-called "junk" she had lifted out of the knitting supplies.

Duct tape. An almost empty roll. Along the sticky edges, Stella could see the fuzz. The blue fuzz stuck to it.

"There's a blue blanket in there, not much of it done," Dolly was saying. "I was going to give it to the next person in town who has a new baby. I hear you've got a new grandchild on the way. So it's yours. I'm sorry I ran out of time. If you know how to crochet, maybe you could finish it, or Savannah or your friend Elsie could. Take those extra skeins of yarn, too. You'll need them to make it big enough for the little one."

Stella lifted the blanket out, fighting the nausea that was rising in her. Not knowing what to do, she removed the blanket and the spare skeins, and replaced the duct tape on top, where she had found it.

As she walked back to the sofa, she found her voice and said, "Thank you, Dolly. That's so kind of you . . . to think of me, of our new baby."

"I used the best yarn I had. Some I've been saving for a special occasion. I'm glad it's going to you, Stella. You and your family are precious to me."

Stella looked down at the blanket and realized her hands were shaking. "It's beautiful yarn. Angora."

"That's the softest kind. It's nice for babies. Soft against their delicate skin."

"I know. Thank you."

For a moment, Dolly's eyes closed, and Stella thought she might have nodded off to sleep or passed out from the liquor. But she quickly opened them again and said, "Okay. You have your present. The other thing is the favor."

"Yes," Stella said, standing there with the soft yarn in her hands and what felt like a cold, hard stone in her heart. "What would you have me do, Dolly?"

Pointing to the rolltop desk in the corner, she said, "On the desk there's a letter. It's addressed to Sheriff Gilford. I want you to give it to him for me as soon as possible. It's very important. Could you do that, Stella?"

Stella walked over to the desk. The first thing that caught her eye was an old photograph in a silver frame, one she hadn't noticed before when visiting Dolly. It was a yellowed picture of an elegant, Tudor-style mansion, much like the one in Atlanta that Dolly had infamously visited every year. But, unlike Atlanta, there were snow-capped mountains in the background.

Standing in front of the home was a pretty blonde woman, holding a curly haired baby in her arms. The woman bore a strong resemblance to Dolly.

"Is it you in this picture?" Stella asked her.

"No, it's my mother. I'm the baby."

Something clicked in Stella's mind. "This was your family home," she said. "It's where you grew up."

Dolly nodded and smiled wistfully. "I miss it terribly. It was so peaceful, so beautiful there. Before. Before everything changed."

"The house you visit every April in Atlanta . . ." Stella ventured.

Dolly sighed. "I know. I know it isn't mine. I saw a picture of it in a magazine, and it reminded me of home. One day, I got drunk and went there and . . ." She shook her head and closed her eyes. "I make a fool of myself when I drink, and every year I drink to celebrate that day."

Stella tucked that information away to share with Manny later.

Looking around, she spotted a letter lying near the picture and picked it up. The envelope was fine parchment with "Sheriff Gilford" typed on the front. The print was dull, the edges blurry, as though the typewriter had been an old one. The tops of the letters were black.

The lower halves were red.

The shakiness in Stella's hands had spread to her knees, making it difficult for her to stand. On unsteady legs she walked over to a chair next to the sofa and sat down, abruptly and hard.

"You can read it," Dolly told her. "I want you to. Now."

"Okay." Stella put the yarn and blanket on her lap and opened the unsealed envelope.

The inside was typed, too, with the same black and red print, and the letter was signed at the bottom with a large, scrawling signature in bold, black ink.

"Dear Sheriff Gilford," Stella began. "I write this letter to confess to the murder of Billy Ray Sonner, a self-proclaimed Nazi, who attacked an innocent girl and did her great harm."

Stella looked over at Dolly and saw that her features registered only grim satisfaction. There was certainly nothing resembling remorse on the woman's face.

Stella returned to her reading. "I understand that Raul Ortez and Franklin Tucker are suspected of committing this crime. I assure you, I did it alone, without anyone's participation or knowledge."

A rush of relief flooded through Stella. The cloud that had been over both Raul and Franklin would be lifted now, from them, as well as their families.

She drew a deep breath and continued, "I killed Sonner the same way we killed millions of innocents, whose memories are now dishonored by fools who deny their sufferings or attempt to rationalize that which cannot be justified by any philosophy on earth, in heaven, or hell. I killed Sonner to stop him from spreading a poison more vile than the deadly chemicals I employed to end his miserable life. His attitudes and words, his attempts to convince others of his vicious lies, are manifestations of an evil that must not be allowed to exist. To my everlasting shame, I witnessed and participated in the horrors born of those attitudes and words. To my credit, I ended him. I leave this life satisfied that I have done what little I could to atone for my sins. Sincerely, Adolpha Brandt."

Chapter 31

"Dolly, is this true?" Stella asked, hardly able to believe the words she had just read.

"You know it is, Stella," Dolly replied, wiping away tears from her cheeks. "In your heart, you know."

"What did you mean when you wrote, 'the same way we killed millions'? Why would you say, 'we'? Why would you say you participated in the horrors?"

"I was a member of the Nazi Party, Stella."

"A lot of regular German folks were. Some didn't have a choice and—"

"I chose. I was a nurse in Ravensbrück. Do you know Ravensbrück, Stella?"

Stella recalled the pictures she had seen when she was younger, the ones that had scarred her soul. Among them, photos of Ravensbrück, a concentration camp for women.

In that moment, in her mind's eye, Stella could see those pictures as clearly as she had as a child, and Stella realized that they weren't scars on her soul after all. They were still open wounds.

Some knowing could never be unknown, and some wounds never healed.

"That's why . . ." Stella choked on her own words, then tried again. ". . . why you were able to save Alma?"

"Yes, I saved your Alma. I wonder, does that take away the sin of one? One of the many that I killed? What do you think, Stella?"

"You killed . . . ?" Stella couldn't believe she was sitting in the same room, breathing the same air as one of the monsters she had read about, had nightmares about.

But she looks so . . . so normal, she thought. *This is my friend Dolly.*

She glanced down at the signature. Adolpha Brandt. Dolly Browning.

How could they be the same person?

"But you brought me tomatoes from your garden," Stella said, knowing it was a ridiculous thing to say under the circumstances. "You bought my granddaughter a teddy bear."

"I'm a person, Stella. We were all just people. Regular people, like—"

"No! You were not!" Stella jumped up from her chair. The yarn, blanket, and letter fell to the floor. "Don't say that! Regular people don't do what you did!"

"Yes, they do! That's what you have to understand. You think people in McGill are different from the little town outside of Dresden where I grew up? They aren't. We rode our bicycles down the streets like children here do. We celebrated holidays with our families, kissed our sweethearts, had jobs, married and raised families, just like you."

"Then you changed!"

"Hate-filled people told us hateful lies, and it served our purposes to believe them. They told us we were stronger and smarter and more beautiful than those who looked different from us. They told us they would put money in our pockets and give us good jobs and enable us to have better things than those ugly, stupid, weak people who didn't deserve them."

"How could you believe lies like that? How could you not question it, resist it?"

Dolly shook her head. "You don't understand. You don't hear the worst lies at first. It's gradual. One lie builds on another. That's why people like Billy Ray have to be stopped, their evil mouths shut for all time. It could happen again, Stella. The human heart doesn't change."

Suddenly, too tired to stand, Stella sank to her knees again beside the sofa. But this time she couldn't take Dolly's hand in hers.

The pictures in the books she'd seen. The medical experiments. Doctors and nurses who weren't healers but torturers. The gas chambers. The endless stacks of emaciated bodies. The crematoriums.

No. She couldn't find it in her heart to offer compassion and comfort to someone who had participated in that hell.

"Billy Ray was a horrible guy," Stella told her, "but you murdered him. Just like you killed all those people in that concentration camp. I don't know how we're supposed to stop people like Billy Ray and his lies. But murder? No, Dolly. There has to be a better answer."

When Dolly didn't respond, Stella reached down, picked up the envelope from the floor and looked at the black-and-red typing. "That letter, the one you brought into the police station, you wrote it and stuck it in your own mailbox to throw us off," she said.

Dolly nodded.

"How did you know Billy Ray would be at Mabel's Motel?"

"At the garage, when they heard me coming, Billy Ray said to them, 'Meet me later at Mabel's.' I knew that meant the old motel, because I lived there when I first came to McGill, while I was buying the house. But I was so rattled when I talked to you and the sheriff there in the restaurant, I forgot all about that. It wasn't until Sheriff Gilford came by later and told me Billy Ray had escaped that I remembered about Mabel's."

"So, you went out there, figuring they'd show up?"

"I did. I parked down the road from the motel among some trees. I was waiting for them, behind the building, hiding in the bushes, when they got there. Deacon and Billy Ray pulled up in Deacon's old jalopy. A minute later, Earle arrived, driving that hideous pickup with the swastikas on its doors. He handed Billy Ray a big, brown bag. Then he and Deacon took off in Deacon's car. They left Billy Ray the pickup."

"The bag would've had his clothes and pistol in it," Stella said.

"It did and some beer," Dolly replied. "I watched through the window as Billy Ray made himself at home there in one of the rooms. He was filthy. I figured he'd take a shower sooner or later. I'd brought the chemicals and tape in case I had a chance to use them."

"You already had them?"

Dolly nodded. "I keep duct tape in my car at all times. It comes in handy."

Stella asked, "But the chemicals? Why would you keep such a thing around your house?"

Dolly toyed with the crystal-studded lace on her bodice, and her face registered extreme sadness as she said, "There have been times I felt I should end myself, Stella. It was the least I could do, considering what I did. And I figured, if I killed myself, I should die the way they did. So, I got the stuff to do it. But I didn't have the courage. To my shame, I wasn't that brave."

Dolly smiled, still sad, but somehow satisfied. "I was brave enough to end him though. I was."

Stella still couldn't imagine this tiny woman doing what Manny had described as a chore that was difficult for him to perform.

"How did you make your way across those beams in the attic?" she asked.

"It wasn't all that hard. I'm spry for my age, and I was careful."

"And you hung that bag of poison from the bathroom ceiling?"

"I certainly did, and I lay there on my belly and watched him die. He was looking up at me, and I was looking down on him when he drew his last breath. That was one of the best moments of my life. That and saving your Alma. I'm proud of both."

Dolly closed her eyes, and Stella heard her whisper, "It won't be long now."

"What? What won't be long?"

"It's working. The pill I took when you got here. It's working. But I need to ask you for one more thing."

Stella's realized with horrible clarity exactly what was happening. "No! Dolly, what did you take? We have to get you to a hospital!"

"It's too late. I'll be gone in just a few minutes. I have to ask you . . . I need . . ."

Stella could tell she was having a hard time breathing. "What do you need, Dolly?"

"Forgiveness. Just in case there really is something over there, on the other side of this, I can't go there without forgiveness."

"Dolly, please let me call an ambulance."

Dolly grabbed Stella's hand and held it so tightly Stella couldn't pull away. "I chose you because you're the best person I know. If anyone can forgive me, it would be you. Please, Stella, forgive me for what I did to those women. I saved some of them. I was a good nurse, too. Like when I saved your girl. But there were others, so many others." She gasped. "Those poor women. Their eyes. Oh, no! Stella, I see them! I see them now!"

Stella tried again to remove her hand from the other's grasp but couldn't. Dolly's eyes, bright with terror, stared into hers.

Desperately, Stella wanted to get away from her, the clawing hand, the piercing eyes, the crushing guilt, and terrible regret for atrocities that could never be undone.

No wonder this woman had lived her life afraid, terrified of unseen enemies.

"I can't forgive you, Dolly," she said. "I just can't."

"I understand. It's too much. What I did. It was too bad."

"It's not just that," Stella told her. "We've all sinned. But the things you did, you didn't do them to me. *I* wasn't your victim. I didn't suffer at your hand. How can I take it upon myself to forgive another person's suffering? So many people? So much suffering?"

For a long time, Dolly stared up at the ceiling and seemed to be considering what Stella had just said. Then she whispered, "I tried to go home again today. It isn't my home. There's no going back. There's no hope. No hope."

"As long as you're breathing, there's hope. I can't wipe it all away and give you a clean heart, Dolly. I'm just a human. Maybe God can. You could ask Him."

Stella watched as Dolly's lips moved in a silent attempt to say something. But Stella had no idea what her friend, the former concentration camp Nazi, healer, and murderer, was saying, if anything.

Stella would never know. Because gradually, the hand that had grasped hers so tightly relinquished its hold, and the lips that may, or may not, have begged for forgiveness stopped moving.

Nearby, Stella heard a movement and a small whimper. She turned and saw that it was Valentine, sniffing his mistress's ankle and then licking it.

Stella felt a hand on her shoulder, a large, warm, strong hand that imparted the comfort she so badly needed at that moment.

Somehow, she knew he had been there, just out of sight but nearby, all along.

"Come with me, Stella," she heard Manny saying, as though from far away. "There's nothing more you can do for her. She's gone."

"I know," Stella said, looking up at him with eyes filled with tears. "But where is she? In the arms of God?"

Manny was quiet for a long time, looking down at Dolly's body, now so curiously empty, the vital, mysterious woman having left it behind.

"I don't know where she is, darlin'," he said at last. "I reckon that's between her and Him."

Chapter 32

Stella sat beneath the magnolia tree in her backyard and watched the people she loved most in the world enjoy the party she had prepared for them. It had been a lot of work, cooking the food, cleaning the house, getting the yard and her garden up to her personal standard. All with a new baby to take care of. But it was worth it.

Now she could rest, at least for a little while, as the tree offered much needed shade from the August sun, both for her and the tiny infant in her arms.

This was what she had been looking forward to for months. Holding her latest grandchild in her arms, enjoying the peace that emanated from a sleeping child, so new to the world that he had no problems to worry about.

In a moment, she would need to get up and mingle, entertain the many friends and neighbors whom she had invited to share this occasion with her and the grandchildren.

But for now, it was just her and the baby, and that was all Stella wanted or needed in the world.

She brushed her pinky across his tiny fist and delighted in how his fingers curled around hers. She ducked her head to kiss his soft, downy hair and breathed in his sweet baby smell.

How could she ever have doubted this blessing or whether or not she would be capable of fully embracing her new responsibilities?

"I've got you," she told him. "Don't you fret about nothin', little Macon Junior. Your granny's got you, and she ain't never lettin' you go."

She looked across the lawn at her younger grandchildren, who were playing freeze tag. Even Alma was fully enjoying herself, running like a maniac when being pursued and "freezing" in the most ridiculous and comical poses when nabbed.

The older ones were embroiled in a highly competitive contest of Twister, which involved a lot of bending, stretching, and shrieking when someone stumbled and fell, taking the others down with them in a human domino–falling crescendo.

The adults were gathered around the barbecue grill, where Manny was flipping burgers and grilling hot dogs. Elsie was giving him tips, and because he was a smart man who knew her reputation as a chef, he was listening attentively.

At the far end of the yard, Raul and Yolanda, and Pastor O'Reilly and Connie were tossing horseshoes with Stella's lifelong friend Magi Red Crow. Stella couldn't help laughing as she watched. Little did the first four know what they were getting into. Magi was a master at tossing horseshoes. They didn't realize the game was over before it had begun.

Stella noticed that the only one who wasn't occupied was Waycross. He, alone, was sitting at the edge of the garden, watching her hold his new baby brother. It was so unusual for the boy to simply sit still that she got concerned.

She crooked one finger, beckoning him to join her. Instantly, he perked up, jumped to his feet, and ran across the yard to the tree.

"Whatcha doin' over there by the garden, grandson of mine?" she asked.

He shrugged. "Nothin'. Just sittin' there with my teeth in my mouth," was his standard reply.

"Don't feel like playin' with the others?"

"Naw. Freeze tag's silly, and I don't wanna get all tangled up with my sisters. A guy can get Girl Cooties doin' stuff like that."

"Hm-m. Wouldn't wanna risk catchin' awful critters like Girl Cooties. I don't even know what you'd have to do to get rid of 'em."

"Steel wool and bleach, I reckon."

"If you're lucky."

Stella saw him glance down at the baby in her arms, and she thought she detected both affection and a bit of jealousy.

Poor boy, she thought. *He waits his whole life for a brother, and now that he has one, he finds out it ain't all it's cracked up to be.*

"How's the, um, baby doin'?" Waycross asked, giving the infant a nod and the briefest of glances.

"Just layin' here," Stella said in her best "no-big-deal" voice.

"No teeth in his mouth," Waycross supplied.

"Nary a one. Not a lotta hair either."

Stella watched as the boy's curiosity got the better of his resentment. He knelt beside her chair in the grass, and gently pulled the receiving blanket back a bit to get a better look at his new brother's face.

"Do you think he looks like me?" Waycross asked. "The sheriff said he can see a family resemblance. Whatever that means."

Stella pretended to study the baby's tiny pink features. Then she pronounced her judgment. "He's not as handsome as you. Won't be for quite a while, 'cause he's gotta learn how. But yes, I think he favors his big brother quite a bit."

Waycross seemed to like the answer, and he brightened a little. "I wish he was big enough to play with. There's not much point to having a brother if they don't do nothin' but lay around."

"That's what all babies do at first. He'll learn stuff though. In fact, you can teach him things, like how to throw a baseball and ride a skateboard and put frogs in your sisters' drawers."

His eyes opened wide. "Really?!"

"Only if you don't tell them I said you could."

"Okay. It'll be our secret. I won't even tell him that you said it. It'll be our secret, just you and me."

Stella reached down and smoothed his copper curls. "You know, Waycross . . . before Macon here was born, you were my only boy. Now, you're my first grandson, the oldest male in my household, and this little guy's older brother. Those are all three very important roles, but I'm sure you're up to the task."

"What kinda things do I have to do now that I'm all those things?"

"Well, you have to be ready to protect the family in any way you can. You need to be strong when a strong guy is needed and a gentle one the rest of the time."

"I can do that stuff."

"I know you can."

"You'll have to look out for this little guy, 'cause he'll probably get in trouble from time to time and you'll have to help him get outta it."

"I'm good at that."

"You certainly are. But right now, there's something very important you can do for him and for me."

"What's that?"

"Feed him."

Waycross seemed shocked at the very possibility. "Really? I can do that?"

"You most certainly can." Stella reached down into the bag sitting next to her chair and took out a bottle. Then she stood and motioned for Waycross to sit there instead.

She could tell he was nervous when she carefully placed the baby in his arms.

"Look at you!" she said. "You're very good at this. You're supporting his little head exactly the way you're supposed to."

For the next ten minutes, she showed her eager student how to give his brother a bottle. In no time, all signs of jealousy were gone, as well as his disappointment at not being able to play ball with the new arrival.

Stella walked a few feet away to give Waycross the illusion of control, while keeping a close eye on the little one for any signs of choking or spitting up.

"Looks like your little man there's got the situation in hand," Manny said as he walked up to her and looked down at the two brothers, who were getting to know each other.

"He's a natural, that Waycross," she said. "A kind heart and a steady hand's all it takes."

Manny moved a bit closer to her and took her hand in his. "This is a nice party you gave to welcome the little guy, Stella," he said. "Everybody's enjoying themselves."

"I hope so. I haven't had much chance to mingle and be a good hostess."

"This gang's capable of entertaining themselves. Look at Raul and Yolanda over there." He nodded toward the horseshoe pit. "That little group's become good friends, it seems."

Stella nodded. "Connie's been spending a lot of time with Yolanda lately. I think it's good for them both."

"I couldn't believe how well Yolanda sang in church this morning," Manny said. "Her voice is beautiful. Strong, too. It filled the sanctuary. I thought she might cause one of the stained-glass windows to shatter."

"I was surprised, too. I remember Raul said she could sing like her momma used to. I swear she's even better."

Stella watched the girl throw a shoe and laugh when she missed by a mile. She seemed to have recovered some of her joy, and her spirit appeared to be much lighter than it had right after the attack. Her new, shorter hairstyle was becoming on her, and at the rate her hair was growing, it would soon be long and beautiful again.

"Have you heard from Macon?" Manny asked.

"No." Stella felt the old, familiar ache in her heart. "Reckon he didn't have a change of heart after all."

"People don't change," Manny said. "Not really. Just in books and movies."

"I think Macon wishes he could. I figure he gets credit for that."

"You're a generous woman, Stella. Most forgiving."

The very word "forgive" brought it all back for Stella, the events of April, and Dolly Browning.

She looked up at Manny and knew he was thinking the same thing.

"I used to think I was a forgiving person," she said. "Now I'm not so sure."

"You are. Take my word for it." He slipped his arm around her shoulders and pulled her against his side. "You honored her, more than she deserved, by not telling anybody what you knew about her past."

"What'd be the point? It wouldn't have made anybody feel better or heal any faster," she said. "It was bad enough that we had to tell folks it was her who killed Billy Ray. Now she's the crazy old woman who lived in the haunted house by the cemetery with all those cats, who killed that bald-headed Nazi guy with the ugly tattoos."

"I'm glad we didn't have to put all that on her tombstone," Manny said.

Stella just laughed and shook her head.

She looked over at her grandson, who was smiling down at his baby brother, his freckled face glowing with pride and affection.

New beginnings. That was the best thing about life, she decided. If you looked for them, you could always find new beginnings.

And just for a moment, Stella could have sworn she saw little Macon Jr. smile back.